PRAISE FOR JACI BURTON'S PLAY-BY-PLAY NOVELS

THROWN BY A CURVE

"The behind-the-scenes inside look at sports and the men who make up the teams is inventive and unique in this series. Garrett is a flesh-and-blood man, not an icon, and Alicia is a strong, confident professional in her own right."   —*Heroes and Heartbreakers*

"I think the Play-by-Play series is one of the strongest sports romance series available."   —*Dear Author*

"As usual, Jaci Burton delivers flawed but endearing characters, a strong romance, and an engaging plot all wrapped up in one sexy package."   —*Romance Novel News*

PLAYING TO WIN

"Burton knocks it out of the park . . . With snappy back-and-forth dialogue as well as hot, sweaty, and utterly engaging bedroom play, readers will not be able to race through this book fast enough!"
    —*RT Book Reviews* (4 ½ stars)

"Has all the characteristics that have put this series high on my must-read list—strong and independent women, emotional depth, personal transformation, and let's not forget smoking hot athletes with rock-hard abs (this is definitely one time you can judge a book by its cover!)."   —*Fresh Fiction*

"An engaging tale . . . Readers will enjoy this heated football romance as the two-minute drill begins."   —*Midwest Book Review*

continued . . .

TAKING A SHOT

"[Jaci Burton] delivers the passionate, inventive, sexually explicit love scenes that fans expect . . . However, *Taking a Shot* isn't just about hot sex. Burton offers plenty of emotion and conflict in a memorable, relationship-driven story."   —*USA Today*

"Ms. Burton has a way of writing intense scenes that are both sensual and raw . . . Plenty of romance, sexy men, hot steamy loving, and humor."   —*Smexy Books*

"For this third Play-by-Play entry, there's no shortage of volatile, steamy sex, but the story development is the key to this thoughtful tale."   —*RT Reviews*

CHANGING THE GAME

"This book is wonderful from beginning to end, even for those who are not baseball fans."   —*RT Reviews*

"*Changing the Game* is an extraordinary novel—a definite home run!"
                    —*Joyfully Reviewed*

"A strong plot, complex characters, sexy athletes, and nonstop passion make this book a must read."   —*Fresh Fiction*

THE PERFECT PLAY

"The characters are incredible. They are human and complex and real and perfect."   —*Night Owl Reviews*

"Holy smokes! I am pretty sure I saw steam rising from every page."   —*Fresh Fiction*

"A beautiful romance that is smooth as silk . . . One hell of a good time, a romance to remember [that] leaves us begging for more."

—*Joyfully Reviewed*

"Hot, hot, hot! . . . Romance at its best! Highly recommended! Very steamy."

—*Coffee Table Reviews*

"The romance sparkles as the sex sizzles."

—*RT Reviews*

FURTHER PRAISE FOR THE WORK OF

JACI BURTON

"Realistic dialogue, spicy bedroom scenes, and a spitfire heroine make this one to pick up and savor."

—*Publishers Weekly*

"Jaci Burton delivers."

—Cherry Adair, *New York Times* bestselling author

"Lively and funny . . . intense and loving."

—*The Road to Romance*

"An invitation to every woman's wildest fantasies."

—*Romance Junkies*

"As always, Jaci Burton delivers a hot read."

—*Fresh Fiction*

"Burton is a master at sexual tension!"

—*RT Reviews*

MELTING
the
ICE

JACI BURTON

BERKLEY SENSATION, NEW YORK

THE BERKLEY PUBLISHING GROUP
Published by the Penguin Group
Penguin Group (USA) LLC
375 Hudson Street, New York, New York 10014

USA • Canada • UK • Ireland • Australia • New Zealand • India • South Africa • China

penguin.com

A Penguin Random House Company

This book is an original publication of The Berkley Publishing Group.

Library of Congress Cataloging-in-Publication Data

Burton, Jaci.
Melting the ice / Jaci Burton.—Berkley Sensation trade paperback edition.
pages cm
ISBN 978-0-425-26298-6
1. Women fashion designers—Fiction. 2. Male models—Fiction.
3. Man-woman relationships—Fiction I. Title.
PS3602.U776M48 2014
813'.6—dc23   201304221

PUBLISHING HISTORY
Berkley Sensation trade paperback edition / February 2014

PRINTED IN THE UNITED STATES OF AMERICA

10 9 8 7 6 5 4 3 2 1

Cover photo by Claudio Marinesco.
Cover design by Rita Frangie.
Interior text design by Kristin del Rosario.

For those who have found love in the strangest places, in people who are polar opposites in terms of profession and interests, and believe that happily ever after comes from finding common ground.

MELTING
the
ICE

ONE

CAROLINA PRESTON'S PENCIL GLIDED OVER THE PAPER like an Olympic figure skater performing an arabesque. Light, easy strokes, the effort behind the task not showing as she created her art, because it was all in her head. But soon, elegant lines appeared, shapes forming on the blank canvas as what she'd visualized became a flowing, sleeveless silk top, followed by a sequined mini. She added a cropped leather jacket to mix hard with soft, sketched in some killer high heels to complete the look, then paused to peruse the finished product, so out of breath her heart pounded.

Nice. Not perfect yet, but as she took a sip of chai tea, she cocked her head to the side and made a few adjustments to the sketch, exhilarated to create her own line of clothing.

It had taken several years of working for someone else, of feeling like a prisoner, unable to stretch her wings. But finally, this fashion season—she was going to fly.

As she worked on her next design, the figure morphed into a

man. Tall, lean, his hands slid into his pockets as he modeled a pair of slacks and a body-hugging shirt. No jacket necessary as the clothes would speak for the body.

She loved menswear, and it would be part of her signature line. She could already picture it on the runway, worn by some chiseled model with raven-dark hair, steely gray eyes and—

No. She wasn't going to go there. She stood, stretched her back, and looked out the window of her Manhattan apartment. For November, it was decent, weather-wise. She should take a walk before the weather changed.

Her cell rang and she smiled as her brother's name came up.

"Hi, Gray."

"Hey, we're in town. Are you busy?"

"Extremely. I'm so glad you called. Come on over. I'd love to see you and Evelyn."

She spent the next hour picking up the disaster in her apartment. She had drawings strewn around her work space, so she picked up as much as she could in there, then closed the door and concentrated on the living area. When the buzzer sounded, she let them in.

She threw her arms around her brother and squeezed him tight.

"You look great," she said to him, then hugged Gray's fiancée, Evelyn.

"Have you two been celebrating Gray's win in the championship?"

Her brother didn't even try to fight his grin. "Overly celebrating, I think."

"It was a big turnaround from how he ended up last year," Evelyn said as they took a seat in Carolina's living room. "I couldn't be more proud of him."

"She's just happy I didn't crash into a wall."

"Or go flying through the air, like last year."

Carolina nodded. "Yes. I think you took at least five years off my life on that crash last year."

"No injuries this year. We raced clean and won a lot, including the championship. Even better, bringing Alex on the team this year was the best move I could have made. He and Donny both ended up in the top twelve. I couldn't ask for more."

The pride in his voice was evident. Her brother had made a success out of Preston Racing.

"You're doing so well," Carolina said. "You must be thrilled."

"I never thought it would turn out like this. When I started out, I just wanted to race."

"I don't know about that. You've always had ambition. And now you have Evelyn at your side, and she's as ambitious as you. Maybe even more."

Evelyn laughed. "That's so true."

"And how about you?" Carolina asked. "Staying busy with my dad?"

Evelyn smiled. "Incredibly. Living the dream here. And so is your father. He's doing a remarkable job as the vice president of the United States, just as I knew he would."

Carolina loved that Evelyn was so dedicated to her father. And so in love with her brother. "How's the separation working out for the two of you?"

Evelyn's gaze shifted to Gray. "Actually, much better than I ever thought it would. We make time for each other, no matter how difficult it is."

"It helps that Dad lets us use the family private jet a lot," Gray said with a smile.

"I'm glad you two reconciled."

"Me, too," Gray said. "Speaking of, will you be coming to Washington for Thanksgiving this week?"

Carolina blew out a breath, thinking about everything she had to do to get ready for Fashion Week in February. The event was the biggest opportunity for designers to show off their lines, and something Carolina had spent the last year getting ready for. "I don't know. I have so much to do now that I've plunged into designing this line. And not a lot of time to do it before Fashion Week. It's kind of mind-boggling."

"I'm so happy for you," Evelyn said. "I want to know everything, and I want to see it all."

"Not much to see right now, I'm afraid. I've got a few things in production, but I'm still trying to decide what's going to go into the line and what's not, and selecting models."

"Can you tell us the focus?" Evelyn asked.

"Right now I'm concentrating on mainly casual fashion for both men and women. I want to keep it along the lines of my own style. Fussy has never worked for me, and I don't think it works for the average woman or man, and that's who I want to clothe. I like movement and ease, and the way clothes make a person look and feel."

She stared out the window, her mind whirling with the possibilities. "With a man, his body has always intrigued me." She turned her attention to Gray. "Since you've played baseball and you race cars, I've watched you over the years. It's helped me gain a keen understanding of movement."

Gray laughed. "So, I've been your study guide for men's fashion."

Her lips curved. "Sort of. I've studied all types of men in various fields. Sometimes I'll just go outside and sit on a park bench and watch men go by. But I keep going back to the sports angle. Surprisingly, I watch a lot of sports."

"Why is that surprising?" Evelyn asked.

She shrugged. "I don't know. Maybe I just surprised myself. At first I did it to watch the angles. All the sports are different, but the way a man moves is always the same. I think a man's body is inherently sexy, and I want to showcase that in my fashion, especially from a sports angle, because I believe that will appeal to a lot of men."

"I think that's a great idea," Gray said. "So where are you on your models?"

She looked at him. "Well . . . if I could get you, that would be a definite plus."

He laughed. "You want me to model for you."

"Sure. You'd be perfect. You're popular, and that will have a certain appeal."

Gray wrinkled his nose.

Evelyn leaned back against the sofa. "Oh, this should be fun."

"I also have a couple models on hold on the female side, but I need a few more guys, and I want to plug in to the sports angle."

"Okay, I could see how that would work."

Carolina grinned. "Great. So you'll do it?"

"I'll walk the runway for you if it's just a onetime thing."

"It will be."

Gray nodded. "You could also ask Drew."

Just hearing his name caused Carolina's pulse to jump. For precisely that reason—and about a hundred others, she said, "No."

"Why not? He plays here in New York, so he'd be the perfect sports figure to tap into. You'd have access to him, and you already know him."

"Gray's right. Drew would be ideal," Evelyn said. "He's good-looking, sexy, and immensely popular. He has a huge fan base. I can't think of anyone who would be better to help launch your line."

The problem was, neither could Carolina. "I don't think that's a good idea."

But Gray was already pulling out his phone. She tried to think of reasons to have Gray stop the call. But apparently Drew had already answered.

"Hey, guess where I am?" He laughed. "No, not at a strip club."

Evelyn shook her head.

"I'm at Carolina's apartment in Manhattan." Gray lifted his gaze to hers. "No, she's not saying bad things about you. Not yet, anyway. We're actually talking about her new fashion line and your name came up. She wanted to know if you'd be interested in being a model for her."

No, she did not want him to be a model for her. Anyone but Drew. In fact, he was the last person she wanted in her head, or to see in person. He'd distract her in so many ways.

"You are? Great. Why don't you come over?" Gray shot her an innocent smile, then gave Drew Carolina's address. "We'll see you soon, buddy."

He hung up. "He laughed and said he'd model, but only if you promise he doesn't have to go naked."

She rolled her eyes and tried not to think about Drew showing up. "How about something to drink?"

She headed to the bar and fixed everyone cocktails. She sure needed one. By the time she served the drinks, her doorbell sounded, so she went over to the door and buzzed Drew up.

When he knocked, she opened the door, abruptly wondering if her hair was combed and how long ago it had been that she'd put her makeup on.

And immediately felt ridiculous for even thinking those things. Why would she even care?

Suddenly, there he was, looking cool and casual in faded jeans that hugged his muscular legs, his light jacket hiding what she knew to be a spectacular torso.

"Hello, Drew."

He smiled at her. "Hi, gorgeous." He kissed her cheek before she could create distance. "You look stunning, as always."

She swallowed, her heart picking up a fast rhythm she had no hope of tamping down. "Thank you. Won't you come in?"

"Hey," Gray said as he came into the foyer. "I'm glad we got a chance to meet up before Evelyn and I have to leave the city."

They shook hands. "Me, too," Drew said. "Congratulations on the championship. You kicked serious ass, especially on that last race."

"Thanks."

Drew took a seat.

"Can I fix you something to drink, Drew?"

He smiled up at Carolina. "A beer would be great, if you have one."

She went to the bar and grabbed a beer out of the fridge, then brought it back to him.

"Thanks. So tell me about your fashion design. What's going on?"

She took a seat in the chair across from him. "I left the designer I was working with and I'm starting my own line."

His brows rose. "Big move for you."

"Yes. But I felt if I didn't make the move now, while I had all this inspiration, I might never do it."

His gaze never wavered from hers. "Yeah? So tell me what's inspiring you, Lina."

His nickname for her never failed to make butterflies dance in her stomach. Or infuriate her, reminding her the way that nickname sailed from his lips that one night they'd spent together. That one and only night, before he'd walked out of her life as if she'd never existed. As if what they'd shared had never meant anything.

Because it hadn't. Not to Drew, anyway.

But that was a long time ago, and she was a lot smarter now. She gave him a cursory overview, telling him much the same thing she'd told Gray and Evelyn.

"So . . . clothes. Sounds fun. And you want me to model some of those for you?"

"Yes. Sort of. But you don't have to do it if you don't want to.

I'm sure you're busy with hockey season gearing up. I can find someone else."

His lips curved into a smile that made her pulse dance. "Trying to get rid of me before we even get started?"

"No. I'm just giving you an out if you want one. Not a lot of sports figures enjoy modeling clothes. And this would require print ads, as well as runway."

He took a long swallow of beer, then shrugged. "I'm game. I figure I owe you."

"You don't owe me a thing, Drew."

"Then I'll do it for the fun. And hey, if your fashion stuff is successful, it'll draw attention to me and to the team, and that's good for hockey, right?"

"That's the way I'm looking at it, too," Gray said.

"Speaking of exposure," Evelyn said, standing, "the vice president has a meeting I need to be present for. We need to get going."

Carolina laughed. "Give Dad a hug for me and tell him I'll see him soon."

She walked Gray and Evelyn to the door. "Thanks for stopping by. I'm sorry we couldn't spend more time together."

"We'll see you at Christmas, for sure," Gray said, giving her a pointed look that told her he wouldn't take no for an answer. "Right?"

"Definitely. I should have a lot more work done by then, and I'll need to take a breather. I promise not to miss Christmas."

After hugging them both, she shut the door and headed back into the living room.

"Well, thanks for agreeing to help me out." She hoped he saw that as a sign that their meeting was over.

Drew stood. "Have you eaten yet?"

"No. I've had a busy day."

"Then let me take you out to eat."

"I have an even busier night ahead of me. There's a lot to do to get this line ready, and not nearly enough hours in the day."

"Then we'll order pizza. Or Chinese. I'm hungry."

Obviously, he wasn't grabbing a clue that she was trying to get rid of him. "Fine. We'll have something to eat. Then you need to leave."

"Sure."

And she'd count every second until Drew was out the door, because having him in her apartment was disconcerting.

She had no idea why she'd allowed this, when he was the one man she didn't want to see or spend any time with. Instead, he was sprawled on her living room sofa, his long, lean body looking incongruous on her short, white designer sofa.

Taking a deep breath, she grabbed her phone.

"Chinese or pizza?"

"Either one is fine with me. I'm just hungry."

She punched in the number of her favorite take-out Chinese place and called in an order. They delivered faster than the pizza place, so she'd get Drew out of her apartment that much sooner.

She went back into the living room to find him outside on her balcony. She poured a refill on her wine and wandered out there. It was cool outside, but not unbearable. He was looking out over Central Park.

"Nice place, Lina."

Cringing at his use of the nickname, she stepped up beside him. "I love it here."

"I can see why."

"Where do you live?"

"I've got a place over on the Upper West Side."

She turned to face him. "I didn't know you lived here."

He gave her a smile. "I do play here, remember?"

He did. She just tried her best to forget that. "Of course."

"I only live here during the season. During the off-season I take off and head back home to Oklahoma."

"That's nice. Do your parents still live there?"

"Yeah, but it's not like I live with them. I'm a big boy now, babe."

Again with an endearment. "I'm not your babe. I never was."

He laid his beer on the table and turned around. "Still mad at me about that night, Lina?"

"It's Carolina. And no, I'm not angry at all. I've never given it another thought."

"I'm sure you haven't. Because that would mean what happened between us mattered. And we both know it didn't. Right?"

He'd taken a step forward, getting into her personal space.

"Or did it matter?" he asked, his voice going low and soft as he swept one of her curls behind her ear.

She shuddered, as always, lost in the stormy gray depth of his eyes.

He'd always been able to do this to her, to make her forget her resolve and turn her into the inept college girl she'd been all those years ago.

The doorbell rang, and Drew took a step back. Carolina pivoted and went inside to answer the door. Drew was right behind her, surprising her.

"I'll take care of this," he said, his wallet already open as he paid for the food and tipped the delivery guy.

"I could have done that," she said, following behind him after she shut the door.

"I know you could have, but since I'm the one who insisted on dinner, I figured I should be the one to pay."

"Fine. Let's eat." She was starting the countdown. Fifteen minutes for food and conversation, another fifteen for after-dinner talk, then he was gone.

She grabbed plates and laid out the cartons of food on her table. Drew had gone out to the balcony to grab his beer.

"Can I fix you something to drink?" he asked, obviously comfortable enough to open her cabinets and grab himself a glass.

"I'll just have a glass of water."

He ended up taking down two glasses. "I'll take care of that for you."

She didn't want him to be nice. She wanted to think about him as he'd been in the past, like that night in college when he'd slept with her and dumped her the next day, effectively ruining her girlish fantasies about him.

But that was in the past. She was a grown-up and a lot of time had passed.

She was over it. Over him.

Right?

Except he was even more gorgeous now than he'd been in college. He'd filled out in places, slimmed down in others. He still wore his hair a little long and shaggy, which she found irresistibly appealing. His cheeks were more chiseled now, his jaw more angular, making her focus on those spectacularly sexy eyes of his that had always drawn her to him. Eyes that right now were zeroed in on her like a hawk zeroed in on its prey.

Yeah. Not gonna happen.

So instead, she scooped some chicken teriyaki and sesame noodles onto her plate, concentrating on the food instead of Drew.

"So what made you decide to launch your own line?" he asked as he lifted a forkful of rice up to his mouth.

Which of course made her raise her head just as he closed his mouth over the fork, which made her focus on his lips. Drew had very full lips, and despite all the years that had passed since—since they'd been intimate, she could still remember what it felt like when his mouth had pressed against the side of her neck, and what he had tasted like, and how gentle he'd been with her, since it had been her first time.

She'd lost herself in that night, that only night with him. And it had taken a goddamned eternity to get over him.

"Carolina."

She jerked her head up. "What?"

He smiled at her. "What made you decide to launch your own line now?"

"Oh." That's right. He'd asked her that question and she'd zoned out, slipping into the past so easily, like she always did whenever he was near. "I couldn't handle working for David Faber any longer."

"What didn't you like about working for him?"

After swallowing, she took a sip of water and laid her fork down. "Where to start? He's demanding, which I can handle. Designers often are. The difference with David is that he's high-strung all the time, which creates such a nerve-racking workplace. And he's such a jealous bitch, treating his designers like slaves, refusing to let them provide any input. It was stifling working for him, which was why I accelerated my move to designing my own line. If he'd once taken any of my suggestions rather than treating me like nothing more than a seamstress, I might have stayed with him, because the man is truly brilliant. But he's so neurotic and so afraid someone's going to steal his designs, he's impossible to work with."

Drew studied her. "Hard to work in an environment where your contributions aren't appreciated."

And just like that, he'd nailed it, when she'd thought for sure he'd just nod and say "uh-huh" or something like that. "Yes, it was. Not that I expected to take over or anything, but I had good ideas, dammit. Ideas that would have helped his line. Not myself, but him."

"I understand. And it's his loss, isn't it? Because you're going to create your own line now and kick his ass."

Admittedly, she was shocked by the compliment. "I don't know about that. But taking that step was freeing in a way I never thought it would be. At least initially."

"And now you're nervous because you're on your own now and you don't know if you'll succeed."

He was also annoyingly keen at identifying her biggest worry. "Maybe."

"Don't be worried. You'll be great."

She pushed her half-empty plate to the side. "How can you be so confident, when you know nothing about me?"

"Easy," he said, standing and moving into the living room, where she'd shoved her sketches onto one of the side tables. He picked them up. "This. And this. They're good, Lina."

She took a deep breath as his gaze caught and held hers. "You're hardly knowledgeable about fashion, Drew."

"Maybe not. But I know what looks good on a woman. You've always dressed well. I think you have a keen eye for what makes a woman feel great about herself. And I'd bet you could do the same for a man. You've never lacked for confidence." He gave her a wicked grin. "Hell, you even threw yourself at me back in college."

Ugh. She couldn't believe he'd brought that up. "Don't remind me."

He came back into the kitchen. "Do you know how much courage that took? It was a huge turn-on, and it showed me how ballsy you were. You were just a girl back then. You're a woman now. I don't think anything can stop you from having whatever you want." He brushed his knuckles against her cheek, forcing her to meet his gaze again.

She lifted her eyes to his and, with him so close, the heat that always seemed to emanate from him surrounded her, enveloping her in a haze of not-so-forgotten lust and longing.

"That's a nice thing to say." He'd always said nice things to her—when he wanted something. Which made her wonder exactly what it was that he wanted now.

She studied him, the woman she was now not nearly as naïve as the young girl she'd been back then.

"Exactly what are you after here, Drew? A repeat performance from college?" She pushed her chair back and stood, creating distance between the two of them. "Because if you are, I can assure you it's not going to happen."

She made sure to keep eye contact with him, so he understood clearly her meaning. "Never again. Ever."

TWO

DREW FOUGHT THE URGE TO SMILE AT THE LOOK CAR-
olina gave him. Man, she was fierce and determined to not show
that she gave a shit about him, while her body and her eyes betrayed
her, just like they had back in college.

If there was one thing he could do and do well, it was read a
woman's body language, and Carolina was all tight with tension
and nerves. She always had been around him.

And he'd been a class-A douchebag back then, had taken advantage of a young woman who'd had an obvious crush on him, had
used her and discarded her in the dickhead way young guys did. He
still felt like shit about it all these years later.

"I'm not here to seduce you, Lina," he said, though when he'd
walked through her front door and seen her again, she still managed to gut punch him like she always had. She was even more
beautiful now than she'd been back then. Her light brown hair was

cut chin-length and framed her face, and her stunningly sharp blue eyes, as always, just about struck him dead.

"I can't believe you agreed to do this. It doesn't seem like it's something you'd be remotely interested in doing."

He caught the edge of anger in her voice. "How would you even know what interests me? Maybe I like fashion."

She let out a snort. "I highly doubt that. You seem more like the bar-brawling, beer-swilling, sweatshirt–with-a-logo-on–it-wearing, sports-watching type to me."

"Hmmm. I have been guilty of all those things. But I also like to dress well. See, you don't know me at all, Lina."

She looked away. "Stop calling me that."

"Why?"

"Because it's not my name."

He moved closer, breathing in the subtle scent of her perfume. "Because it reminds you of that night."

She stepped away. "No, it doesn't." She lifted her head and gave him a look that showed her pain. "You're trying to piss me off."

Now it was him who took a step back. "No. I'm really not. I just want to be friends."

She laughed. "We can't be friends, Drew."

Maybe she hated him because of what he'd done. He'd always managed to stay friends with the women he slept with. He was nice to them and never lied to them. He never made promises he didn't intend to keep. Hell, he never made promises. He'd never promised Carolina anything that night, either. But maybe she'd heard something he hadn't said. Or maybe he'd said something that night he couldn't recall saying.

"This isn't a good idea." She closed up the boxes of food.

He stopped her, laying his hand over hers and forcing her to turn and look at him. "What's not a good idea?"

"This. You and me."

"Working together?"

"Anything . . . together."

"Come on, Li—Carolina. You need this for your work, right?"

She shrugged. "I can get models."

"Oh, but you need me. I'm a hot commodity."

She shot a look at him. "Modest as always, aren't you, Drew?"

"Well, you know me."

"Yes, I do know you."

He figured if he could joke with her, tease her like he'd always done, she'd snap out of this sad, reflective mood. Mad Carolina he could deal with. The sad one he couldn't handle.

"Come on. It'll be just like old times. Only you get to tell me what to do. You can even be mean to me. It'll be like payback. Think of all the fun you'll have ordering me around."

She straightened and cocked a brow. "Why do you want to help me? Surely you have better things to do with your time. Like playing a hockey game, or picking up some woman."

"Not really. Annoying you has always been one of my favorite things to do."

"Yes. I remember that well."

"Think of it as a nostalgia trip, then. And besides, I come cheap. I won't even charge you for my time, seeing how I'll get all that free publicity."

"How generous of you."

"I know, right?"

She took a deep breath and let it out. "Fine. We'll do this."

"Great."

"And can you get me tickets to see some of your games?"

Now it was his turn to give her the once-over. "I didn't know you liked hockey."

"Now who doesn't know much about whom? I actually do like hockey, Drew. Plus I want to study your lines while you skate."

"Huh. Okay, sure. There's a preseason game tomorrow night against Denver. Do you want to come to that one?"

"Tomorrow night? Let me check my calendar." She went over to her desk and grabbed her phone, doing some scrolling with her thumb. "What time is the game?"

"Seven thirty."

"Yes. That'll work. I should be finished up by then."

"Okay. I'll have a ticket set aside for you. Are you going to bring someone?"

She looked up from her phone. "No. It'll just be me."

"You can pick up the ticket at the box office. Just give them your name."

"Thanks. This will really help with my designs."

"Anytime."

She looked around. He hated to admit he found her discomfort amusing, but he did. If she was uncomfortable, then it meant she felt something. And he wanted her to feel something.

For him. About him.

"So . . . you'd like me to leave."

She lifted her gaze to his. "I didn't say that, but I do have work."

He stepped over to her, deliberately getting close. "You should just say what's on your mind, Carolina."

She didn't say anything, but her eyes said it all. Confusion, that slight irritation that always made him smile, and then her eyes darkened, a flash of desire she tried to hide before she moved away.

But he'd seen it, and it made him tighten.

He took a deep breath. "Hey, I can take a hint." He grabbed his jacket and put it on.

"Thanks for coming over," she said as she walked him to the door.

"I'll see you tomorrow night at the game."

"Sure." She held on to the door and gave him a stiff smile. "Good night, Drew."

"Night, Carolina." Before she could shut the door in his face, he brushed a brief, soft kiss across her lips, taking in her slight gasp of surprise. "Don't work too hard."

He turned and walked away and she shut the door.

He smiled as he pushed the elevator button.

Yeah, he got to her. Surprisingly, she got to him, too. He'd always enjoyed teasing her. After all, she was Gray's little sister. Until she'd become more than that in one night that had rocked his world.

She'd thought he'd walked away as if she hadn't meant anything.

But she'd meant a lot more to him than she would ever know. And that had scared the shit out of him. That one night with her had brought out feelings he hadn't been ready to deal with. Not when he'd had a new career ahead of him and his entire life had been about to change. He couldn't have handled falling in love all those years ago.

Now? Now was a different story. Now he was settled, with a good career and a stability in his life he hadn't had before.

Except Carolina wouldn't give him the time of day.

He aimed to change that.

THREE

CAROLINA TOOK A CAB TO MADISON SQUARE GARDEN, went to the box office to pick up her ticket, and made her way to her seat, surprised when she realized it was in the middle and down low.

Great seats. She'd have an amazing view of all the action and the players. She took out her sketchbook and readied for the game.

When the players came out, which happened to be right near where she was seated, she shifted in her seat to watch them take the ice.

It was just as she'd imagined, only so much better seeing it in person. Despite being loaded down with heavy uniforms and protective gear, they glided across the ice, as breathtaking in form as a figure skater who wore the lightest of costumes. Carolina settled in and watched the players warm up, the grace and fluidity of motion they used to slide the puck back and forth as graceful to her as any skater she'd ever seen.

When the game started and the referee dropped the puck between the two opposing players, she leaned forward, her gaze already trained on Drew, one of the forwards. He and his teammates struck fast, grabbing the puck and driving ahead toward Denver's goal.

Drew was lightning fast. Carolina no more than blinked and he had skated down the ice toward the goal and taken a shot. It missed, but his teammate had scooped it up behind the goalie and shot it toward another one of the Travelers players.

The interplay fascinated her. She'd watched a lot of games on television, but there was nothing like being at a game. The action was fast paced, and she found herself leaning forward, her pencil clutched tightly in her hand. By the time Denver had snatched the puck and moved to the other side of the ice, she realized she hadn't sketched anything because she'd been too absorbed in the game.

Time to change that. She focused on Drew, the way his body moved when he skated. Of course she wouldn't be able to get a decent sketch of his body, but she drew the lines to give her an impression of movement.

"Hey, whatcha doin'?"

She looked up at the man sitting next to her. He was maybe in his late forties, wearing a Travelers jersey and clutching a beer in his hand.

"Sketching."

"You a reporter?"

She smiled at him. "No."

"So why you drawin' pictures?"

She really didn't want to get into why she was doing this. "I just like to draw. It . . . brings the game alive for me."

"Oh. I get it. Better than takin' a picture with your camera, huh?"

"Yes. Something like that."

He slapped her on the back. Hard. "Good for you, honey."

She winced and went back to watching the game, flipping the page so she could sketch some action shots with more than one player, wanting to get the speed of the skates, the teamwork involved, and the way the puck seemed to disappear when they all crowded around it.

Men at work. This was Drew's job, and as she zeroed in on him, she highlighted his face, glad now that he'd gotten her these seats so close-up. She depicted the fierceness of his features as he concentrated on fighting for the puck. And when he was slammed against the boards right in front of her, she saw the ends of his hair peeking out from his helmet. His hair was wet from sweat despite how cold it was in the Garden. Not surprising, considering there wasn't a moment he was on the ice that he wasn't moving.

Movement. Men were constantly in motion, which meant they needed style and comfort. While she wanted the men's clothes in her line to look amazing, she also knew men placed a high premium on freedom and ease in their wardrobe. Carolina jotted down some notes, her mind whirling with the possibilities of what she could create. She could write faster than she could draw, but she already had five or six ideas she wanted to sketch later, including underwear.

She grinned, wondering if Drew would model those for her, then forced that thought aside. Fitting him for underwear might be more than she could handle.

But wouldn't he look magnificent in a print ad? She could already envision it in her mind, the angle of his body, the way they'd set up the shoot.

It was perfect. Now she'd have to drum up the courage to ask him to do it.

DREW'S ENTIRE BODY KNOTTED UP WITH TENSION AS Boyd Litman shot the puck at him. He raced forward and fought one of Denver's defenders for it, wrestling it away and skating toward the opposing goal.

Tied one to one in the third, the last thing they needed was a tie. This had been a tough game already and he knew everyone was beat-up and exhausted. There were two minutes left in regulation. Time to end this thing.

He passed the puck to Ray Sayers and skated past the defender, getting himself into position by the goal, fighting with the defender to stay where he needed to be while Sayers and Litman fought to keep the puck away from Denver's defender.

When the puck came toward him, he jostled with Marquette on Denver's team, one of their toughest defenders. He took a shot and missed.

Dammit. A quick glance at the clock showed they were down to the final minute. With renewed determination, he fought for possession and gained it back, and made a tricky shot toward Litman who was right at the goal.

Litman slid it past the Denver goalie and it went in.

Drew had never seen anything sweeter than when the goal lit up. He raised his stick in the air and skated toward his teammates while the fans in the Garden went wild.

That had been a great victory, hard-won because Denver was a tough team to beat.

As they worked the line to shake hands with their opponents, Drew searched the crowd and saw Carolina, standing and clapping along with everyone else.

He liked seeing that smile on her face. He skated over to the boards and motioned for her to come down. She did.

"You played very well, though I wasn't sure you were going to finish it off in regulation."

"Neither did I. Will you stay and wait for me?"

She looked uncertain. "I have some work to do."

"Did you eat?"

"Well, no."

He shook his head, then smiled at her. "Have dinner with me."

"I suppose I could."

"Great. I won't be long. Just wait right here."

"Okay."

He stayed long enough to sign a few autographs for some of the fans, then headed to the locker room to take a shower. He hurried out of there before he got stuck doing media interviews, which would likely piss off his coach, but he wasn't in the mood tonight.

Not when he'd convinced Carolina to go out to dinner with him.

She was still waiting in her seat, her knees drawn up, her sketch pad on her lap. She hadn't seen him, so he watched her. She was so engrossed in her work that nothing could shake her out of it.

She had her hair pulled behind her ears and she was worrying her lower lip with her teeth, which brought his attention to her mouth. It might have been eight years since that hot night in the dorm, but he could still remember the sweet innocence of her taste, how she'd flung herself wholeheartedly into sex with him.

She might have been a virgin, and she'd known nothing about sex, but she'd wanted to sleep with him, had been eager to rid herself of what she'd referred to as the unpleasant yoke of virginity.

He'd been surprised that, at twenty, she'd still been a virgin. When she was a teen she'd been a little overweight, but she'd always been beautiful, with her dark hair and stunning blue eyes. What was wrong with guys that they hadn't leaped at the chance to be with her?

Then again, what the hell had been wrong with him that he had missed out on her the two years they'd been together in college? He'd been so wrapped up in sports and his friends and screwing every girl he'd had the chance to be with that he hadn't noticed her. Or maybe he had noticed her, but she'd been Gray's little sister, and you didn't screw your best friend's sister. That was one of the rules.

Or it had been, at least until graduation night, when he'd been plenty drunk and Carolina had been plenty brave enough to ask him to take her to bed.

He'd broken the rule. And had never regretted it.

When she finally looked up and saw him, she tucked her sketch-book into her bag and came down the stairs.

"Took you long enough," she said, her gaze scanning his face and hair. "Did you use extra gel and a blow-dryer?"

He liked that she gave him a hard time. "Yeah. It was a rough night. Plus, I wanted to look pretty for you. Did it work?"

She held her gaze on his awhile. "I won't need to put a bag over your head, so I guess you'll do."

He laughed and grasped her hand. "Come on. I must have burned a thousand calories on that game. I need a big steak."

He led her out through the side door, where he'd already arranged to have a car.

"Ooh, a private car, huh?"

He laughed as he held the door for her and then climbed inside. "Hey, I get some perks, ya know."

The car drove them to Sparks, one of his favorite steakhouses.

"I love the food here," Carolina said as Drew helped her out of the car.

They were seated right away and presented with a wine list.

"Wine?" he asked.

"I shouldn't. I have so much work to do."

"Think how relaxed you'll be and able to work after you have a nice meal and some wine."

She cocked a brow. "I think you're full of it. A full stomach and wine and all I'll want to do is climb into bed and fall asleep."

"Then think how productive you'll be tomorrow after some rest."

She laughed. "You might be right about that. I've been working nonstop for months."

"You needed a night off, then. Too much work muddles the brain cells and you can't think clearly."

"I did get some sketches drawn during your game."

"Yeah? Can I see them?"

He read the hesitation on her face.

"Oh. I don't know."

"Are they secret sketches?"

"Not really. They're just difficult to explain."

He gave her a look. "So, you think I'm an idiot."

"I didn't say that."

He held out his hand. "Then let me see them."

"Fine." She dug her sketchbook out of her bag and flipped to a page, then handed it to him.

He looked at them, stunned by her talent as he reviewed the pages she'd drawn of him and some of the other players. She'd caught everything about the game and the players. The speed, the intensity in their expressions. He could feel the action and the emotion on these pages. He lifted his gaze to hers. "Wow, Carolina. These are really good. I had no idea you had talent like this."

He saw the blush creep across her cheeks as he handed the sketchbook back to her.

"I had to do them fast. They're just messy drawings."

"No, they're . . . amazing. You captured the fast pace and passion of hockey like nothing I've ever seen."

"What I really wanted to do was show how you all move."

"I'd say you did that perfectly."

Their waiter showed up. Carolina deferred, so Drew ordered a bottle of wine for them.

"What's your intent in doing the drawings? Obviously you're not looking to design hockey uniforms."

She let out a short laugh. "Uh, no. But I am thinking about sports when I design for men. How to take movement into consideration. And comfort. Men don't like to feel restricted or weighed down in clothing. You want to feel comfortable, even in"—she looked around and leaned forward—"underwear."

"So you're going to create a line of men's underwear, too?"

"Yes." Her lips tipped upward at the corners. "How do you feel about modeling underwear?"

He shrugged. "I feel fine about it, but how do you know I've got the goods to do it? Maybe you want to use some dude who does that for a living."

"I suppose you have a point. I'd have to . . . see your body again."

He smiled. "Now we're getting somewhere."

She rolled her eyes. "Look. You're going to have to be a professional about this if we're going to work together."

"Hey, I can get naked and not think about having sex with you. Maybe."

"Can you?"

"I'm not twelve, babe."

"Or twenty-two, drunk, and unable to remember my name?"

He leveled a not-quite-happy look at her. "I knew exactly who I was sleeping with that night."

"Maybe you did. It was the day after you forgot who I was."

"Yeah, I screwed up big-time that night, and the day after. I could give you a lifetime of I'm sorry's, but that can't change what happened or the fact I treated you like shit afterward. But I'll still say it, as many times as you need to hear it—I'm sorry, Carolina."

FOUR

THEIR WAITER BROUGHT THE WINE, AND TOOK THEIR
food order, so Carolina didn't have time to respond to Drew's apology. Probably a good thing, since she had no idea what to say to him.

She'd waited years for that apology, had played over and over in her head what she'd say to him if he ever said he was sorry.

She'd planned to throw his apology back in his face. She'd tell him she'd cried over and over again for months after he walked out on her and never called her. She'd felt worthless and used and in love with someone who obviously felt nothing for her.

But that was the twenty-year-old, brokenhearted Carolina who'd had all those feelings.

Drew had never once made any promises to her that night, and all her feelings had been just that—*her* feelings—the ones of a very young girl who'd wrapped all her hopes and dreams in fantasy, none of which had been his fault. She'd known he was leaving campus, that he had a promising career ahead of him with a hockey team. Instead, she'd manufactured some love story in her head that had nothing to do with reality.

Which, again, hadn't been his fault at all. It had taken her a long time to come to grips with that. But she'd moved on, finished college, and had become an adult. She'd had other relationships and had shoved Drew into a drawer of the past.

Sometimes love taught very painful lessons, but she'd long ago decided she wasn't equipped for that whole falling in love thing.

"Apology accepted. I'm sorry I brought it up—again."

He took her hand. "You're entitled to bring it up as many times as you want to. I was a jerk that night. And a lot before that. I didn't notice you when I should have."

He wasn't making this any easier. "You weren't supposed to do anything other than be who you were. I was the one who threw myself at you."

He smiled at her. "You did. Thanks for that. It was good for my ego."

"As if your ego needed any more stroking. You had girls lining up to crawl into bed with you all through college. For as long as I can remember, you were the hot stud every girl wanted to get with. And you were oblivious to most of them, or you strung them along, choosing the best ones and discarding the less attractive ones."

"Ouch. Was I really that bad?"

"Yes. You were really that bad. As far as I know, you might still be."

"Trust me. The only thing keeping me busy these days is hockey."

"Uh-huh. Somehow I find that difficult to believe. A leopard doesn't change its spots, Drew. And you haven't suddenly become a monk."

"Okay, maybe not. But I'm an adult now, and chasing after

women like there's no tomorrow isn't high on my priority list anymore."

She wasn't sure she bought his reformed-bad-boy speech, but as they ate dinner, she noticed he focused only on her, despite several very attractive women trying to get his attention. Okay, points for him on that one. She'd been out on dates with plenty of men who had a roving eye, who seemed to think that they'd been placed on earth to have women service them.

Generally, those were the one-date-only types. A man who couldn't pay attention to her for the duration of a date didn't deserve her, and the one thing she'd learned over the years was that she deserved to have a man who wanted her—really wanted her.

Maybe she had Drew to thank for that, since she'd endured a lot of misery because of him, and she'd grown up during those months she'd spent crying over him and mourning the loss of her fantasies about love and happily ever after.

"You're quiet over there."

She lifted her gaze to find him staring at her. "Just enjoying my dinner."

"The steak is that good?"

"You wouldn't have brought me here if it wasn't, isn't that right?"

The waiter took their plates and Drew leaned back in the chair. "Right. So you've had some wine, and you've been fed. Feeling better now?"

"I was feeling fine before."

"No you weren't. You wanted to rush home and do something about those sketches you made during the game."

"Maybe."

"Now your face is flushed and you don't seem as . . . frenetic."

"Oh, you know big words."

His lips curved and she watched them as he finished off his glass of wine. "Yeah. I went to college, you know. Got a degree and everything."

"So I heard. And what have you done with that degree in business you got? Anything useful?"

"Nah. Just pissing the money away on booze and women."

She didn't believe that, but then again, what did she really know about what Drew had been doing with his life in the years since he'd left college?

"Seriously?"

He gave her a slanted smile. "Sure. I'm single and carefree. What else am I going to do with the money?"

"I don't know. Invest it. Give some of it back to your community, to those less fortunate."

"Now you sound like your dad."

"And that's a problem? What's wrong with my father?"

"Nothing. He's a great guy. Smart. Successful. Vice president of the United States and everything. And he likes hockey. What's not to like about him?"

"You didn't mention his politics."

"I make a point to never mention politics."

"Why? Afraid you can't handle political talk?"

He leaned forward. "Are you baiting me, Ms. Preston?"

"Not at all. I'm just curious about what you do like to talk about."

"That's easy. Hockey. And sex."

Now this was the Drew she remembered, the one who teased her and did his best to irritate her.

It was working.

She rolled her eyes. "Amazingly enough, two of my least favorite subjects."

"I know you're lying about the hockey part. I saw how excited you got watching the game. So, you don't like sex?"

"I didn't say that."

"I think you just did."

She should have just gone home after the game. Despite his apology, Drew was obviously only interested in annoying her. He hadn't changed all that much in the years since college. "I think it's time I leave."

He laughed. "You never could handle a good argument, Carolina. And I thought as a politician's daughter, you'd be one to hang in there for at least a little longer." He waved to the waiter, who asked if they wanted coffee and dessert. When Drew looked at Carolina, she shot him a glare.

"Guess not, Daniel. We'll just take the bill."

He sat back and finished up the last of the wine, then paid the bill while Carolina fumed silently.

He'd gotten to her, and Carolina had been certain he didn't have the capacity to do that any longer. She didn't know if she was more irritated with him, or with herself. They stood and headed outside, and she was half tempted to grab a taxi rather than share a car ride with him.

But that would be petty and childish and she'd outgrown those emotions. She could certainly endure the ten-minute ride back to her place.

"You're irritated," he said after a few minutes in the car.

"No, I'm not. I'm just tired and thinking about how much work I have to do tonight."

"Are you on a schedule?"

"Yes. A very tight one."

"Then maybe you should have said no when I invited you to dinner."

She shot him a look, then realized she couldn't blame him. He was right. She was an adult and capable of making her own decisions. It wasn't like he'd kidnapped her or in any way forced her to come to dinner with him. It was her own weakness where he was concerned that pissed her off.

"Maybe I should have. Next time I'll say no when you invite me out."

"What makes you think I'll invite you out again?"

Refusing to take the bait this time, she sat silently while the car took them to her apartment. She reached for the door handle, but Drew stopped her.

"I'll walk you up."

She let out a short laugh. "I don't think so."

Ignoring her, when the driver opened the door, he stepped out after her, his long stride bringing him alongside her.

"I don't want you coming up with me."

"I'm going to see you to your door. It's the way I was brought up."

She stopped. "Oh . . . so *now* you're being a gentleman?"

Apparently, he wasn't taking the bait, either, because he merely smiled and held the door for her while she went inside and to the elevator. Clearly she wasn't going to be able to get rid of him, so she stepped into the elevator and rode with him to her floor, then walked to her door. Key in hand, she unlocked her door and turned to him.

"Thank you for dinner."

"Why don't you invite me in for an after-dinner drink?"

"I might be dumb, Drew, but I'm not stupid."

"Not sure I know what that means. Can I use your bathroom?"

She rolled her eyes at the obvious ploy. "No."

"Come on, Carolina. It's kind of urgent. I had a lot of wine and it's a long ride back to my apartment."

"Fine." She stepped in and closed the door while he made his way down the hall. She hung up her coat and went into the kitchen to put the kettle on to boil to make tea.

"What are you doing?"

She jumped, her thoughts lost in what she was going to be working on tonight, along with the tea. She turned to face him. "I'm making tea."

He wrinkled his nose. "No coffee?"

"I do have coffee."

"Good. I'd love some." He shed his coat.

Drew was the worst guest ever. She followed him into the living room. "Don't you have a car waiting?"

"Yeah."

"Don't you think you should go downstairs and get in it?"

He blew into his hands. "No. He'll wait. Do you want me to make the coffee?"

She let out a frustrated sigh. Drew was either utterly dense or deliberately trying to piss her off. He wasn't stupid, so she was going with the latter. Surely he knew she had work to do and that she wanted him to leave.

She should just ask him to go. Damn her upbringing. Her mother would kick her butt if she found out she'd thrown out a guest, even if it was Drew. The Prestons always treated company with a smile. They were always polite.

Ugh. She wanted to boot his annoying ass right out the door. "No. I'll make the coffee."

She put water in her brewer and stuck a brew cup in, then pressed the button to start the warming process and grabbed a cup.

"Cream and sugar?" she asked him.

"Black is fine for me."

She prepared her tea, then his coffee. "Why don't we go into the living room and sit down?"

"Okay."

She mentally relaxed her jaw, which had tightened when Drew had invited himself to stay. Thinking of all the sketching and notes she had to make, she forced her shoulders down and tried to relax.

Always be a good hostess. That was the Preston way. After all, he couldn't stay all night long.

Could he?

She glanced at her watch. It was eleven thirty.

And it was going to be a long night.

DREW SHOULD HAVE BEEN A GOOD SPORT AND LEFT Carolina at the door, but there was something about this woman that got under his skin.

He couldn't just let it go—let her go.

Besides, she was just so damn polite. She should have stopped him downstairs. Or at the door. She should have been rude to him and told him to take a hike. Instead, she'd been gracious, letting him come in when he'd given her that bogus excuse about needing to take a leak. Then she'd even made him coffee, when any other woman would have kicked his ass out the front door.

Typical Preston manners. He'd seen it plenty in Gray's parents, especially his mother. God knew Gray didn't have the same manners. Gray would kick your ass if you needed it, though he still possessed elements of etiquette—more so than any of the other guys, anyway.

But Carolina—she was a piece of work. He'd done his best to annoy her, and she still gave him the Preston stiff upper lip and air of politeness.

He'd really like to ruffle her feathers a little, to bring out the passion he knew lurked just under the surface. He'd made her burn once, had turned the ice queen into a molten, bubbling volcano of sexual lava. He'd seen glimpses of her today, when she thought he wasn't looking. The glances she leveled at him, the way her body turned in his direction. It was like she wanted him, but she resisted.

He wanted that erupting volcano of a woman again, not this cool, reserved specimen of polite society.

He took a seat on her sofa, which he knew irritated her. She wanted him to leave. He wanted to talk to her. "Are you going to Washington to be with your family for Thanksgiving?"

"I don't think I am. I have so much work to do. Are you going home?"

"No. I have a game right after, so I'm just going to hang out here. A bunch of us are going to serve the homeless for Thanksgiving."

She leaned back. "That's . . . really nice of you."

He shrugged. "Better than hanging out in the apartment playing video games."

"I have to admit, this surprises me."

"Why?"

"I don't know. It just does."

"I have a heart, Carolina. Despite what you might think about me."

She took a sip of tea. "I don't think anything about you."

"Don't you?" He smiled at her.

"No. I don't."

"Why don't you spend Thanksgiving with me and the guys?"

He loved the way her eyes widened, the look on her face like a cornered animal, searching for a way to escape.

"Oh. I don't think so. Like I said, I have to work."

"It's Thanksgiving. No work that day."

"That's the reason I'm not going home. I need to be productive."

"You need to be thankful for everything you have that day. Or show your appreciation to others for everything you have. Work the rescue mission with me and my friends."

He had her now and she knew it. "Okay. Fine. I'll do that for a few hours, then I'll come back and work."

"Sounds great." He laid his coffee cup down. "Speaking of work, I'm sure you have some you'd like to do, so I'll get out of your way."

She stood up so fast she created a breeze. "I'll walk you to the door."

She opened the door. Drew leaned in and brushed a kiss on her cheek. "Thanks for coming to the game, and hanging out with me at dinner."

Again she wore that surprised look, which made him happy. He liked keeping her off balance.

"Thanks for inviting me to the game. It'll help with my line."

He gave her a smile. "Anytime, babe. I can't wait 'til we work on the underwear."

FIVE

CAROLINA HAD INTENDED TO SPEND THANKSGIVING immersed in her work, not elbow-deep in gravy. Yet here she was at the mission, surrounded by a half dozen men a foot taller than her and a crowd of people hungry and waiting to be fed.

It was amazing. The mission was filled with people, and instead of being alone and lonely, she was facing smiles and listening to raucous laughter, both behind and in front of the counter where she was serving up turkey dinner.

She supposed she had to be grateful to Drew for dragging her out of her apartment today. She would have likely eaten a salad and spent the day watching the parade and missing her family. Instead, he'd picked her up at seven a.m. and she'd met four of his teammates, who'd immediately hugged her and told her she was now one of the Travelers. Drew even brought her a team jersey to wear today, though it was miles too big for her. But Colin Kozlow, one of Drew's teammates, had told her she looked cute.

Cute. Just great. Avery Mangino, the goalie for the Travelers, had asked her if she was Drew's girlfriend, since the jersey she wore had Drew's name and his number. She vehemently said no, which had caused Drew to smirk and all the guys to give him a hard time.

She liked the hard time part, and as long as they weren't hitting on her, which they weren't, she was fine with it.

Actually, they were a great group of guys, all missing their families as much as she missed hers. Most of them had stayed in the city for Thanksgiving because their families lived too far away to visit.

"We're getting short on gravy," Carolina said to Lakeesha Divant, the director of the mission.

"I'm on it," she said. The woman was like a general, shouting orders to some of her staffers.

Carolina had been in awe from the moment they'd walked into the mission this morning. Everything had been set up and ready to go, the food had been prepped the night before, so all they had to do was start serving when they opened the doors. It saddened Carolina to see that even at seven thirty in the morning a line had already formed outside.

People were homeless and hungry, and they knew today would be a good day for a full, hot meal. Of course the mission provided a hot meal every day, but there would be a big crowd on Thanksgiving, and the regulars wanted to be sure to get in line early.

"Here's a refill on the gravy." A big burly guy brought the container out.

"Thanks, Jim." She'd familiarized herself with all the staff this morning, making it a point to get to know everyone who worked there. Some of them were formerly homeless themselves, and now were thrilled to have jobs working at the mission. Lakeesha made them work hard at it, too, and they were all grateful to be earning their keep.

"Just workin' up an appetite for that great lunch we're all gonna eat later."

Carolina grinned. "My stomach is already growling."

She served for another couple hours, until the crowd began to thin around one thirty.

"Not even one complaint," Drew said, who'd come up behind her. He'd spent most of his time in the kitchen, so she hadn't seen much of him other than when he helped Jim with restocking.

She moved out of the way as another of the staff took her place. "Why would I complain?" she asked as she untied and removed her apron and swiped a loose hair from her eyes.

"You worked hard today."

"It was worth it. Just look at how happy everyone is."

"Yeah. For some of them, it's the only meal they'll eat today."

She hated thinking that.

"And I'm hungry, so how about we eat?" he asked.

She nodded. "I've been smelling that delicious food for hours. I'm ready to grab a plate."

They did, and found a seat with Lakeesha and a group of older men who made room for them at their table.

"These are our veterans," Lakeesha said, introducing her and Drew to Ronald, Oscar, Lewis, and Bailey.

"It's a pleasure to meet all of you," Carolina said. "Thank you for your service."

"Ma'am," Ronald said. "Thanks for serving up the meal today. It's mighty good."

"I think you can thank Lakeesha and her staff for all of the work that went into preparing the meal. I just helped serve."

"But without all of you who give up your Thanksgiving, we'd never be able to do all this," Lakeesha said with a smile. "And our people would have to wait in even longer lines. So thank you."

Carolina looked over the men, unable to imagine what they'd

been through in their lifetimes. "I can't think of a finer group to spend Thanksgiving with."

"Me, too," Drew said, then asked them all when and where they served. The men launched into a discussion of their military service, and while Carolina ate, they fascinated her with war stories, some from Vietnam, some from the Gulf. She noted they avoided anything unpleasant, preferring instead to share positive, fun stories about brotherhood and good times shared.

She didn't blame them. She was sure there was plenty of unpleasantness that stayed with them at all times. Otherwise, they wouldn't be living on the street. Today was a day to share happiness and fond memories, and she was delighted to be part of it.

After a while the men, and Lakeesha, wandered off, leaving just her and Drew at the table.

"Where are the other guys?" she asked, looking around.

"They took off. They ate during an earlier shift and they're going to congregate at Avery's place to watch football."

She arched a brow. "And you didn't go with them? I thought that was a guy thing to do on Thanksgiving Day."

"I brought you here. I'll see you home."

Again with the acting like a gentleman thing. She didn't know what to make of him. "You didn't have to do that. I can make my own way back home."

"I'd never abandon you like that, Carolina." At her look, he said, "Not this time."

"No, really. Feel free to abandon me. I'm fine with it."

He gave her a look, then a sly smile. "Not a chance."

"You know I have to work today."

"I thought we'd hang out."

He really was relentless. "I said I'd help out here at the mission today. Now I'm going home to work."

"Today's a day to relax and have some fun."

She rolled her eyes and stood, then walked away from him. He'd taken up her entire evening earlier in the week, setting her behind on her deadlines. She'd given up going home for the holiday so she could catch up. No way she'd allow him to monopolize her entire day.

If she wasn't going to be with her family, she was going to get some work done, not play around with Drew.

After she said good-bye to Lakeesha and her staff, she walked outside. Drew had once again picked her up this morning in a private car, claiming a taxi on Thanksgiving Day would be nearly impossible. The car was still waiting for them.

"I can't believe you made the driver wait," she said as she slipped inside.

"I didn't make him wait. He came inside and had turkey dinner. Didn't you see him?"

Actually, she hadn't, but then again she'd been busy all morning.

She leaned back, tired and feeling more like she needed a nap. She wasn't sure how she was going to get through the afternoon.

Her eyelids had actually started to drift closed when the car came to an abrupt stop. Jerking her eyes open, she realized they weren't anywhere near her apartment.

"This is Rockefeller Center."

He grinned. "Yeah. Thought we'd do something fun before I dropped you off. You did work hard this morning."

"No, I need to work hard this afternoon."

The driver opened the door and Drew stepped out, holding out his hand. "Plenty of time for that."

"You go have fun. I'll go home and work."

"Carolina. Come on. An hour. Then I'll take you back home."

"Drew. Absolutely not. I have things to do."

"But it's Thanksgiving."

"I don't care if it's the end of the world. I have a deadline."

He shook his head. "You really need to set some parameters and take some downtime."

"Good-bye, Drew." She reached for the door handle.

He squatted down in front of the car door, giving her an incredible view of his amazing thighs encased in denim. Strong and muscled, just like the rest of him.

"Would it help if I told you that this detour is at your mom's suggestion?"

She paused. "What?"

"Gray and I talked last night, and when he found out I hadn't gone home for Thanksgiving, and that you were going to serve meals for the homeless with me, he said he was grateful you weren't going to be alone for the holiday. I guess your mother was nearby, because she got on the phone with me after that."

Carolina would believe that. "And she said what?"

"She asked me if I wouldn't mind forcing you to go out and have some fun today, and I quote, 'instead of letting her imprison herself in her apartment for the duration of the holiday.'"

That did sound like her mother. "She worries too much. I love my work."

"I'm sure you do. But the thing is, I promised her I would. And you know how formidable your mom can be. You don't really want me to tell her I let her down, do you?"

Carolina frowned. "That sounds an awful lot like blackmail, Drew."

"It does, doesn't it? So let's go." He took her hand and pulled her out of the car.

As they walked along, she looked up at him. "This is why you're not with your friends watching football."

"Huh?"

"Because of some sense of obligation you feel toward my brother and my mother."

"Oh. No, that's not it."

"I can assure you, Drew, that you don't have to feel obligated. I'd even lie."

He stopped and turned to her. "You'd lie to your own mother?"

"To make this deadline? Yes. So we can go back to the car now, and your conscience would be clear. You can hang out with your friends, and I'll go to work."

She pivoted, but Drew grasped her arm. "Not so fast."

She wanted to scream out her frustration. "What? Surely you haven't suddenly dredged up some long-lost Boy Scout sense of honor, have you?"

"No. But I did promise your mother. And besides, I agree with her. Gray and your mom both told me you've been working non-stop on launching your line for the past two years, even before you quit working for whatever-his-name-is designer."

"David Faber."

"Yeah, him. So is that true?"

She stopped, enjoying the feel of warm sunshine on her face, despite the chilly day. "Mostly."

"That probably explains why you're so cranky."

Her jaw dropped. "I'm cranky?"

"Sure you are. Because you're working all the time and you don't remember how to go out and have fun."

She wanted to kick him right in the balls. "I know how to have fun. I have fun all the time."

He led her up the stairs. "Yeah? What was the last fun thing you did?"

"I . . ." She stopped and thought. "I shopped for fabric."

He shook his head. "That's work-related. Something not related to your job. When was the last time you went to a club, or a movie, or to a friend's party? Or went out on a date."

She opened her mouth to give him an answer, then realized one didn't immediately come to mind. Okay, so she had been focusing a lot on work. But that was by choice, and sacrifices had to be made when the prize was her own fashion line. "I can't remember."

"Uh-huh. That's what I thought. And that's why you're cranky. You probably haven't gotten laid in at least a year."

She couldn't believe she was having this conversation with him. Besides, it was more like a year and a half, but she was not admitting that, especially not to Drew, the hot stud who probably got laid four times a week. "That's so not true."

He gave her a wry grin that spoke volumes about how he didn't believe her.

Damn him.

She thought they were going to stop at a bistro for some coffee and conversation, so when he took her to the ice rink, she stopped and tugged her hand from his.

"Oh, I don't think so."

"Why not? It'll be fun."

"Yeah, for you. You skate for a living. I haven't skated in a very long time."

"Come on. It's like riding a bike. You never forget how."

"Wanna bet?"

"You're chicken."

"I'm also not twelve. That ploy isn't going to work on me, Drew."

"Fine. You hang here. I'll skate."

Oh, sure. And he'd be mobbed by all the attractive women currently skating on the rink, and it would be college all over again.

No way.

"Okay, I'll do this. But no laughing when I fall on my ass."

"I don't intend to let you fall on your ass."

She followed him inside and they rented skates. The teenager working the counter recognized Drew immediately.

"You're Drew Hogan from the Travelers."

Drew gave the kid a wide smile. "I am." Drew looked at the kid's name tag. "And you're Justin."

Justin grinned. "So cool. And you're going to skate here?"

"I am." Drew paid and Justin reverently handed over the skates to Drew like they were a prized trophy.

Carolina rolled her eyes.

They headed to a locker and she took off her boots, grateful that she'd worn jeans today. Maybe they'd cushion her fall.

The walk on the carpeted area seemed easy enough, but she hadn't been lying to Drew when she'd told him it had been a really long time since she'd skated.

He took her hand and led her to the entrance of the rink.

"So how long has it been?"

She tried to recall the last time. She'd gone with a group of friends to a park rink. "Three years, maybe?"

"Not that long."

She slanted him a look. "An eternity."

He laughed. "We'll start out slow."

He stepped out onto the ice first, then flipped around and held his hands out.

She hesitated.

"I promise I won't let you fall, Carolina."

She was being ridiculous and she knew it. As she surveyed the rather thick crowd of skaters, several people slipped and fell, then laughed, got up, and tried again.

She had no idea why she was being such a baby about this.

Maybe because she'd humiliated herself once in front of Drew by getting drunk and throwing herself at him.

The ice was his home. This was where he was the most comfortable. The last thing she wanted to do was appear to be a novice.

Which she absolutely was.

She should have just stayed in the damn car.

Instead, she gripped his hands and took a tentative slide onto the ice. Her ankles wobbled and she fought for balance.

Drew was right there, wrapping his arm around her to hold her upright. "Take a deep breath and relax. I've got you. You're not gonna fall. Just listen to the sound of my voice."

Still holding on to her, he moved in front of her and tipped her chin up. "Don't look down at your skates. That'll screw up your balance. Look straight ahead. And don't forget, there's no way you'll fall, as long as I'm holding you, so just enjoy this, okay?"

He finished off with a confident smile. She nodded. "Okay."

"Then let's skate."

His calm assurance helped her focus. He moved beside her, his arm securely wrapped around her as he slowly skated forward while she tried to remember how to skate instead of walk.

In the beginning, Drew mainly dragged her along, but she realized she was never going to get proficient at this if she didn't at least try, so she moved her skates forward, and it all started coming back to her. It helped that Drew had a strong hold on her.

And he was right. With his firm grip on her she wasn't going to fall, so that gave her confidence to try. Soon muscle memory took over, and she remembered what it felt like to glide across the ice.

"Now you've got it. Just like that."

He was so patient with her, not once going too fast. And when she wobbled, he'd tighten his hold on her and slow things down.

After about twenty minutes she felt like she had a handle on it, so she pushed out, gripped his hand and separated them.

"You sure?"

"Yes. Just don't let go."

His gaze met hers. "I won't. I promise."

They made a full circle around the rink, and as she began to relax, she finally had a chance to look around at the other people.

They had drawn a crowd of onlookers, both on the rink and those looking over it.

Or, rather, Drew had. It didn't surprise her that he had been recognized, especially on the ice.

And when a boy about eight years old skated up to them, Drew immediately pulled in close to her and came to a stop.

"Hey. You're Drew Hogan, forward for the Travelers."

Drew smiled at the boy. "I am. And what's your name?"

The boy revealed a gap-toothed smile. "I'm Henry. I live in Long Island, but we're here visiting my grandparents. They have an apartment here and we watched the parade and had turkey and dressing and cranberries and stuff."

Carolina looked up and saw people who had to be Henry's parents standing behind him, wide smiles on their faces. Drew noticed them, too, and gave them a wink.

"That sounds like a fun day, Henry. So, do you like hockey?"

"Yeah. A lot. The Travelers are my favorite team and you're my favorite player."

"Thanks."

"Hey, would you autograph my jersey? I wore it under my coat today."

"No kidding. Let's see it."

Henry unbuttoned his coat to show off the green and white colors of the Travelers jersey, and sure enough, there was Drew's number twenty-two jersey.

"Nice. And I just so happen to have my Sharpie with me." He opened his coat and pulled out his pen, which he'd used earlier today to sign autographs. He signed Henry's jersey with it, and Henry went wide-eyed.

"Wow, that's so cool. Wait'll my friends find out I met you. They won't even believe it."

"If your parents have a camera on them, we can take a picture."

"Really?" Henry asked.

"I can take a picture," Henry's mom said, pulling out her phone.

Drew kneeled next to Henry while his mom took the picture. Carolina wasn't sure if she'd ever seen a kid look happier.

After the family moved off, there was a surge of fans. Carolina made her way over to the side of the rink. Drew looked her way, but she nodded and waved, and he took the time to meet with all of them, sign some autographs and take pictures. She was certain his fans would have liked him to skate with them, but he finally excused himself and made his way back to her.

"Sorry about that."

"It's no problem. It's nice you take time with your fans."

"I forgot about it being Thanksgiving. I didn't even think about the possibility of the rink being so crowded. Or of being recognized."

"Please. You, on the ice? I think it was obvious."

He laughed. "Maybe so. Let's take another few turns before we hop off."

He slipped his arm around her and glided her around. By then, people were taking pictures of both of them, and a few of the kids skated nearby. Most hot athletes were chick magnets. Drew was definitely that, but he was also apparently a kid magnet, which he took in stride. He made sure to skate slow enough, and even held a little girl's hand as she floated up beside him, gave him a bright grin, and wobbled her way around the rink with them, her parents hovering in front of them snapping pictures the whole time. Drew chatted with the little girl the entire way.

Which didn't endear him to Carolina in the least.

Much.

By the time the break bell sounded, she was more than ready to get off the ice.

"How about some hot chocolate?" Drew asked.

"That sounds fabulous. My toes are cold and my legs feel like Jell-O."

He laughed. "We need to work on your skating endurance."

They removed their skates and headed upstairs. "Since it's highly unlikely I'll be ice skating regularly, I don't think I need to worry too much about building up my endurance."

Drew ordered two hot chocolates for them. "Oh, you never know. You might decide you love it."

"It's doubtful."

"What if I give you season hockey tickets?"

She cracked a smile. "First, thank you for the offer. I do enjoy hockey. Sadly, I won't have time to see all your games, because I'm kind of busy right now. And why would you do that?"

"Always nice to have someone you know in the stands."

She shook her head. "You need a girlfriend."

"I do, don't I? Care to apply for the job?"

She wasn't sure if he was teasing her or not. "Uh, no, thanks. I think that ship has sailed."

"Has it?" The way he looked at her melted the last of the ice on her formerly frozen toes. So direct, so purposeful, the way he had been that night so long ago. She might have been inebriated and she'd definitely consumed enough wine for liquid courage to embolden her to invite him to her place after the graduation party. But he'd latched onto her at the party and hadn't let go of her the rest of the night. He'd danced with her, had held her close, whispering in her ear about how beautiful she was, and how he'd asked himself why the two of them had never gotten together before that night.

And then he'd taken her back to the quiet of her dorm room when everyone else had been out partying . . .

"Carolina."

She lifted herself out of that trip to the past and met his gaze. "Yes?"

"You were off in a fog somewhere."

"Thinking about work."

"Time to go?"

"Yes, I think so." Before she did something foolish, like travel too far down that path of yesterday and fall down the rabbit hole again.

With Drew right beside her.

Which would be a huge, huge mistake.

SIX

DREW WATCHED THE PLAY OF EMOTIONS CROSS CARO-
lina's face as they climbed into the car. One of the things he'd
always liked most about her was how smart she was, how she was
more than what you saw on the surface. In college, he'd often run
into her on the quad, and she was always sketching, or had her nose
in a book.

Beautiful women were a dime a dozen. He knew, because he'd
had plenty of them chasing him through college. But try to have a
meaningful conversation with some of them and it was like coming
up against a brick wall. A lot of them wanted to get their hands in
his pants, and hey, as a young stud, he'd let them. But after you got
out of bed, you had to have something to talk about besides where
the next party was.

A beautiful, intelligent woman? Now that was something special.

He'd always kept his distance from Carolina because she was
Gray's little sister, and that had made her off-limits.

Until the night of graduation, when he'd had a little too much to drink—okay, he'd had a lot to drink. And Carolina had given him an invitation that had been too hard to resist. He'd forgotten all about her being his best friend's sister then.

He hadn't known then that she'd never been with a guy before. He figured as beautiful and as smart as she was, that she'd had a boyfriend or two.

Stupid move on his part, but he couldn't say he regretted being her first. He'd only regretted turning tail and running after that. One of the most cowardly moves he'd ever made.

Now that he'd run into her again, this was his chance to maybe do it all over—the right way this time.

When they pulled up to her apartment, she turned to him. "Thanks for the ride."

"You're welcome. Thanks for coming along to help today."

She got out, and so did Drew.

"What are you doing?" she asked as he moved in step beside her.

"Walking you up."

"Again, this is not necessary."

"Do we have to have this conversation again? I'm walking you to your door, and you know why."

He could tell she was bugged that he walked with her to her door. Admittedly, he enjoyed this aspect of annoying her, liked seeing the high rise of color to her cheeks.

She fished her keys out of her bag, then whipped around with her back to the door. "Thanks for taking me ice skating."

"You're welcome."

She was guarding the door like a wolf protecting her young. In other words, she wasn't going to invite him inside.

Good thing he enjoyed a challenge, because he'd promised her mom and Gray that he wouldn't let Carolina work today.

"How about you show me what you're working on?"

"How about you let me actually get some work done?"

"I'd like to see what your plans are for me."

She arched a brow. "Why?"

He laughed. "What do you mean, why? Because if I'm going to be involved in this line, I'd like to know what it's about."

"You saw some of the sketches."

"Not all of them. Show me what you have in mind."

With a resigned sigh, she turned around and unlocked the door.

"If I show you the line, then you'll take off, right?" she asked as she stepped inside.

He followed her in. "Absolutely." Not.

"Okay."

"Have I mentioned how much I like your place?" he said as he shrugged off his coat.

"No, you haven't, but thank you. I like it, too. Good thing, since I spend so much time here."

"So you're a hermit."

She laughed. "Sort of. Designers don't exactly get out much."

"I'll have to change that."

"Uh, no, you won't. Not if I want to be able to show my work for Fashion Week." She went to the kitchen and put on the teakettle. She automatically went to her coffeemaker and added water, then turned it on.

He smiled. It meant she was thinking of him. He liked that.

She handed him a cup and took her own.

"Come on up to the workroom with me."

Her apartment had a loft, so he followed her up the stairs. Here, it was open, with a wide floor-to-ceiling window. Lots of white, from a wall-to-wall desk to a drafting table and a bulletin board that covered one entire side of the room. Tacked onto the bulletin board were sketches of clothes. All different kinds, from men's to women's, fancy attire to casual. On the desk were more sketches, but all in order, like Carolina had placed them that way.

"You do it all on paper?"

"It starts that way. My mind works best in freehand. Then I transfer each sketch to a digital notepad so I can add color and refine the shape."

"Show me how you do that."

She sat at the table. "For example, when I went to the game the other night, I did this sketch." She pulled out one of the sketches of him skating. "I liked the movement, the fluidity of it. It made me aware of a man's body. The way a man is in motion."

She turned on her notepad and scrolled through several designs. One was a suit, another slacks and a long-sleeved shirt, another casual wear. Different colors, patterns, and styles, each more impressive than the last.

"You got all these from going to a hockey game?"

She looked up at him. "Inspiration comes from amazing places."

"Do you show these to anyone?"

"Only my assistants who are helping me create the line."

His lips curved. She frowned.

"So why show me?"

"I . . . don't know. Because you asked, I guess."

"Thanks. Your process is fascinating to me."

She pushed up and he straightened. Drew walked along and stared at each sketch, Carolina staying right by his side as he perused each one.

He looked to her as he reached out for one. "Is it okay if I touch?"

"Yes."

He picked it up and studied it, a penciled drawing of a man wearing casual attire. Workout pants, a henley, and tennis shoes.

He looked relaxed, dressed in something Drew would wear on a weekend.

He tilted his head to look at Carolina. "I like this."

"Really?" She worried her lower lip, which pulled Drew's attention to her mouth.

"Yes. I'd wear it."

"Are you just saying that so you don't hurt my feelings?"

He laid the drawing down. "I don't say what I don't mean, Carolina. The reason I picked it up was that it caught my eye. It's something I'd wear on the weekend."

He saw the joy on her face. "Thank you. I haven't shown my work to anyone, outside of my assistants, of course. And I pay them. It helps to get an outside opinion."

He moved along the other sketches. Women's clothes, of course, didn't mean a whole lot to him. But the men's did. She had a definite feel for men's clothing. None of it was stuffy or buttoned up. It was all casual.

"I like all of it. I'd wear all of it."

She laid her hand on his upper arm. "Seriously. You're not just saying that?"

"I'm serious. I think you have an eye for what makes a man comfortable, and for what looks good. Maybe in my college days I didn't mind looking like shit, but now when I go out I'd like to look put together." He motioned to the sketches. "These would make me feel comfortable and fashionable. It's a marriage of both."

She threw her arms around him. "That's exactly what I'm going for. I can't tell you how relieved I am to hear you say that."

When she pulled back, she wore an excited grin on her face. "And you're not even a fashion critic. You know nothing at all about fashion."

"Gee, thanks."

"That's not what I meant and you know it. Your observation was wholly without prejudice. That makes it even more wonderful. You've made my entire day."

"Awesome. We should celebrate."

"Yes. I should celebrate by getting to work."

"Or . . . we could go get some pie. I didn't have pumpkin pie earlier."

She rolled her eyes. "And whose fault is that?"

"Mine. You didn't have pie, either."

"I had hot chocolate. And a giant plate of food at the shelter. That's plenty of calories for me for the day."

He gave her the once-over. "You do have to eat again today."

"Nothing's open."

He laughed. "There are tons of places open today. I know the perfect place. And they have pie. Come on."

"Drew. I have to work."

"Not today, you don't. It's Thanksgiving. And I promised your mom."

"Seriously?"

"Come on. We can go get a sandwich and pie. And by the time we get back, it'll be late, the day will be over, and you can sneak in some work if you feel you need to. I won't even tell your mom."

She gave him a look, as if by glaring at him she could get him to back down.

Not likely.

"I cannot believe I'm agreeing to this," she said.

"It's because you're hungry."

"No. It's because of my mother. She was disappointed that I wasn't going to be with the family for Thanksgiving. And she's worried that I'm working too much."

He leaned against her desk and crossed his arms. "Probably because you are?"

"No, I'm really not. I've got some very tight deadlines. I should be working today."

Her gaze scanned the sketches.

"One day won't matter that much, will it?"

With one last lingering look at her desk, she lifted her gaze to his. "I suppose it won't. Let's go eat."

SEVEN

THE DAY HAD NOT TURNED OUT LIKE CAROLINA expected. Then again, she should have known Drew would be a force to be reckoned with.

So was her mother. Even from afar, Loretta Preston was formidable. It didn't surprise her at all that she'd enlisted Drew's cooperation in getting Carolina to take a day off. Considering she'd done no work today, she could have flown down to D.C. and had Thanksgiving dinner with her family. She could have flown out tomorrow and still had the rest of the holiday weekend to dig in and work on her designs. She'd at least have had some family time, instead of spending the holiday with Drew.

Though she had to admit, instead of spending Thanksgiving alone working, this had been a great day. She'd loved giving out meals at the shelter today, and ice skating had been fun. She just wondered what it was going to take to get rid of Drew, who didn't seem to want to take no for an answer.

Her mother would be proud of him.

They ended up at the Gotham Bar and Grill, which surprised her.

"We're never going to get in here. You do realize that to eat at a restaurant on Thanksgiving, you have to make reservations in advance."

He gave her a smile as they exited the car. "Don't worry. I know people."

She knew people, too, but it didn't matter what connections you had on a holiday. You weren't getting in.

He walked them right past the front door and entered through the side, by the kitchen, waving at the staff, who all waved back as if he did this on a routine basis.

"I suppose you eat here a lot."

"You know, there are a lot of hockey fans in New York."

She rolled her eyes as the waiters waved at them, too.

"Hey, Drew. Are you here to eat?" asked one of the guys, whose name tag read Heath, as he shook Drew's hand.

"Yeah. I know you're busy today, and we only want a sandwich and some pie, so we won't take up a table for too long."

"No problem. We'll make room for you." They followed along as Heath found them a small table in the corner that a couple had just vacated. He cleaned it up and they sat.

Drew looked at her. "What do you think? Turkey sandwich and some pumpkin pie?"

"That sounds perfect to me," Carolina said, not wanting to inconvenience the staff or the patrons who'd made reservations. Obviously, Drew didn't, either.

"Great," Heath said. "What would you like to drink?"

"Iced tea for me," Carolina said. Drew ordered a cup of coffee.

"Not a beer?" she asked when Heath was gone.

"Nah. Got a game tomorrow, which means warm-ups and practice early. I need my head clear."

"So I can come disrupt your day tomorrow?"

He gave her a smile. "Sure. Come on by. You're also welcome to come to the game."

"Not a chance. I'll be buried in fabrics tomorrow."

"But you'll watch the game, won't you?"

"Uh, sure. Wouldn't miss it."

He laughed. "You weren't planning on catching the game. I can tell. Now I'll be sure to quiz you about it the next time I see you, so be sure to watch."

The next time he saw her? Did he plan on making this a regular thing? They weren't dating. They weren't . . . anything. She had no time for a man in her life, especially not now. She was going to be knee-deep in designs and fabric and fittings until after Fashion Week.

She definitely did not have time for Drew in her life. Though she'd drawn him into her life by asking him to be one of her models, hadn't she?

Or rather, her brother had. Damn Gray for doing that. She could have selected another model. She could have been alone today. She was already thinking about all the work she could have gotten done.

Then again, as she leaned back and assessed Drew, his angular looks and athlete's body, who would be a better showcase for her work? She could already picture him in some of her designs. His body was perfect for them. Not too bad a sacrifice to make for one day's lost work.

"You're staring," he said.

"I was. I was picturing you in my clothes."

The corners of his mouth lifted, a sexy half smile that sent a jolt to all her female parts.

"I would look terrible in a bra and lace panties. But I'd like to see *you* in them."

She laughed. "Not *my* clothes. My designs for men."

"Oh, those. Got anything for me to try on?"

A thought hit her. She hadn't put any clothes on her models, hadn't brought any of the designs to life yet. That might really spark her creative juices . . .

"Actually, yes I do. Could you stop by my place tonight before you go home?"

"Sure."

"I have a few things I'd like you to try on. They're not exactly finished, but if I could get your measurements and fit you, it would help propel me forward in the process."

"Happy to do anything I can to help."

"Great."

Heath brought their sandwiches and they dug in. Suddenly in a hurry, Carolina wasn't even embarrassed about wolfing hers down. One, she hadn't realized how much time had passed since they'd last eaten, and two, with the promise of inspiration on the horizon, she was eager to get Drew into her designs.

Unfortunately, he seemed to savor every bite of his sandwich. After that, there was the pie, which he seemed to delight in slowly sliding into his mouth bite by bite, while she tapped her foot and looked around the room.

"We should probably hurry so Heath can give this table to people who have reservations," she said.

"You just want to leave so you can get me back to your place and out of my clothes."

She gaped at him, then scanned the tables nearby to see if anyone had heard. Thankfully, the people at the other tables were too engrossed in their families to eavesdrop. "You do realize we're in a packed restaurant."

"So? Did I say anything that wasn't true?"

"Yes."

"What did I say? Aren't you going to get me out of my clothes when we get back to your place?"

"I am not going to be taking your clothes off. You'll be taking them off."

He took a sip of coffee, then gave her a sidewise smile. "So, you want a striptease, huh?"

She rolled her eyes. "Now you're being ridiculous."

"Am I? Or is this just some nefarious plan of yours to see me naked?"

"Are you sure there isn't alcohol in that coffee?"

"Why? Do you think I need to be drunk to tease you?" He wiped his mouth and signaled to Heath. "We'll take the check."

"Let me pay."

He gave her a look. "Why would I do that when I'm the one who invited you out to eat?"

"You've been paying every time we've gone out."

"And?"

And . . . she had nothing, other than him buying all the time made it seem very much like they were dating. Which they weren't. At all. And never would be. As far as she was concerned, Drew was nothing more than a mannequin.

A very hot, extremely sexy, breathing, human mannequin.

Heath brought their check, Drew paid, and they left through the front door. The car pulled up and they climbed in.

"This poor driver has been at your beck and call all day. What a terrible Thanksgiving for him."

"Jason has been very well paid for it, too, haven't you, Jason?"

"Yes, sir. Making all my Christmas money off you today, Mr. Hogan."

Drew laughed and leaned back in the seat.

When they got back to her apartment, Carolina took off her coat and stared at Drew, pondering what she'd like to see him in.

"I suppose the first thing I need to do is measure you."

His eyes gleamed and she could read the dirty thoughts in his head as if he were telegraphing them from his brain directly to hers.

"No, not that. Already seen it."

"Yeah, but one, you haven't seen it in a very long time. And two, have you ever *measured* it?" He waggled his brows.

He was such a . . . guy. "Not necessary. But you could strip for me."

"Now you're talkin'." He undid his belt and reached for the zipper of his pants.

If he thought she was going to balk, he was in for a surprise. In fashion, she dealt with naked or near naked models of both sexes all the time.

"I'll go get my tape measure."

She went upstairs and grabbed her supplies. As she came down the stairs, Drew was out of his boots and slipping out of his jeans.

She stopped midway down the stairs, a sudden vision of that drunken night at the dorm flashing into her head.

Her on the bed, watching as Drew took off his clothes, and vowing to remember that moment forever as every inch of his skin was revealed.

Just like now, as he pulled off his shirt, revealing a body she had spent hours exploring, and years remembering.

Except now that he'd stripped down to his boxers, she realized how much he'd changed since the last time. He'd been gorgeous then, a young man just waiting to fulfill his destiny.

Now he was the man she'd always known he'd become. His body had filled out, become leaner in spots, more muscled in others. And as she forced herself down the stairs and came closer, she realized he bore scars he hadn't before, because she still remembered mapping that body all those years ago, touching every part of him, committing every inch of his skin to memory.

The scars only added to his attractiveness, made him seem more grown-up, and so much more a man.

He had a tattoo now as well, on the inside of his upper right biceps. Two hockey sticks, crossed, with a puck in the middle and flames shooting out from the sides. That hadn't been there before. It added a very badass appeal to a very badass body.

She couldn't help the sigh of pure feminine appreciation. And as her hand curled over the tape measure, she realized how very much she wanted to lay her hands on him.

Her hands trembled as she forcibly relaxed her fingers and straightened the tape measure.

How foolish she'd been to think she could dress him, that Drew was like any other model she'd measured—like any other man she'd had in her house—and that she could be oblivious to his male form as she touched and turned him in every conceivable way so she could get his measurements.

She could have had him come in for measurements when one of her assistants was here to deal with him, instead of now, at night, when they were alone together in her apartment, and he watched her with that predatory gleam she remembered all too well.

But he was here, and unclothed, so she'd just have to suck it up and deal with it.

She ran the tape measure across his shoulders. For someone whose body was so . . . hard, his skin was smooth as she pressed the tape from one end to the other. She remembered that night when the two of them were in a room alone together, both of them naked, his arms coming around her as he tugged her close.

The tape measure slipped from her fingers.

"Everything okay?" he asked.

She shook it off. "Yes. Just fine."

It wasn't fine. It was every memory she'd tried so hard to erase, except she couldn't move in and press her breasts to his chest. He wouldn't slide his lips across her neck, kissing his way across her throat. He wouldn't touch her breasts, awakening her sexuality to raging life.

Not that her sex drive was having any problems at the moment. Her breath came out ragged and heavy as she fought with the tape measure, feeling flustered, this normally easy task taking longer than it should.

Best to get it over with as quickly as possible so Drew could put his clothes back on. Then everything would get back to normal again.

She sized both arms, jotting the measurements down, ignoring that tattoo even though she wanted a much closer inspection. She wanted to ask him when he'd gotten it, and why. But that would be a personal question, and she wasn't going to get personal. Not now. Not ever.

"Lift your arms out a little so I can measure your chest."

He held very still, the room so quiet all she could hear was the sound of his breath, feel the rise and fall of his chest as she wrapped the tape measure around him.

She drew in closer, breathing in his scent. Some soap he used that made him smell just as she remembered. It was crisp and clean, reminding her of wintergreen and the outdoors. She wanted to linger, to slide her lips over that spot on his neck that had given him goose bumps that night. She'd spread her tongue over his neck to get a taste of him, and it had made his cock pulse.

And now she was the one with goose bumps. Her nipples hardened, her sex quivering as she recalled how he had surged forward when she'd shyly wrapped her hand around his shaft and stroked him. He'd given her instruction, had told her how good it felt when she touched him, put her mouth on him.

He'd been her education that night.

And her downfall.

Drew cleared his throat. "Everything going okay, Carolina?"

No. It was a disaster. She let the tape fall from his chest. "Just fine." She wrote down the numbers.

"What's next?"

A hard shot of whiskey, maybe? Followed by a double shot of regret?

"You'll need to spread your legs apart a bit so I can get your legs and inseam."

"Sure."

She couldn't look at him. He had to know how uncomfortable she was. No, uncomfortable wasn't even the correct word.

Lost in the past, and utterly and completely ready to throw herself at him and repeat the same mistake all over again.

She held the tape measure at the top of his hip, then ran it down his leg, quickly standing to make the note on her pad before doing the outside of the other leg.

Almost done. All she had to do now was his inseam. This time, she started at the bottom, sliding the tape measure up toward his thigh.

"I'm going to have to . . ."

She lifted her gaze to his and he smiled down at her. "I've been measured before, Carolina. I know what you're doing."

He was so nonchalant about it. So why was it suddenly so damn hot in here?

Because she brushed his balls and his cock as she measured. And because he wore tight boxer briefs, and the unmistakable bulge grew noticeably bigger.

She decided to ignore it, jotted the measurement down and moved to his other leg.

She could get through this. One more time, and she'd be done. They'd be done. He could get dressed and leave.

And then she was going to have one hell of a glass of brandy to calm her shattered nerves.

She laid the tape down at his feet, lifting it slowly upward, conscious that the bulge hadn't dissipated. In fact, it had grown larger. And when she reached his inseam, once again brushing her knuckles against him—against it—she shot him a glare.

He gave her a smirk. "What? You want me to apologize for getting hard? You're touching my dick."

"In a purely nonpersonal way."

"Honey, any time you touch me it's going to be personal."

She whipped the tape measure away, finished the last of her notes, and took a step back.

"We're finished."

"That took awhile. Were you nervous?"

"Of course not."

He crossed his arms and grinned at her. "You sure about that? I'm pretty sure your hands were shaking."

How nice of him to notice. She glared at his penis. "Is that ever going to go down? It's hard to have a discussion with you when you're . . . like that."

He laughed. "Yeah. It'll go down. Eventually. But seeing you all flustered, your cheeks pink and your nipples beading against your sweater, isn't helping."

She crossed her arms. "Damn you. This is all your fault."

"How could it be my fault? You said undress. I undressed. You said hold still. I held still."

"I did not tell you to get an erection. So do something about that."

"Okay, fine."

He took two steps toward her and pulled her into his arms. She opened her mouth to object, but his lips covered hers, his tongue sliding inside to tangle with hers.

As if they had a mind of their own, her arms twined around his neck, his hand gravitated toward her butt, and every hot fantasy she'd had about him all these years came rushing back to her.

EIGHT

DREW HADN'T EXPECTED THIS TO HAPPEN, BUT AS soon as he felt Carolina's surrender, as soon as she kissed him back, his dick got harder, his heart pumped faster, and he was fully in the game. He wrapped an arm around her, his fingers sliding down to find that sweet spot just above her butt. He didn't want to scare her off, but it felt damn good to hold her again after all this time.

She tasted as amazing as he remembered, the softness of her lips brushing over his a reminder of just how long it had been since he'd held her and kissed her. Only it was different now—they were both adults, and he was going to try really hard not to screw it up this time. She might have been reluctant, but the way she kissed him told him she wanted this as much as he did.

And he really did. Having her hands on him as she measured him, the soft glide of her fingertips along his skin, had been torture.

He'd tried to be good, to treat it as her doing her job, but his dick had other ideas.

He'd planned to ignore it, but apparently Carolina couldn't.

And when she'd told him to do something about it, the only natural conclusion he could come up with was to kiss her, to see where this would go.

Now, her heart beat wildly against his chest, and he raised the back of her sweater so he could feel her skin. She was still as soft as he remembered, and he wanted more.

She moaned against his mouth, nipping at his lips. He groaned, tunneled his fingers in her hair and backed her up to the sofa, both of them falling on it. He held tight to her, keeping his balance as she landed on top of him.

She raised up, her eyes glazed pools of deep blue.

He caught the indecision in her eyes.

"Don't think about all the reasons we shouldn't. Just think about how good it feels between us, Carolina."

But he could tell he'd already lost her, because the heat of a moment ago had been replaced by icy coolness in her eyes.

She palmed his chest and lifted up. "Seems to me we had this same conversation eight years ago. It didn't work out so well for me back then. And I don't need this distraction." She pushed off the sofa and stood.

He swung his legs around and sat up, dragging his fingers through his hair.

Things had been going so well. She'd been into it, until she'd let her brain kick in.

He got up and grabbed his clothes, pulling his pants and his boots back on.

"Sorry," she said, turning away and heading toward the kitchen. "But this isn't going to work."

He put on his shirt and went to the kitchen, turning her around to face him.

"You know, there's no logical reason for the two of us not to be together."

She arched a brow. "Seriously? I can think of several. One, I have a ridiculous amount of work to do, and having a relationship doesn't fit into my life right now."

He put his hands on her arms, could feel how tense she was. "I don't think we need to have a relationship, but sex is a great tension release."

She pulled away and grabbed a tea bag. "That's the oldest excuse in the book for a guy to use to get a girl to have sex with him. You need some new lines."

"Look, Carolina. We've known each other a long time. We're compatible. I'm a reasonable guy and I know what you're up against as far as work and deadlines. I'm working, too. But all work and no play makes for one jumbled-up package of nerve endings and no outlet.

"I can get out of your way when necessary, and I'm not going to expect anything from you other than fun and sex. I'm the perfect guy for you right now."

Carolina stared at him, almost not able to form words. She'd come over here to cool herself off after nearly throwing caution to the wind and repeating the same mistake she'd made in college. Fortunately, Drew's idiotic words had cooled her down considerably. "You really have no clue, do you?"

"I don't understand."

"Yes, and that's the problem. You never did." She walked over and grabbed his coat, jabbed it in his chest and pushed him toward the door. "Thanks for a great day, but really, Drew, it's time for you to go."

"I said something to upset you."

"Really? You? I find that hard to believe." She opened the door. "Good night, Drew."

He turned to her, looking like he really had no idea. "This isn't over, Carolina."

She shut the door in his face, embarrassed that she'd nearly fallen into bed with Drew.

Again.

What was it about that man that made her want to get naked and have sex with him? What was it that made her so easily forget her vow to hate him for what he'd done to her all those years ago? He'd humiliated her once, and yet she was still wildly attracted to him. Today he'd made her forget that she had all these plans for her future, plans that hinged on her having laser focus and tunnel vision.

Only one thing in her life was important right now, and it wasn't sex and a complicated relationship with a man that, despite all her protestations and determination, still seemed to linger in her heart and all over her body after all these years.

Even now she could smell him on her, and as she took a deep breath, lust filled her and she regretted throwing him out. Right now they could be having hot, passionate sex.

He was right about one thing—she was tense, and she could use a release. Her body pulsed with need and she'd been so close to having him, to feeling his hands and his mouth on her again.

Would that have been so bad?

She dragged her fingers through her hair. God, yes, it would have.

He weakened her resolve. He weakened her—everything. As strong as she knew she was, she became nothing more than a quivering mass of . . . *female* whenever she was around him.

And that just wasn't acceptable.

She needed to steer clear of Drew Hogan, not only for the next few months, but forever.

NINE

THE QUIET OF THE HOLIDAYS—AFTER CAROLINA HAD
gotten Drew out of her house, if not out of her head—had given her
the opportunity to make some serious progress on her line. She'd
buried herself in work, mainly because she needed to, but also
because she wanted to forget the mistake she'd almost made.

Again.

He touched her so easily, slid past her defenses as if that hurt
had never happened. Though it was her hurt, not his, so she had to
stop blaming him for how he made her feel.

And if it was light and simple to him, again, that was on her. He
wanted her, and she supposed she should feel flattered instead of
insulted.

As she rolled her head around her neck to get the kinks out, and
lifted her shoulders up and down, she realized Drew had been right
on one count.

She was tense, could feel it in every muscle as she worked on hour ten of this day, which had started far too early and would likely keep going until she couldn't see the thread or her eyes grew so tired the lines on the fabric patterns started to run together.

Today she was in her work studio, a space she rented so she and her assistants could sew and bring in the models for fittings. She was fortunate that she'd made a good living working as a designer for David Faber, and that she had family money to start her business. But that's as far as the family money went. Now she was on her own, and she wanted to succeed—or fail—on her own merits. She didn't want to rely on Preston money year after year to fund what others would think of as a hobby project. The pressure was on.

This line had to be a success.

At least she was seeing some progress, and that made a little of the tension ease.

"It's coming together, Carolina."

She nodded at Edward, one of her assistants, a talented designer in his own right. She'd hired him as soon as she knew she was going to design a line of her own. He'd been an invaluable asset, with a critical eye for what looked good on men, and sewing skills that she treasured.

"Yes, it is. At least there are finished products going up on the racks."

He put an arm around her and hugged her close. "And beautiful finished products at that. One step at a time, is what you always tell me."

She turned and smiled at him. "I know. I know. I just want it all to be done right now."

"But it isn't, and you need to have patience. Just breathe and take it one day at a time. The reward will be yours at the end, love."

She laughed. "Quit throwing my own platitudes back at me and get back to work."

Edward moved off. Carolina went to the rack, checking the

finished products against her tablet so she knew what had been completed and what was left to be done.

Too many things left to do and not much time to accomplish them.

She fingered one of her dresses, a simple cotton shift she'd worked hours on designing. She slid her fingers along the scalloped edges. The hint of lace had been a perfect touch. The beige was subdued. She loved its simplicity and hoped the audience would, too.

But maybe it was too simple. Maybe if she amplified the color or changed to a print . . .

"You're second-guessing yourself again, boss. It's perfect just the way it is."

She shifted her gaze to her other assistant, Tierra, a gorgeous, raven-haired beauty and the best seamstress a designer could ever ask for.

"You're right. That dress is perfect."

"It is," Tierra said. "So leave it alone and come talk to me about how you want this shirt stitched. I also have a question about the fabric for this dress. The patterns aren't matching up like they should."

The next couple of hours were a flurry of activity. By the time they ended for the day, it was nearly eight p.m. Carolina headed back to her apartment, mentally and physically exhausted.

She changed into yoga pants and pulled a sweater over her long-sleeved shirt, then fixed a frozen Chinese microwaveable meal and sat on the couch cross-legged. She grabbed the remote, needing some mindless television to wind down her brain after today's intense work session.

She surfed channels, not finding anything that suited her. When she landed on tonight's hockey game, she stopped, set the remote on the arm of the chair, and watched the game while she ate.

The Travelers were tied one to one with Nashville's team going into the second period.

After her not-so-stellar showing on the ice skating rink Thanks-giving Day, Carolina watched the ease with which the skaters raced across the ice, sticks in hand. She couldn't help but focus on Drew as he fought a Nashville player for the puck, always so impressed with his skill on his skates. He'd been so calm and patient with her that day when he could have just as easily blown her off to showboat his superior skating prowess. Instead, he'd put his arm around her and slowly made his way around the ice with her.

Okay, so he wasn't the jerk he'd been in college. At least he hadn't been that day at the rink. But he'd still tried his best to get in her pants.

Then again, she hadn't exactly been throwing off *stay away from me* signals, had she?

Pondering that thought, she focused again on the game. She hadn't heard from Drew since she'd asked him to leave her apart-ment that night. When he'd told her it wasn't over.

Yet he hadn't called her and hadn't been back.

She rolled her eyes and took her bowl to the sink, rinsed it and put it in the dishwasher.

Did she expect him to follow up, to chase her down like he'd promised?

"What is wrong with you? You don't want or need him in your life except to model your clothes."

She marched into the living room, determined to change the channel. But her phone rang and she picked it up, smiling when she saw who it was.

"Stella. What's up?"

"I'm downstairs. Are you busy?"

"Not at all. I just came home and threw on sweats. Long day."

"I'm coming up. Buzz me in."

Stella was Carolina's best friend, and you just didn't say no to her. Besides, she could use the pick-me-up, and since Stella was a fireball of energy, she couldn't think of a more perfect time for a visit. She buzzed her up and went to the door to let her in.

"Hello, love," Stella said as she breezed through the door and shrugged off her short leather jacket.

"Your style always kills me, Stell," Carolina said.

Stella looked down at herself. "What's wrong with what I'm wearing now, oh fashion maven?"

"Not a damn thing. You're stunning as always." Carolina looked at Stella, always marveling at her friend's fashion sense. Stella was tall, so the black leggings showcased her amazing dancer's legs. She wore a gauzy top that rode to her hips, and finished the look with distressed combat boots. With her spiky short blonde hair and her sexy, killer blue eyes, the woman was a man magnet.

Stella waved her hand. "Stunning, my ass. And you look like shit. Have you slept yet this year?"

"And to think I wanted to see you so you could brighten up my day."

"No you wanted to see me because you know I'll bitch slap you with the truth. You're working too many hours. And I brought beer."

Carolina wrinkled her nose. "When have I ever liked beer? And you know I have to work a lot right now."

"Whatever. I'm putting the beer in your fridge. And because I know you're a beer hater, I also bought wine. The good kind—not even from a box."

Carolina laughed. "You're so sweet to think of me. Let's get to drinking."

Stella popped a beer, then fumbled through Carolina's gadget drawer for the corkscrew and drew the cork out of the wine bottle while Carolina grabbed a glass from the cabinet.

"And you bought a cabernet. You remembered."

Cocking a hip, Stella waved the corkscrew at her. "Of course I remembered. We've been friends for almost six years now."

"I know. But you'd be surprised how many self-absorbed people I know."

Stella handed Carolina the glass, then lifted her beer and clinked it against Carolina's wineglass. "Honey, I work in the dancing world. I know all about self-absorbed."

Carolina led her into the living room and they sat on the sofa. Stella's gaze strayed to the television and she cocked a brow. "Hockey? You're watching hockey?"

She knew she should have turned off the television before she let Stella in. "It's . . . research."

"I'll say. Hot men, fast skates, all that adrenaline. Yum." Stella propped her feet on the coffee table and took a sip of beer. "Which one's your favorite?"

She should've just blown it off and made up someone. "Actually, I went to the same college as Drew Hogan. He's going to do some modeling for the new line for me."

Stella looked at the TV, then leaned forward. "No shit? You know him that well?"

"Remember that guy I told you about, the one I had the drunken interlude with during college?"

Dragging her gaze from the television, Stella looked at her. "Virginity guy?"

"Yeah."

"That was Drew?"

"That was Drew."

Stella laid her feet on the floor and put her beer down. "You have got to be kidding me. And you're still speaking to him?"

"It was a long time ago, Stella."

"Yes, and he was a big dick to you that night. Correction. He gave a big dick to you that night, and then he acted like a douche."

Carolina shook her head. "We were both drunk."

"And he took advantage of you. Then dumped you. Asshole."

Carolina loved that her friend was so fiercely protective of her. "It wasn't exactly like that. Did I make it sound like that?"

"You didn't need to make it sound like that. That's how it was, wasn't it?"

She shrugged. "Not really. I mean yes, I was a virgin, but God, I chased after him. Lusted after him. He just gave me what I'd wanted. What I asked him for. It wasn't his fault that he couldn't—didn't love me like I wanted."

Stella sighed. "And you're still speaking to him. You're way more forgiving than I would be."

"Clearly, you're a mean bitch. Who broke your heart so badly?"

"No one, because I won't let a guy get within a mile of it. I've seen too many of my friends messed up by men. They're all vicious heartbreakers. Best not to fall in love, that way you won't get hurt."

Carolina shifted on the sofa. "Seriously? But you date a lot. In fact, you're always going out with guys."

"Exactly. Different guys. They're fun, and they have penises, and if they know what to do with them, they might get to hang around for a while. But keeping them, long term? No way. As soon as I think I might be developing feelings for one, he's out the door."

After all these years of knowing Stella, she had no idea her friend felt this way about men. And she could deny it all she wanted, but some guy had broken her heart. Why else would she protect it so fiercely?

She was so gorgeous. Tall and lithe, with a killer figure and a man's attitude about sex and dating. She could quite possibly be every man's dream.

"So who broke your heart, Stella? Seriously."

Stella picked up her bottle of beer and took a long swallow. "I'd rather hear about the hot and studly hockey player who's back in your life again. You should tease the hell out of him, then leave him high and dry."

Carolina laughed. "You have a mean streak."

Stella grinned. "I know. But that's me. So tell me about you and—oh shit, he just scored. Goddamn, he's good."

Carolina jerked her attention to the screen and caught Drew's score on the replay. He'd skated past the defender and caught a pass from a teammate, shooting the puck past the goalie and into the net.

It had been a magnificent shot, so filled with power she had felt it zing all the way through her television.

"Hello? Did you just orgasm watching the replay?"

She rolled her eyes at Stella's comment. "Not funny. It was a good shot, though."

"So how much are you seeing this Drew Hogan guy?"

"I'm not seeing him at all. We did spend Thanksgiving together, but only because I stayed here to work, and my mother and brother conned him into dragging me out of the house. So I worked the homeless shelter with him. Then he took me ice skating. And we went out to eat later that day."

"So, you spent the entire day with him. Did you get him naked? Did he get you naked?"

"He most definitely did not get me naked that day."

Stella laughed. "So he got you naked another day."

"I had to get his measurements."

"Ohhh, so you *did* get him naked."

"Not naked. He had his boxer briefs on."

Stella glanced at the television again, then pulled her attention back to Carolina. "I'll bet he has a killer body."

"He's ripped, for sure. Even more so now than he was in college."

"And you want to fuck him again?"

"Honestly, Stella. You're so . . . blunt."

"So? What's wrong with women loving sex? When was the last time you got laid?"

She had a point. "Too long."

"Okay, then. Go jump hot stuff's bones, then dump him, hard. You'll get a great release and it'll be nice payback. But hey, first we should go to a game. I love hockey. Can you introduce me to some of the players?"

"Why? Do you want to ruin one or two of them, leaving them well satisfied but crying in your wake?"

Stella laughed. "Maybe."

"I'll see what I can do."

"Good. Since they're in town, send hot stuff a text message. We can go party with them after the game."

"Uh, it's a little late, don't you think?"

"It's Friday night. What else are you going to do?"

"I was going to work tomorrow."

"You can start a little later. Let's have some fun tonight."

She narrowed her gaze at Stella. "You're a very bad influence."

Stella laughed. "No, honey. I'm the best friend you've got. The one who's going to prevent you from turning into a sweater-wearing cat lady who owns a rocking chair. Now send the text. They're deep into the third period now and up by two goals, and I'd wager your guy is going to be ready to party after the game."

Carolina could not believe she was doing this, but she grabbed her phone and sent the text.

"You're going to make me regret this."

"No regrets. Just fun."

Carolina didn't know about the fun part. But the message had been sent.

And she already regretted sending it.

TEN

AFTER A GRUELING GAME THAT ENDED WITH A THREE-to-one win, Drew was ready to let off some steam. So were some of the other guys.

He was shocked when, after showering and getting dressed, he grabbed his phone and found a text message from Carolina.

My friend Stella and I want to meet up with you after the game for drinks. Are you and your teammates heading somewhere?

Huh.

He wondered who Stella was. A fan, maybe? Either way, he was happy to hear from Carolina. He texted her back the name and location of the bar he and a few of the guys were headed to, and told her to meet them there.

McGill's Bar was dark and packed, a typical hangout for the before, during, and after-the-game crowd. Drew always felt comfortable coming here because the fans were respectful and didn't give them a hard time. They could hang out, drink a few beers, play some pool, and unwind. The big-screen TVs to watch the games didn't hurt any, either. Since it was mostly guys, he didn't have to deal with the hockey groupies.

So when Carolina walked in, looking cool and sexy in a brown leather jacket and dark jeans that hugged her slender legs, she definitely got the once-over from all the guys in the bar. And the tall blonde with her was gorgeous. Drew moved from the back of the bar to meet them.

"Hey," he said, winding his arm around Carolina. "Glad you could make it."

"Drew, this is Stella Slovinski. Stella, Drew Hogan."

Drew shook her hand. "Nice to meet you, Stella."

"Same here. Good game tonight."

He arched a brow. "You're a fan?"

"I love hockey. Carolina and I watched the game at her place."

He shifted his gaze to Carolina's. "You watched my game, huh?"

She shrugged. "It was on while I was eating. Then Stella dropped by, and she likes hockey."

Drew grinned. "I love a hockey fan. Come on back. We're playing pool."

He led them to where the guys were in the middle of a game. He introduced Carolina and Stella to the six other guys who'd come with him to the bar.

"Nice saves at goalie tonight," Stella said, striking up a conversation with Avery.

"Thanks."

"Can't believe you let that one in the third period slide by you, though. Were you napping back there?"

"Oh, tough critic," Trick, Drew's fellow forward said with a wide grin. He signaled the waitress. "Beer, Stella?"

"Definitely. And you have room to talk, Trick. You missed an easy pass from Drew while you were an inch from the goal."

Trick laughed. "I like her. She has balls."

"Well, no, I don't, but I don't mind busting yours."

Drew laughed, then turned to Carolina. "What can I get you to drink?"

She grabbed a chair. "I'll have a glass of wine. Something red, if they have it."

"Coming right up." He went up to the bar and ordered a glass of cabernet for Carolina, watching as Stella engaged the players. Deep in conversation with them, Stella seemed right at home while Carolina observed.

Actually, her gaze tracked back to him at the bar. But as soon as she saw he was looking at her, she slipped off her chair and joined Stella in conversation with the other guys.

Okay, he liked that she didn't want him to know she was watching him.

She liked him. He knew it, and he understood the history between them and why she was wary.

His fault, really, but he was the one who was going to have to do something to change that.

He handed her the glass of wine.

"I was just telling your friend Trick here that he'd better get his ass in gear if he wants his stats to be as good as yours before the season starts," Stella said.

"Oh, a statistician in our midst," Drew said.

"Yeah, but I think she has her math wrong, because I've outshot you three to one."

"My math is never wrong, Trick. Just ask Carolina."

"I'm afraid Stella is right on that," Carolina said.

"Yeah? How would you know?"

"She's a hard-core hockey fan, and follows every player on the Travelers. She probably knows your stats better than you do."

Trick leaned back to observe Stella. "No shit. Are you some kind of mathematician?"

Stella laughed. "No. I'm a dancer. But I'm very good at math."

"So, you're smart and beautiful. Score two for you, Stella."

Avery moved over and pulled up a chair next to Carolina. "And you're some kind of . . . designer, right?"

Carolina smiled at Avery, surprised he remembered her at all from their brief meeting at the mission on Thanksgiving. "That's right."

"What kind of designer was it again?"

"Clothing."

"Oh. So you're big into fashion and stuff."

Carolina smiled. "Yes. You could say that."

"And you're friends with a hockey stats geek."

"Hey," Stella said, giving Avery a glare.

Avery laughed. "Touchy, touchy. Sorry. A beautiful, dancing, hockey stats genius."

Stella nodded. "Better. And now you owe me a beer for the insult."

"Consider it done. But how good are you at pool?"

Stella slid off the stool. "I'll kick your ass at pool. Especially after that geek comment."

Carolina shook her head and watched Avery rack the balls. Stella shrugged off her jacket, much to the admiration of all the guys.

"Get over here, Carolina," Stella said. "You're going to play, too."

"I haven't played pool since college."

Drew came up next to her. "So? Afraid you'll get beat?"

"Not a chance." She took off her jacket and went to pick out a cue. "Stella, let's show these boys how it's done."

Two hours later, she had won two games and lost two. All in all, not bad. Stella, of course, was kicking major butt, not surprising considering how good she was at pool.

"Your friend is a hit with my friends," Drew said as they stood and watched Stella line up her shot.

Carolina grinned. "Men love Stella. And she's a natural with them, always so comfortable around guys."

"And you're not?"

She shrugged. "Men don't naturally gravitate toward me."

He laughed. "You must be blind, babe, because every set of male eyes in this place has been on you since you walked in the door."

She looked around, and caught several gazes quickly darting away.

Huh.

"Plus the guys on my team. I've had to glare at all of them to keep them away from you."

She turned back to him. "And why would you do that?"

He leaned in closer. "I think you know why."

She warmed as he looked down at her, his gaze direct, his intent obvious.

"I don't pay much attention to men."

"Maybe you should. Because they sure as hell pay attention to you. I sure as hell pay attention to you."

And then it got hotter in there and she lost herself in the beauty of his face, the way his shoulder brushed against hers. It was like they were all alone in the bar despite the shouts of his friends and Stella's raucous laughter.

"Why did you text me tonight?"

"Because Stella wanted to come meet the guys."

"Is that the only reason?"

"Yes. Of course."

He cocked a brow. "You didn't want to see me."

"Why would I want to do that?"

He tucked her hair behind one ear. "Because you missed me."

Her eyes held his. She should step back and go hang out with

Stella, but something about him, about the way he looked at her, held her there.

"I didn't miss you. I've been working."

"And not thinking about me—at all."

"No. Not at all."

He leaned closer and wrapped an arm around her, tugging her closer. "I've been thinking about you, Carolina. A lot."

"Don't."

"Don't what? Don't hold you like this, or don't think about you?"

She didn't know which way to answer. She didn't know what to think. Right now she wasn't thinking, because Drew's hard body pressed against hers. She reached up and palmed his chest.

"Don't—"

"Hey, are you two going to stare into each other's eyes all night, or are you going to play pool?"

Thank God for Stella. Drew moved away, and Carolina took a breath.

"Definitely play pool," Carolina said, picking up a cue and moving back to the table.

After she took her shot, she moved alongside Stella.

"So what was going on over there?" Stella asked.

"We were just talking."

"With what? Your tongues?"

Carolina laughed. "There were no tongues involved."

"I don't know about that. I could feel the heat transfer all the way over here. You two have something hot going on."

"We have nothing going on."

"But he wants to *get* it on."

Carolina rolled her eyes. "Honestly, Stella. I think you're the one who needs to get laid."

Stella eyed Trick's butt as he bent over to take a shot. "You're right about that. But it has nothing to do with you and Drew." She took a long swallow of beer, then turned to Carolina. "Don't hesitate, honey. Take what's so obviously being offered. Sex is fun, you know."

She did know that. Sex *was* fun.

And oh, so complicated.

But maybe it didn't have to be. After all, Drew had offered her a no-strings romp. So why not take it and ease some of the tension tightening her muscles? She already knew how good it could be between them. This time she wouldn't be timid and inexperienced. She'd be relaxed and could enjoy herself.

She didn't have time to cultivate a relationship with someone new. And actually, the last thing she needed right now was something complicated.

With Drew, she'd know exactly what she was getting—or rather, not getting. He was easygoing, and he didn't want a girlfriend. He wanted to get in her pants. She would certainly enjoy getting in his again. Then she could get back to work, a lot more relaxed.

She searched the room and found him at the bar, chatting it up with one of the guys from his team. As if he had some kind of psychic connection to her, he lifted his head and turned it her way, then smiled at her, as if he knew what she'd been thinking about.

She took a deep breath and smiled back.

It was on.

ELEVEN

THE GROUP HAD STARTED TO THIN OUT AS THE NIGHT wore on. It was late, and some of the guys headed out.

After a while it was only Drew and Carolina and Stella and Trick. It was obvious that Trick was into Stella, and Drew got the feeling Stella was into him, too, since they had hung together since the start of the night. Though he hadn't paid all that much attention since his focus had been on Carolina.

Now Stella and Trick were huddled together at the bar, their foreheads nearly touching as they talked and laughed, which left Carolina and Drew to stick it out together, since it was obvious Carolina wasn't leaving without her friend.

Though, knowing Trick as well as Drew did, he didn't think Stella would be leaving with Carolina tonight.

"Need another glass of wine?" he asked.

Carolina shook her head. "No, I'm already woozy enough and

I'm going to have one hell of a hangover tomorrow while I work. I should have said no to the last . . . two glasses."

She wasn't slurring, so she held her liquor well enough. He signaled for the bartender. "Maybe a club soda?" he asked her.

"Great idea."

He ordered one for her and another beer for himself.

Stella slid from her stool and came over.

"I'm heading out."

"Oh," Carolina said. "Let me get my coat."

Stella grinned. "No, you stay here. Trick is going home with me tonight."

Drew liked Stella. Very straightforward. Nothing coy about this woman.

He stood and held out his hand. "Great meeting you, Stella."

"You too, Drew. I trust you're going to take care of my girl and see that she gets home okay?"

"You can count on it."

Carolina hugged Stella. "Call me tomorrow?"

"Of course. You two have fun and be safe."

"You, too."

Stella laughed. "Honey, I'm always safe."

"Later, Trick," Drew said.

Trick dipped his head and smiled. "Later."

Trick threw an arm around Stella and they headed out the door.

"Surprised?" Drew asked.

"About what?"

"Stella hooking up with Trick."

She took a sip of her club soda. "Not in the least. Stella knows what she wants and goes after it with a vengeance."

"Jealous, then?"

She laughed. "No. Well, maybe a little. She's very confident and always has been."

"You're always confident. It's one of the things I like most about you."

She took another drink. "I wasn't always that way."

"Yeah? When were you ever not confident?"

"Like . . . always."

"You were bold enough to come after me in college. I liked that so much about you. So many girls back then . . . I mean they were bold, but not in the way you were."

She leaned back against the stool and swiveled around to face him. "Care to elaborate on that one?"

"Yeah. They flirted, but they expected me to be the one to do the chasing, to ask them out, to coax them into bed. It had to be my idea, you know? It was nothing more than a game. But with you, it was so different."

"Don't remind me."

He laughed. "No. It wasn't like that. At least not for me. You were like the only drop of water in a desert. You stood out to me because you were so fresh and so beautiful. There was no pretense with you."

"You do realize I was drunk off my ass that night."

"So? You were honest. You didn't slide up to me and rub your breasts against me, and then act all innocent. You boldly asked if I'd take you to bed."

He saw her grimace, knew that memories of that night made her uncomfortable. But he wanted her to have good memories, not bad ones. "Carolina, I loved everything about that night. I still remember every minute of it."

She lifted her gaze to his. "So do I."

"But how do you remember it?"

"What do you mean?"

"I remember it as a hot, sweet night where this beautiful young woman propositioned me and gave me a gift I'll never forget. She was so sweet, so innocent, and yet oh, so sexy. And we spent an amazing night together, a night I've thought about a lot over the years."

She took a deep breath, looked away for a few seconds, then met his gaze again. "For a while I tried not to think about it at all. I felt like I'd made a mistake. I was so heartbroken. But that was youth, and fantasies. After a while I got past it. And yes, I do think about that night."

"I'm sorry I hurt you."

"I know you are."

He signaled to the waiter, who brought the tab for him to sign. He grabbed her jacket and held it for her while she slid her arms in. They headed outside and he hailed a taxi.

"Your place or mine?" he asked.

"Isn't yours closer? I'd like to see it."

He nodded and gave the driver his address. It was a short ride to his brownstone, especially this late at night with less traffic on the streets. He paid the driver and they got out.

"This is nice, Drew."

"Well, it's not your place, so don't expect much."

She laced her arm in his. "I'm not expecting anything."

He could tell she was buzzed and a lot more relaxed than the last few times they'd been together.

Which he liked. He wanted her to have a good time. He just hoped he'd remembered to pick up the place before he left for his game.

They walked up to the second floor. Drew took his time. He liked Carolina leaning against him. He pulled out his keys and unlocked the door, then flipped on the light, exhaling as he saw the place. That's right. He'd just had it cleaned yesterday, so it wasn't its normal disaster.

She slid out of her coat and hung it on the rack by the door. "This is nice, Drew."

"Thanks. Just a one-bedroom. Kind of small. Like I said, nothing fancy like your place."

And it wasn't. It was a simple, one-bedroom apartment. He had some basic furniture, a sofa and a couple chairs. He had a killer TV and gaming system, of course, but this wasn't home to him. It was where he stayed during the season.

"You want something to drink? I have water, pop, and . . . beer. No wine. Sorry."

"Water would be great, thanks."

Drew grabbed two bottles of water from his refrigerator, opened the tops and handed one to her.

"Thank you," she said.

Carolina walked around his living room, then down the hall, opening the door to his bedroom.

Okay, they were going there. He was going to ease into it, maybe turn on the television or play some music.

She stared at his king-size bed. There wasn't room for much else in the small apartment, but there was no way in hell he was sleeping on some cramped, tiny bed, so he'd opted for the bed and a nightstand and shoved the dresser in the closet.

"Big bed."

"I'm a big guy."

She glanced at the bare walls before turning to face him. "And I love how you've decorated the place."

"Thanks. It's my specialty." He took a long swallow of water, then leaned against the doorway. "I don't spend a lot of time here. Just sleeping, mainly."

"This place isn't home to you."

She was observant. "No."

She was also holding back, hesitant. He wanted to go to her, touch her, pull her into his arms and kiss her. Oh, man, he really wanted to kiss her. But he wanted her to come to him, to feel comfortable about being here with him.

This had to be her call. He knew how resistant she had been to him, and her sudden turnaround had surprised the hell out of him. If she had any reservations, the last thing he'd do was push her into doing something she really didn't want to do.

She wandered into the room. "The bed is the focal point."

"Yeah. I don't need a lot of furniture." He smiled at her. "I'm a guy. I just need a place to crash."

She walked along the side of the bed and traced the tips of her fingers across the comforter. "It's a nice bed, Drew."

"It's comfortable."

She set her water down on the nightstand and climbed up on the bed, then unzipped her boots, letting them drop to the floor. "Care to join me on it?"

He pushed off the doorway and came toward the bed, then sat next to her, putting his water on the table. He picked up her hand, held it in his. "Warm."

She lifted her gaze to his. "Hot, actually."

"Just how much have you had to drink tonight?"

She let out a soft laugh. "I've had some. I'm not drunk, if that's what you're asking, so I know exactly what I'm doing here."

He toed off his boots and shifted, sliding onto the middle of the bed. He grabbed Carolina by the waist and pulled her on top of him, liking the feel of her soft body against his. "Yeah? And what are you doing here?"

She wriggled against him, resting her arms on his chest. "Getting comfortable."

He wrapped an arm around her and rolled her over, putting her under him. "I'm not sure I want you so comfortable you'll fall asleep."

"Mmm, I like this." She threw her legs over him, tightening her thighs around his and arching upward.

His dick went from semi-hard to full-on, oh-yeah-let's-do-this-right-now erect. He cupped her face and brushed his lips across hers. "So, you want me to make you uncomfortable?"

"Yes. Very uncomfortable."

He put his mouth on hers and this time, took the kiss he'd wanted to take since the minute he'd seen her walk into the bar tonight. Deep, satisfying, locking tongues with her.

And she gave back, with no hesitation, wrapping her arms around him to tug him closer. He wound his fingers into her hair, loving the way the strands felt like silk, the way her body seemed to fit his perfectly, the way she moved against him as he kissed her.

His heart pounded as hard as his dick and he lost himself in her scent, the way she felt as he moved his hand along her rib cage to slide under her sweater. He needed the feel of naked flesh under his hand, and when she moaned against his mouth, he couldn't hold back the primal surge of hunger that made him rock his cock between her legs.

He slid his hand upward to cup her breast over the soft satin of her bra. He waited for her to tense, to let him know in any way she wasn't ready for this. All he got was another moan and an arch of her back as she filled his hand with the soft mound.

He raised her sweater and moved down her body so he could touch his lips to her skin. He kissed her stomach, unable to get enough of her scent, breathing her in as he snaked his way up her rib cage. He bunched up the sweater and she grabbed it, raising it over her head and discarding it, then lifting up on her elbows to watch him.

"We should get naked," she said. "This will go much faster."

"Are you in a hurry?"

"You might say that."

He pressed her down against the bed. "Relax. We've got the rest of the night to touch each other."

She shuddered out a breath and reached for him, pulling him down for a kiss that made his cock press tight and hard against his jeans. And when she reached between them to rub her hand against his shaft, he was the one groaning this time.

Maybe he should be in a hurry, because the thought of being inside her slick, wet heat was all he could think about right now.

But he wanted to do it right for her, wanted to take his time.

"You know," he said, sweeping his hand over her bare stomach. "The first time we were together we were both drunk. This time I'm stone-cold sober."

"You had beers tonight."

He laughed. "A few. But not a lot. I don't get drunk anymore."

She lifted up on her elbows again. "Why not?"

"I like to know what I'm doing. Being drunk was fun in college, when I was a kid. I'm not a kid anymore."

"So you're all mature and responsible now?"

He sensed she didn't believe him. In him. He wanted to change that. "I intend to be responsible for your pleasure tonight." Once again, he eased her shoulders back down on the bed, then reached behind to unclasp her bra.

"As I recall, I had a pretty good time that night in college."

"Good to know. I'll give you a better time tonight."

"You keeping score, Drew?"

He pulled the bra away and tossed it to the foot of the bed. "No, Carolina, I'm not. Are you?"

She didn't answer, but her nipples puckered and tightened into sweet buds. He circled one with the tip of his finger. Her breath caught, and he bent and captured a nipple in between his lips.

Soft, just like the rest of her skin. He flicked the bud with his tongue, then pulled it into his mouth, sucking gently.

"Oh, God," she whispered. "I like that."

It had been a long time since he'd been with her, and he might have been drunk that night, but he still remembered how responsive she'd been, and how sensitive her nipples were.

He focused on them, cupping them, licking them, until she wriggled against him, arching her back to feed them into his mouth. And when she dug her nails into his arm, he knew he had her, wild and out of control.

He released her, looking down at her, at the way her nipples were tight, hard points, wet from his mouth. It made him shudder, his balls tight and pounding.

He swept his hand between her breasts and down her belly, then reached for the button of her jeans and popped it open.

"Let's get these off."

He slid off the bed only long enough to pull her jeans over her hips and down her legs. She wore black panties and knee-high socks, surprisingly sexy, actually. He rolled the socks down, then laid his hands on her hips, liking the way she watched him, her eyes stormy, dark, and filled with desire.

He reached for the tiny strings holding her panties on her hips and drew them off, then cupped her ankles, sliding his hands up to her calves, spreading her legs as he reached her thighs.

Her sex was moist, pink, and as he kneeled on the floor in front of the bed, he breathed in her scent, musky and sweet. He pulled her to the edge of the bed and cupped her butt, drawing her pussy toward his mouth.

"Drew."

His name floated from her lips like a begging whisper. He knew what she wanted. He kissed the inside of her thigh, then licked along the curve of that hollow, pressing his lips to her sex, snaking his tongue out to draw along her sweet center.

She shuddered. He moved upward, and put his mouth over her sex, flattening his tongue over her clit.

She said his name again and he licked her, the whole length of her, tasting her and putting his tongue inside to lap at her flavor. He rolled his tongue over her, finding the spots that made her lift against him.

"Yes, there," she said, and he stayed there, giving her what she needed to come. He wanted her to climax, to fill his mouth with her juices.

His dick pounded, so hard it ached. Her body vibrated as she writhed against him. He held on to her hands as she gripped him tightly, moving her hips up and down as he sucked on the tight bud and took her right to the edge. He slid a finger inside her to give her more, to make it better for her.

"Oh, Drew, I'm going to come," she said, and he flicked his tongue faster over that spot that seemed to make her quiver and slid his finger in deeper.

She cried out and he held her as she thrust her pussy against his face, lifting and shuddering through her orgasm. He held on to her while she rocketed through a long climax until she eased and dropped down to the mattress.

She was breathing heavily, so he waited, kissing around her sex, knowing she'd be sensitive there. He rose and pulled off his shirt, undid his belt and pants and dropped them to the floor, along with his socks and underwear. He climbed onto the bed next to her and pulled her into his arms.

She rolled to her side and looked up at him. "That was much better than I remembered."

He laughed. "Thanks. Good to know I've gotten better at it."

"I don't think you were ever bad at it. But, wow, Drew. That was intense. It's been awhile for me. Maybe that's why it felt so good."

"I'm glad."

She sat up, looked down at him and patted him on the chest. "Well, thanks for the orgasm. Gotta go now."

He dragged her back down and pulled her into his arms. "Nice try."

She laid her hand on his chest, then drifted it down over his stomach. "Are you trying to imply we're not finished here?"

"Not even close. That was just a warm-up."

Her hand drifted lower, then wrapped around his cock. "So, you're saying there's something you want."

He sucked in a breath. "Yeah, there's definitely something I want."

"Maybe a return of the pleasure you gave me?"

"Babe, if you put your mouth on me, we'd be done in a hurry."

Her eyes gleamed. "Oh, that's a definite challenge if I ever heard one."

She slid down his body, kissing his chest, his ribs.

"Tell me about the tattoo. It wasn't here before."

"I got it when I was drafted by the Ice."

She traced it with her finger. Even her light touch on his biceps made his dick twitch. "And yet, this one has flames."

"Yeah. I liked the design, and I didn't want it to be team specific. You never know when you're going to be traded. But the hockey part—that's forever."

She continued to run her fingers over his skin. "It reminds me of you—of how you look when you're skating. So fast, like you're on fire."

"Thanks."

She continued her digital mapping of his body, stopping at his stomach.

"Have I mentioned how mesmerized I am by your abs?" she asked.

"Uh, no."

She splayed her hands across them. "I am. They're magnificent."

"Now the truth comes out. You're using me for my body."

"Absolutely."

She pressed a kiss to his lower abdomen, then moved her way down, her hair tickling his skin along the way. She rested her head on his hip, then gripped the base of his shaft in her hand.

"You were hard all the time you were licking me, weren't you?"

"Yeah."

She lifted her head and propped up to look at him. "How uncomfortable for you. We should do something about that."

"We can. I can put on a condom and we can fuck."

"Pfft. Now who's the impatient one? Didn't you say we had all night?"

"That was earlier. Now I'm in a hurry."

"Too bad. Most men love blow jobs, you know. I don't understand why you're so reluctant."

"I'm definitely not reluctant. I just don't want you to feel like you have to do this."

She got up on her knees, and goddamn, that was a sight to behold. Her breasts swung back and forth, and she had a beautiful ass.

"I never do anything I don't want to do, Drew. Now relax and enjoy this. After all, we have all night long, right?"

She leaned over him and put her lips over the head of his cock. He held his breath as her soft mouth touched the crest, and nearly died when her tongue wrapped around him to draw him into her hot, wet mouth.

"That's so fucking good." He reached out to slide his fingers in her hair, and arched up to encourage her to take more.

She did, engulfing him inch by slow inch into the warm cavern of her mouth. Watching his shaft disappear between her lips made his balls quiver, made him want to shove into her, hard. He had to exercise all the patience he had and let her take the lead, which was damned difficult, because he was primed and ready to go off as soon as she'd put her mouth on him.

But this sensation was too sweet, the visual too erotic to let go of just yet, so he leaned back and watched as she took him deep, then slowly rose up, his cock wet from her mouth. She rolled her tongue over the tip, then licked the length of him, all the way down to his balls.

"Christ," he said, his voice gone hoarse as she wrapped her hand around him and stroked him, then fed him into her mouth again, tightening her mouth around him, squeezing him as she sucked him. He jammed his heels into the mattress to hold on, gritting his teeth as she used her hands and her mouth to give him the greatest pleasure.

Sweat broke on the back of his neck and he knew he wasn't going to be able to hold on.

"Carolina, I'm going to come." It was the only warning he was going to be able to give her, because he was pumping into her mouth just as the first spurts of come burst from him.

She didn't flinch, just went down deeper on him. He let go, thrusting hard into her waiting mouth. She held on to his cock as he groaned and came, releasing everything he had into her mouth. It was the most beautiful thing to watch her throat work to swallow. He tightened his grip on her hair and held her there while he emptied.

Spent, he fell back against the pillows while Carolina licked and kissed his cock, then climbed back up to lay against him. He was out of breath for a few minutes and couldn't even speak, so he wrapped his arm around her and held her.

"Wow," was all he could manage.

"You're welcome."

His lips curved and he tipped her chin up to brush his lips

across hers. He grabbed their waters from the nightstand so they could both take a drink. "For a warm-up, that was pretty good."

She took a drink, then climbed over his lap to lay the water down. "I'll say. Now let's get on to part two."

She straddled him, and his cock rushed to take notice. And when she cupped his face and kissed him, he really liked that, loved the softness of her mouth, the way she brushed her lips back and forth over his. And when she playfully nipped at his lower lip, he grabbed her and planted a deep kiss on her that told her exactly how much he enjoyed what she was doing.

She pulled back and looked at him. "It turns me on when you do that."

"Do what?"

"Make that sound. Like a growl, only it's deep in your throat."

"I wasn't even aware I made a sound."

"You definitely make a sound. It's . . . animalistic."

He cocked a brow. "Really. If it turns you on, I'll try to do it again."

She laughed, then pulled him toward her again for another kiss. Though he had no idea what type of animal sounds he made, he sure as hell liked kissing her, liked the way she kissed him. And she sure brought out the animal in him. He grasped her hips and moved her over him, sliding her pussy over his shaft. He went from semi- to full-hard in seconds.

"Condoms are in the nightstand," he said.

She gave him a wry smile. "I like a man who's prepared."

"Always."

She leaned over and opened the drawer, giving him a great view of her ass, which he couldn't help but smooth his hands over.

Carolina pulled out a condom and tore open the wrapper, then slid the condom over his cock.

"I like your hands on me, Lina."

This time, she didn't complain at his use of her nickname. Instead, she gave him a hot look that shredded him, and lifted, fitting his cock at the entrance to her pussy. He watched his shaft disappear inside her and let out a low groan as her body squeezed him, surrounding him with her heat.

It was the best damn feeling.

She arched her back and gave him a view of where they were connected, and then she rocked back and forth, riding him. He gripped her hips and gave them both the rhythm they needed.

"You feel good inside me, Drew."

The last time had never been like this. She'd been a virgin and tentative, a little bit scared. She hadn't talked much, and he'd probably talked too much, trying to reassure her. He had been careful and slow so he wouldn't hurt her. They'd both fumbled a little, and yeah, it had been hot and enjoyable, but nothing like this all-out, bodies-connected free-for-all.

Carolina had been a young girl then, enjoying her first time. He'd tried to make it good for her, but he'd known it wouldn't be all that great.

Now, she was a woman, fully taking charge of her pleasure, controlling how she wanted it. She was beautiful like this, and as her pussy pulsed over his cock, he realized what he'd missed by walking away from her all those years ago.

Though he hadn't been ready for her—for any woman—back then.

Now, he was more than ready to take her on, to show her he was man enough to give her what she needed.

He reached between them and found her clit. She let out a moan when he coated his fingers with her juices and swept them over the hard nub, heightening the sensation for her.

"Yes, touch me," she said, lifting, then coming down on him, using her muscles to grind against him. He rolled over her clit and drove into her, and her eyes widened.

"Like that?" he asked.

"You're going to make me come."

"Yeah," he said, then held on to her, pumping hard into her, giving her the friction and the thrusts she needed to climax.

And when she did, when she threw her head back and let go with a long moan, he did, too, releasing as she tightened around him.

She fell forward, shuddering against him while he wrapped his arms around her and pumped his release into her.

Their bodies were slick with sweat, Carolina breathing hard against his chest. He stroked her back as they both came down from that amazing high.

It had been good. More than good. Better than he'd anticipated. And now he was wrecked and exhausted. So was she, apparently, because she made no move to climb off him.

He rolled her to her side and went into the bathroom for a minute, then came back and pulled the covers over them both and turned off the light.

"Tired?" he asked.

"Mmm," was all she said as she snuggled against him.

He smiled, wrapped his arms around her and closed his eyes.

He woke in a daze, the sunlight streaming in through the half-open blinds in his bedroom. For a few seconds he felt disoriented, until he remembered last night.

And then he smiled.

He'd really conked out after he and Carolina had sex. She'd exhausted him, and herself, too.

His mouth was dry. Really dry. He reached over for the water on his nightstand and took a couple long gulps before rolling over.

"Lina. You want a—"

She wasn't there. Huh. He threw off the covers and went into the bathroom. Not there, either.

Her clothes were gone, too. Maybe she'd gone into the kitchen to make coffee.

Coffee sounded like such a good idea right now. He climbed into his jeans and went into the kitchen.

Not there.

She was gone. She'd left his apartment without saying a word.

She'd left him.

Just like he'd left her that night in college after they'd slept together.

He shook his head, dragged his fingers through his hair and leaned against the kitchen counter.

Well, that felt shitty.

And now he knew how Carolina had felt. He leaned against the kitchen counter, shaking his head and smiling at the thought of the payback she'd given him.

A payback he'd damn well deserved.

Well played, Carolina. Well played.

TWELVE

"THIS HEMLINE NEEDS TO COME UP TWO INCHES. JUST above the knee, so each tier of the skirt has movement."

"I can take care of that," Tierra said, kneeling in front of the model to mark where the cut in the hemline would be.

Carolina walked down the line, surveying her clothes on the models. So different than viewing them on a hanger. Now they had life.

She twirled her finger, and the next model turned and walked the length of the room.

"This one's good just the way it is."

"I totally agree," Edward said. "Love the color and the way it clings to her body."

"Just one thing, though," Carolina said, squinting as she observed. "The color. It's too muted. We need to change the fabric. Flesh it out a bit. Maybe more of a deep coral rather than a peach?"

Edward studied the model, too, then finally nodded. "I think you might be right. I like the peach, but the coral would be stunning, especially with Felicia's skin tone."

Carolina nodded and jotted down the change in her notebook. "Let's do that."

Edward made a note as well.

They spent the next hour going over textures and fabrics and design, watching the way each piece of clothing moved and the way they looked under the lights before making some changes. All in all it was a good fitting.

She'd spent the past few weeks immersed in the line. It had been a furious undertaking and she'd worked nonstop, seven days a week, burying herself in her designs as the clock ticked on finalizing everything.

Since that night she'd spent with Drew, she hadn't had a moment to think about him.

Much.

She'd woken early that morning after and gotten up to use the bathroom and had come back into the bedroom, planning to slide under the covers with him.

But something had stopped her. Maybe it was the way he looked, the covers drawn down, covering only his lower half. He'd been sprawled on his stomach, his hair wildly unkempt, his arms thrown up over his head. His lashes, so sinfully long, nearly brushed against his upper cheek. His full lips were closed and she'd held her breath as she watched him sleep.

God, he'd looked so sexy at that moment all she'd wanted to do was grab her sketch pad and draw him looking just like that.

Before the inspiration left, she'd gotten dressed and hightailed it out of there, grabbing a taxi and heading home. After she'd spent an hour getting the angles and shadows just right, she was satisfied she'd gotten the sketch as she'd envisioned it.

It was beautiful. Perfect.

Exhausted after that burst of creativity, she climbed into bed and slept for two hours. It wasn't until after she woke up, showered, and made a cup of tea that she realized she'd just up and left Drew without a word.

She thought about calling him, even picked up her phone, her finger hovering at the button, then laid her phone down.

After that night, it was probably best to just leave it alone. They'd had a good time. Or at least she had. The sex had been phenomenal. Not that it had surprised her that they would be good together. Their first time had been more than she'd fantasized about. This time? Even better.

She warmed thinking about how he'd touched her, how many times he'd made her come. She wished she were back in bed with him right now.

But just once. Only that one time. That was all there could be between them. It wasn't going to happen again.

Diving headfirst into work had been the best way to keep herself from contacting him.

And he hadn't called her, so that was a good sign he'd thought much the same thing.

Then again, maybe he was pissed she'd walked out on him. She really did owe him an explanation. Or maybe she should just leave well enough alone and call it another great one-night stand with Drew. They seemed to do one-night stands really well, only that night had been the last night.

The only problem was, she needed to start calling in her male models for fittings. Christmas was right around the corner and she needed to finalize sizings before the holidays shut everything down and she wouldn't be able to get in contact with everyone.

Gray told her he'd come in for a fitting, and that meant she needed to get hold of Drew and figure out who would be wearing what. Then she needed to start an advertising campaign, a tease for her line.

After doing that sketch of Drew asleep the morning after their night together, she already had a fantastic idea for advertising the underwear line. She could get another one of the models—a professional—to do the shoot, but the problem was, her vision was dead-set on seeing Drew in that spot.

Any hot, sculpted body would do. Logically, she knew that. But logic didn't always fit with her inspiration. She just couldn't see anyone else in her men's underwear but Drew.

She took a deep breath and grabbed her phone, hoping he didn't answer and she'd get his voice mail.

Success. After several rings, Drew's voice mail picked up.

"Hey, Drew, it's Carolina. I'd like to arrange a time for you to come by and try on some of the clothes you'll be modeling for me. Plus, we need to start talking about how you'll fit into my advertising plan for the line. If you could give me a call back, or just shoot me an email with your schedule for the next week, we can work something out. Thanks."

She hung up, satisfied that she'd sounded completely professional.

Now all she had to do was wait until he—

She jumped when her phone buzzed in her hand. She looked at the display, then relaxed when Stella's name came up.

"Hey, Stell."

"Hey, yourself. How's work going?"

"Good. Crazy busy. How about you?"

"It's going well. Rehearsals are intense and my calves are cramping, but I'm excited about doing this show."

"I can't wait to come see it."

"I called to tell you I have a few hours' break. Can you take a little time off and have some lunch with me?"

She hadn't seen Stella since that night at the bar, either. The problem with having a deadline was shutting herself off from everyone. But she hadn't eaten yet and things were running smoothly. "I'd love to."

"Great."

They made plans to meet at a bistro not far from the theater district. She gave some instructions to her staff, then hopped in a taxi. Stella was waiting outside the restaurant.

"It's cold out here," Carolina said as she slid her arm through Stella's and they headed inside.

"I'm still hot from rehearsals. The fresh air felt good."

It was a little after the regular lunch hour rush, so the place wasn't crowded. They were seated right away and Carolina ordered an iced tea and a chicken salad.

"I want all the details on how rehearsals are going."

Stella took a deep breath and shrugged out of her coat. "Great, but the choreographer is a bastard. He works us all until every muscle in our bodies is screaming. I both love and hate him. I'm learning so much, but oh, my God, I'm so sore at night that all I want to do is go home, ease my body into a hot bath, then fall face-down on my bed and pass out."

"But it's good, right?" Carolina asked as the waiter brought their drinks. "It's going to be a good show?"

"It's going to be a great show, and really amazing exposure for me. I'm so lucky to be with the company. You know how much I literally squealed like a damn girl when I got a spot."

Carolina laughed. "I know. You've been working so hard to get in with a good troupe."

"Yes. So no matter how much I complain about how hard they're working me, it's just the best job. And we have to rehearse hard because the show opens right after Christmas."

"I'll be there."

Stella grasped her wrist. "I know you will. And I love you for that, considering how insane with work you are right now."

Carolina laughed. "Well, my insanity is coming up, but I always have time for you."

The waiter brought their food and they sat and ate. Stella dove into her salad just as eagerly as Carolina did.

"Are you eating well?"

Stella nodded. "Yes. I have to. I'm burning calories like crazy. I'd die if I didn't replenish. How about you?"

"Trying to. Edward and Tierra ride me worse than my parents about eating. One or the other of them is always fetching me food. It's unlikely I'm going to starve to death."

"I'll be sure to thank them both next time I see them." Stella stopped to take a sip of tea, then looked at her. "And how about hot guy Drew? Seen him lately?"

She popped a crouton into her mouth and shook her head. "Not since that night in the bar. How about hot guy Trick? How did that go?"

Stella grinned. "That went very well. And he is very hot. But like you, I don't have a lot of time for hot men in my life, and he's had several road games. But we have done some long-distance sexting."

"That sounds fun."

"It has been. And it relieves some of that excess tension. He's a great guy."

Carolina studied her. "You like him."

Stella shrugged. "As much as I can like any guy. He's good in the sack, and I might want to do him again."

"You try so hard to make it seem like he doesn't matter."

"Please. We only had one night. And you're avoiding the subject of you and Drew. How did that go after we left?"

"I went to his place."

Stella laid her fork down. "And?"

"And I . . . left the next morning."

Stella's eyes widened. "Ohhh, so you slept with him. Yay. You needed to get laid."

"I really did."

"Anything since then?"

"Nothing at all. I actually left before he woke up. And I've been so busy I haven't had any time to talk to him. Plus, he hasn't called me."

"So, you walked out on him without a word. Good for you."

She loved Stella's smug smile. "You know I didn't plan to dump him. I had this . . . well, this is going to sound bizarre, but when I got up that morning, he looked so beautiful sprawled out on the bed, I was inspired to draw him just like that. Unfortunately, I didn't have my drawing pad with me, so I dashed out of his place, raced home and sketched that image I had of him before I could lose the visual."

Stella just stared at her.

"I know. I told you it was bizarre."

"No, I'm just thinking. So you weren't out to get revenge on him for dumping you in college."

"No. Of course not."

"Not consciously, anyway. But maybe subconsciously?"

Carolina took another bite of salad, studying Stella. Finally, she waved her fork at her friend. "I think you have a vindictive streak in you."

Stella laughed. "You think?"

"I still think some guy broke your heart and you never got revenge."

"And you think I'm projecting my need for revenge onto you."

"Yes."

Stella laughed. "Trust me. If I wanted revenge, I'd go get it for myself. I just think Drew did you wrong, and I figured you took your opportunity to get him back."

"I wasn't out to get him back. What happened between us just . . . happened."

"And then you ran out on him and haven't spoken to him again. So what does that mean?"

Sometimes her best friend irritated the crap out of her. "It doesn't mean anything, other than we've both been busy."

"Or, it means that you got exactly what you wanted from him, and now you have no more use for him."

Frustrated, she shook her head. "That's not what it means at all."

"So you do want to see him again."

"I didn't say that, either."

"So you're done with him."

She laid her head in her hands. "You make me crazy, Stella."

"It's a particular talent of mine."

Carolina lifted her head. "It just happened between us. It didn't really mean anything other than we slept together, had one night together, and now it's probably over. Except I am using him as a model for my line, so I guess I'll be seeing him again."

Stella leaned back and sipped her tea. "And how do you feel about that?"

Carolina let out a sigh. "Stella, spending a lunch hour with you is a lot like talking to a therapist."

"So, you do feel something for him," Stella said with another victorious smile.

"You're a giant pain in my ass."

"That's what best friends are for."

TWO WEEKS OF ALMOST NONSTOP ROAD GAMES WERE taking their toll on Drew. They'd had one series of home games, but it seemed as if he'd blinked and they were back on the damn road again.

He was cranky. They'd lost three games and he wanted nothing more than to get back to the Garden and the home crowd again. This new season wasn't starting out the way anyone on the team expected, and if they didn't turn it around soon, it was going to be a dismal one.

Even worse, after practice today he'd found a voice mail on his phone from Carolina. Using her most professional voice, she'd asked him about meeting with her. Not to see him personally, but to get together to meet about her line.

There wasn't a single word or phrase she'd used in that voice mail that had been personal in nature. It was like that night they'd shared hadn't even happened. Couple that with the disappearing act she'd pulled, and his lousy mood had increased, if that was even possible.

"You practicing your scowl for the game tonight?"

His gaze shot up and he glared at Trick. "What?"

"Hey, that's an even better one. You should try that one on Vancouver tonight."

"What the hell are you talking about?"

Trick shut the door to his locker. "Man, you're grumpy. You need to get laid."

"Fuck you, Trick."

Trick just laughed. "That mood has got to do with a woman. A certain pretty brunette I met at the bar a couple weeks ago?"

"I don't want to talk about Carolina."

"So it is her." Trick took a seat on the bench next to Drew. "Did she dump you?"

"No, she didn't dump me. Well, maybe. I don't really know."

"You don't know? What the hell, man? Has it been that long since you've been given the boot by a woman you can't tell when you've been dumped?"

"Actually, I've never been dumped."

Trick let out a snort. "Every guy has been kicked to the curb at least once. You either didn't recognize it or didn't care. And now you have, and you do care, so you don't know what the hell to do. Like now, with the hot brunette."

"Her name is Carolina."

"That's right. Carolina. So Carolina dumped you."

Maybe she had. He'd never been with a woman he liked enough to care whether she wanted to see him again or not. He searched his memory to try and remember if any of the women he'd dated in the past had ever given him any signals about not wanting to see him again.

Maybe there had been a few in his past, and he just hadn't read the signals. Nothing like being self-aware.

But with Carolina, he had no idea. He dragged his fingers through his hair. "I don't know, Trick. With the road trip, I haven't had a chance to talk to her. But she does want to see me. She left me a voice mail."

"That's a good sign then, right?"

"It's about the modeling thing for her fashion line."

"Oh." Trick slapped him on the back. "Start there. If you like her, it at least puts you in front of her."

"I guess. I don't know. Women are a lot of work."

Trick stood and grinned. "But so much fun to play with."

THIRTEEN

CAROLINA FINISHED UP SOME PAPERWORK AND LOOKED at her phone, answering a few text messages and emails.

She cleared several off her phone, leaving the one she'd gotten from Drew three days ago.

Out-of-town games. Back on Friday. Will call you.

Terse. Noncommittal. And decidedly not warm or friendly.

Then again, she hadn't exactly told him she'd missed him in her voice mail, or that she'd had a great time that night they'd spent together. Her voice mail had been cool and professional. So what had she expected in return?

She set her phone aside and went back to her paperwork, wrinkling her nose at the prospect. Design was fun. It fired her blood and fueled her excitement. The accounting and paperwork and everything else that went into starting up her business? Not so much fun. She had accountants and lawyers to handle the finances and legalities, but she was the CEO of Carolina Designs, and as such, it was up to her to go over every detail, including the drudge work she didn't enjoy.

After two hours of poring over numbers, she was satisfied they were on track.

Her phone buzzed.

Drew.

She picked it up and pushed the button.

"Hi, Drew."

"Hey, yourself. How's it going?"

"Busy. How about you?"

"Finally back in town."

"Away games?"

"So, you haven't been watching?"

"I'm sorry. I've been a little distracted lately. How did it go?"

"Buzz me up and I'll tell you."

"You're downstairs?"

"Yeah."

She rolled her eyes and headed to the door. "What if I hadn't been here?" She pressed the buzzer.

"Then I'd have gone out to dinner alone. Hanging up now."

And now he expected her to just drop everything and go to dinner with him? That was ballsy. And more than a little annoying.

She opened the door and waited for him to show up, which he did a minute later, looking gorgeous as always in relaxed jeans and a navy blue peacoat. He even wore a scarf. Damn, but the man was infuriating, attractive as hell and even worse, he dressed well.

Other than his arrogant attitude, she had nothing to pick apart.

He stepped in and looked around, zeroing in on her coffee table. "Paperwork explosion?"

"Something like that. Would you like to take your coat off?"

"No. I'm starving. I thought maybe you'd want to get dinner."

"I'm kind of busy. And it's eight thirty."

His lips curved. "You're always busy. So you ate already?"

"I did. Hours ago."

"That's fine. I'll just go grab something."

"No. Don't leave. I can fix you something." He was here and she didn't want him to leave. She wanted to get him in her clothes and back out of her apartment again.

He cocked a brow. "You cook?"

"I cook."

"Great." He took off his coat and hung it up, then followed her into the kitchen.

"What would you like?"

"I don't know. How about some eggs?"

She wrinkled her nose. "I hate eggs. I don't even keep them in the house."

"That's like . . . un-American, Carolina. Everyone likes eggs."

"No, everyone doesn't. I don't."

"Fine. What do you have?"

"How about some chicken? I made it for dinner and have some left."

"That'll work."

She took out the chicken and rice she'd baked earlier and warmed it in the microwave.

"Something to drink?"

"Water would be fine."

He made his way into the kitchen and came up beside her as she prepped the plate.

"This looks good. Thanks for fixing it for me."

"It's no trouble."

She sat at the table with him while he ate. Or, rather, while he wolfed down the meal in what seemed like less than five minutes.

"Hungry?" she asked.

He laid down his fork and wiped his mouth with the napkin.

"Starving. It was a long flight and they don't feed you shit on the plane." He took the plate to the sink, rinsed it and put it in the dishwasher. "Thank you again for this. I feel human again."

"You're welcome."

He downed the glass of water and refilled it, then came back to sit next to her at the table.

"How was your road trip?"

"Long. Painful. We lost three games. It sucked."

"I'm sorry."

He shrugged. "It's over. We'll regroup. And we have several home games now. That'll help."

"Will it?"

"Yeah. The home crowd always motivates us to do better."

"I hope so."

"You should come to a game or two."

She leaned back in the chair. "And you think that would help you win?"

"I know it would."

She laughed. "I doubt that, but I'll see what I can do."

"Bring Stella. I'm sure she'd like to see a game."

"That's probably true, but she's busy getting ready for a show. I'll check with her and see if she's available."

He looked around her apartment. "How's the work going?"

"Good. I've gotten a lot done, which was why I called you. I'd like you to try on a few things."

"Okay." He pushed back the chair and stood. "Where do you want me?"

She tilted her head back and looked at him. Ridiculously, her first thought in response to that question was, in her bed.

She shook that off and stood. "We need to head over to my work studio. That's where all the clothes are."

"All right."

They put on their coats and headed downstairs to hail a taxi. It was a brisk night, cloudy and overcast, with the threat of freezing rain forecast. Carolina was cold and the taxi's heater wasn't exactly in working order. She shivered.

"You cold?" Drew asked.

"A little."

"Come over here." He pulled her over and put his arm around her.

She wanted to resist, wanted to keep that line of distance and professionalism between them, but who was she kidding? She was freezing, and Drew's body was warm. She snuggled in closer.

"Better?" he asked, putting his other arm around the front of her.

"Much. Thank you."

As soon as the chill wore off, they arrived at the building.

Damn. She dug into her purse to pay the driver, but Drew had already taken out his wallet.

"Please let me pay. I'm asking you to do this for me."

He gave her a look. "Are we going to have this conversation again?"

The driver gave them an exasperated stare, as if he wanted them out of his cab so he could go grab his next fare.

"Apparently not."

"Good. Then let's go."

She shook her head and dug for her keys to enter the building, then led Drew onto the elevator to the tenth floor where her studio was located.

She flipped on the lights.

"Wow," Drew said as he made his way inside. "You have a lot of space here."

"I need it for all the work we do." She slipped off her coat and wandered the room, turning on lights and heading toward the racks of clothes.

She studied him, then the clothing, already deciding the more formal wear was out. Suits just didn't, well, suit his physique. She went to the rack and started pulling clothes.

"This one. Definitely this. I want to see you in these pants and this shirt." She started throwing clothes on the table, then stopped and stared at him. "Don't just stand there. Strip."

"I love when a woman talks dirty."

She rolled her eyes and went back to the rack. When she turned around, Drew was pulling off his shirt. Her gaze may have lingered a bit on his abs while his shirt covered his head.

And she might have sighed in pure feminine appreciation.

He flipped the button on his jeans, and she found herself staring. She caught the curve of his lips.

"Are you sure we're just trying on clothes, or is this some nefarious plan to get me naked so you can sex me up on your worktable?"

As soon as he'd said it, visuals of climbing on top of him and riding him on her oversize worktable filled her mind.

"Of course not."

"Good. Because I'd like to bend you over that window seat and take you from behind."

Her gaze immediately shot to the window. "Seriously? At the window? Where people could see us?"

"Come on, Lina. Living dangerously is half the fun."

She could already feel him behind her, pounding into her while she planted her hands on the window seat, wondering who'd be looking in from outside.

Heat flared through her body. She pushed it aside.

"That's not going to happen."

"Too bad. Just the thought of it made my dick hard."

He shrugged out of his jeans, his erection very evident against his boxer briefs.

"Well . . . unharden it."

He laughed. "Kind of difficult since it's all I can think about now."

It was all she could think about, too, damn him. She made an about-turn. "I'm going to get clothes. You work on that problem."

"So, you want to watch me jack off?"

She pivoted in a hurry. "No. Absolutely not."

"Your cheeks are pink. I'll bet you'd like to see that."

"Dammit, Drew, I didn't bring you here to have sex with you. Now get serious about this."

"Oh, I'm very serious, Lina."

She stared at him—at his face this time, to let him know just how not funny she thought he was being.

"Okay, fine." He stared at the ceiling.

"Now what are you doing?"

"Counting ceiling tiles."

She tapped her foot and waited, trying not to stare at his cock. It took about a minute, but he finally nodded. "Okay, let's play dress-up."

She took the first outfit out of the garment bag. She'd chosen a pair of workout pants and a tight-fitting T-shirt. He put them on.

"Shoes?"

"I have some. Hang on." She started into the other room, then stopped. "Oh, I need your size."

He told her, then she dashed in and came out with shoes. He put them on.

"Now, walk," she said.

"Walk, where?"

"Back and forth, like you'd be walking on the runway."

"How?"

Of course. He was a guy and had likely never seen a fashion show. "Like this." She demonstrated, walking the length of the room, pivoting, then walking back.

He smiled. "You have a great ass."

She rolled her eyes. "Now you do the same."

"I hope you don't expect me to walk all girlie."

"I don't. I expect you to walk like a man."

He slid his hand into the pocket and took a stroll.

God, he was a natural. Some models took years to perfect a walk like that. Drew took seconds to head down the room, stop, turn, and head back.

Women would be falling at his feet.

And even better, the outfit looked magnificent on him. He was tall, lean, with chiseled looks that would serve him well on the runway.

Or in a magazine.

Or on a billboard.

He was perfect for her line.

"How did I do?"

"Great. Stand there for a second." She ran and grabbed her notebook and took a photo of him in the clothes. "Now put this set on." She handed him the next outfit. He undressed, put it on, and did the same walk. She made notes and took photos while he tried on six different outfits.

He wore them all incredibly well. And didn't complain once about being bored or irritated.

"Thank you for doing this," she said as he climbed out of the last outfit.

"We're done already?"

"Yes. Why? Did you enjoy it? Thinking of hanging up your skates and becoming a model?"

He laughed. "Not on your life. But for you, I don't mind."

He'd been so great about this. Even the professional models hated trying on clothes. Dressing them in an outfit and sending them down a runway at a packed show, fine. That's what they were paid for. But they found fittings tiresome.

"You were awesome."

He stepped toward her. "So does that mean I get some kind of reward?"

"Uh, like what?"

He wrapped an arm around her and tugged her close. "I was thinking we could go make out on the window seat."

"And I think you can get dressed now."

Surprisingly, he let go of her and took a step back. "Okay, if that's what you really want."

The feel of his rock-hard body against hers made her want him.

And then he'd let go of her. So easily. Shockingly, actually, as she watched him climb into his jeans.

She was surprised by her disappointment. "Seriously? You're getting dressed?"

He looked up at her. "Isn't that what you want?"

"Yes. No. I mean, yes, of course. We should go."

"What do you want, Carolina?" he asked, his jeans still unzipped, hanging on his hips and making him look sexier than he did when he was standing there in his briefs. She could sketch him, just like that, the hint of his hipbone shadowed by the denim . . .

God, she was insane. Drew did this to her. Somehow this was all his fault.

"I need to get back to work. Make some adjustments to the clothing, line out the models."

He walked over toward the door. Confused, she frowned. He wasn't fully dressed yet. What was he doing?

When the lights went out, she was disoriented.

"Drew?"

"I'm right here." He whispered, his body coming up to nestle behind hers. He wrapped his arms around her, then kissed her neck.

She shivered, closed her eyes, and tilted her head to the side, giving him access. Maybe it was seeing him mostly unclothed, or seeing him in her clothes. Maybe it was his cooperative spirit and the way he'd given himself over to modeling for her.

She didn't know, and right now, right here, in the dark, with his body so close to hers, she stopped questioning it, stopped questioning herself. She only wanted Drew, only wanted his lips gliding along the column of her throat, pulling her sweater aside to nip at her shoulder.

She shuddered, and when he walked them forward, toward the window, her body pulsed with excitement.

"I've been thinking about you—about this window seat—since we walked in here tonight."

He raised her sweater, spreading his hand across her stomach. Ripples of desire quivered throughout her body.

"I missed you while I was gone, Lina." He whipped her around and cupped her chin, then kissed her, a searing hot kiss she felt through every nerve ending. She wanted more, wanted to be closer to him. She leaned into him, tunneled her fingers into his hair and moved her body against his.

When he groaned and cupped her butt, she knew she wanted him inside her. She'd missed him. That one night together—the night she thought would be the last time between them—hadn't been enough.

She pulled back. "We could go back to my place."

He smiled at her, a dark, dangerous smile that thrilled her. "Where's your sense of adventure, Lina?"

"Uh, back in my apartment? In my bedroom?"

He laughed and turned her back around. "Look out the window. No one can see us. It's dark in here. But you can look down at them."

He popped the button on her jeans and drew her zipper down. His hand was warm as he slid it inside.

Her breath caught as he slipped his hand under her panties, cupping her sex.

"You're wet, Lina."

"Yes."

"Do you want me to make you come?"

How could she not when she was a tight knot of nerve endings ready to burst?

"Yes."

Arousal beat a furious dance, her pulse pounding as he tucked a finger inside her and rubbed the heel of his hand against her clit.

He cupped her breast over her sweater, caressing her nipple as he continued to pump his finger and roll his hand over the bud of her clit. The sensations were maddening. She thrust her sex against his hand, gripping his wrist to help him find the rhythm she needed.

"Your pussy grips my finger," he said, flicking her ear with his tongue. "Tight, hot." He thrust into her. "Makes me want my cock inside you, Lina. I want you bent over so I can watch it go in and out of you."

His words, spoken in the darkness while he was behind her, only fueled the fire within her that raged nearly out of control. She was so close, hovering a breath's whisper near the edge of falling.

"Come for me, Lina."

His words were a heady caress, tantalizing her, making her tighten and reach for the climax she knew was right there waiting for her. And when he gently rode her clit with his hand, then tucked another finger inside her, the rush of orgasm took her breath. She laid her head back against his shoulder and rode it out, moaning as he held her tightly and she rolled with the waves of euphoria that rocked her senseless.

He waited for her to come down, his fingers still gently sliding in and out of her, taking her up that stepladder of coiled need and fierce desire. He pressed against her, his erection profoundly reminding her of where she wanted to go next—where they'd go together.

She wasn't nearly finished with him. She wanted him inside her.

"Yes," was all she managed before she heard the rustle of his jeans as they hit the floor. He drew her jeans and panties down to her knees, then bent her over so her hands rested on the window seat.

She heard the tearing of a condom wrapper, smiling and also relieved that he'd thought to bring one.

He smoothed his hands over the globes of her butt, then she felt the warmth of his lips there.

"You have a magnificent ass, Carolina."

She took a deep breath.

"And I'm going to enjoy watching it while I fuck you."

He swept his hands over her butt, then slid his hand between her thighs, cupping her sex.

"Yes. Touch me like that."

"You want me to make you come again?"

She could, if he continued to caress her clit in that gentle back and forth motion. But this time, she wanted to release with him.

"I want you inside me."

With his hands on her hips, he eased into her. The sensation of his cock swelling inside her was overwhelming.

"Look outside, Lina. Do you think they can see us?"

"No."

"What would you think if they could?"

Breathless, she rose up and braced her hands on the window, giving him deeper access to her. "I don't care."

Drew laid one hand on the window above her and thrust into her. "Good. Because this is just about you and me, in the dark. I want you to feel me."

He withdrew partway, then slid back in. Her pussy tightened

and she felt every glorious inch of him. And when he reached around and found her clit, it was a burst of pleasure that made her whimper. She both hated and loved that he made her feel so needy, so desperate for this orgasm, but the feel of him, coupled with his fingers stroking her was like nothing she could do on her own.

She wanted this. With him and only him.

She arched, pushing against his cock. "More."

He grasped her hand and dragged them both down, bending her from the waist so he could plunge deeper, never once losing the rhythm he'd found on her clit.

"You're close," he said. "I can feel your pussy gripping me."

She laid her head on her arm, her body and mind lost in the sensation of Drew driving into her, of the way his fingers danced over her sex. She immersed herself in the sounds of their lovemaking, lost herself in his warm breath on her neck, the scent of sex filling the air around them.

"Oh. Oh, Drew. I'm going to come."

He strummed her clit faster. "That's it. Squeeze my cock. Make me come with you, Lina."

His words were the last she needed to crest the wave. She cried out and shattered, her entire body rocking as her climax shook her. Drew groaned and pumped fast into her, kissing her neck as he orgasmed along with her.

Her legs were shaking. Without Drew's tight hold on her, she wasn't certain she could have stood upright. He pressed kisses along her shoulder and back, the aftermath just as sweet as the act itself.

When he withdrew, he turned her around and cupped her face, then kissed her, a long, slow deep kiss that curled her toes and warmed her from the inside out.

"There's a bathroom down the hall," she said.

She led him to the bathroom and they cleaned up and straightened their clothes. Drew hit the lights and helped her put all the clothing back on hangers and racks. Then they grabbed some water out of the refrigerator and took a seat at one of the empty tables.

She was surprised and a little touched that he dragged her chair right next to his and pulled her legs onto his lap. Some men weren't into being close after sex.

She was learning a lot about Drew.

He looked around her studio. "You've made a lot of progress. Or maybe you already had all this stuff here before."

"We had some. But we've been working hard the past few weeks. With Christmas coming, we're going to be faced with some downtime. I wanted to get ahead, because we'll be pushing full steam after the holidays."

"What? You're giving your people time off for the holidays? No playing Scrooge and forcing them to work in an office with no coal to heat their frozen little fingers that are stiff and sore from all that sewing?"

"Funny. Yes, they get the holidays off. I'm not that driven."

"Yes, you are. If you had your way you'd work straight through Christmas and New Year's. Except your mother would drive up here and have the Secret Service drag you by the hair and make you come home with her."

She laughed at that. "You're probably right. I might have been allowed to skip Thanksgiving with the family, but no way in hell will I be permitted to skip Christmas, too."

"I can see that about your mom."

"I'm sure yours is the same."

"Actually, not so much. My parents are going on a cruise for the holidays."

She stared at him. "Really? Where to?"

"Some Mediterranean thing or the Greek Isles or something

like that. They've been talking about it for months. I can't believe she convinced my dad to go."

She crossed her arms. "Your father isn't one for cruises?"

"It's hard to get my dad to leave Oklahoma. But Mom has been after him to slow down and take a vacation for years. This is the year for them, and he's the one who suggested it, surprisingly. Mom jumped all over it before he changed his mind."

Carolina smiled. "That's sweet. So what are you going to do for Christmas?"

He shrugged. "I don't know. I'll hang around here, I guess. No reason to go home since no one else will be there."

She knew she shouldn't say anything, but it tugged at her that Drew would be spending Christmas alone. "Come home with me."

He arched a brow. "What?"

"You heard me. Gray would love to see you, and so would my parents. Come and spend Christmas with us at the ranch."

"Seriously. You do realize you just invited me to spend the holidays with you."

"Yes. Well, with Gray and with the entire family. Not just with me."

He smiled at the qualifier. "Okay."

She wasn't sure what can of worms she'd just opened, but the idea of Drew spending Christmas alone didn't sit well with her.

And now he was going to spend the holidays with her. And her family.

That should be interesting.

FOURTEEN

DREW HADN'T BEEN TO GRAY'S FAMILY'S RANCH IN Oklahoma since over a year ago, in the summer, when Gray had invited him to come for a family barbecue. It had been the first time he'd seen Carolina in a long time.

She'd given him an icy chill and he'd known then she still harbored resentment over what had happened between them in college.

Now, though, it looked like things were beginning to thaw between them.

He hoped so. He liked spending time with her. She was smart and ambitious. And beautiful and sexy and different from any woman he'd been with before.

Now that he was going to be spending time with her—and with Gray—he was going to have to walk a fine line, because Gray didn't know what had gone down between Drew and Carolina all those years ago in college. Gray didn't know how much Drew had hurt Carolina.

And Gray sure as hell didn't know what was going on between Carolina and him now.

He probably should have had a conversation with Carolina before he arrived at the ranch, discussed how much, if anything, to tell Gray about the two of them. Big brothers had a tendency to be overprotective toward their little sisters. And Gray of all people knew about Drew's reputation with women. But he had to know Drew would never hurt Carolina.

Or, at least, wouldn't hurt her again like he had before.

He dragged his fingers through his hair as he sat in the back of the car Carolina had arranged to bring him from the airport to the ranch.

The Preston Ranch name greeted him as they reached the gates. Drew took note of the black SUV parked there. They stopped and he had to give the Secret Service agent his ID before they were allowed to pass through.

Gray was outside waiting for him when the car pulled in front of the huge house.

He grinned when he got out. "I'm so glad you're here."

Drew smiled and gave his best friend a quick hug. "Yeah, well, it's your sister's fault. She didn't want me to be alone for the holidays. You know how women are about that stuff."

"If I'd known your parents were going on a cruise, I'd have invited you myself. Come on inside."

He thanked the driver for the ride and grabbed his bags, following Gray up the stone steps and inside. The place was just as he remembered it from the last time he'd been here—high ceilings, polished wood floors, and so many rooms a person could get lost and never find their way out.

The only difference was that now Secret Service were all over the place because Gray and Carolina's father was the vice president of the United States.

"You can leave your bags by the stairs. Someone will take them up to your room."

"Okay, thanks. How do you like having the suits with guns and earplugs hanging around?" Drew asked as Gray led him into the kitchen.

Gray laughed. "Hey, as long as they're not following me around, I'm fine with it. And they keep the press away, so it works for me."

"I'm sure it does. Where's Evelyn?"

Gray grabbed a beer out of the refrigerator and held another one up for Drew. Drew nodded, and Gray handed it to him.

"Out doing some Christmas shopping with my mom and Carolina. Carolina flew in late last night and Mom dragged her out of bed this morning to hit the city for all-day shopping."

"Bet she loved that."

Gray shrugged and took a swallow of beer. They took seats at the table near the back door. "I don't know. They were going to have breakfast, then start shopping as soon as the mall opened, and according to Mom, all the way through dinner, so we aren't supposed to expect them back until later tonight."

Drew grimaced. "Better them than me."

"Amen to that. How was your flight?"

"It was good. How are things with you and Evelyn?"

"Great. Adjusting to our crazy schedules, but, man, it's going well. She's busy as hell with my dad, of course, and we weren't sure in the beginning how it was all going to work, but we find the time to be together."

"I guess when you're in love, you find a way to make it work."

Gray grinned. "I guess so."

"Where's your dad?"

"In his home office, on the phone, of course. He and I had breakfast this morning that lasted all of twenty minutes before he was pulled away by a phone call."

Drew leaned back in the chair and took a long swallow of beer. "Well, he is kind of a busy guy."

"Yeah, he is. I'm happy for him, though, and for my mom. She's thrilled to be able to push her literacy agenda at the national level, and my dad—well, he's changed. A lot. Surprised the hell out of me, but he's a much better man than he used to be."

"I'm glad the two of you have found common ground."

"Me, too. Life is pretty damned perfect right now. And how about you? You had a few shitty games. At least you started turning it around when you got back to the Garden."

The one thing Drew could always count on from his friends was blunt honesty. Ever since college, when he, Gray, Garrett, and Trevor had roomed together and become friends, they'd always been honest with each other about their shortcomings, especially in sports. When they rocked it, they all gave each other pats on the back. When they sucked, they were the first to tell each other.

"Yeah, we had a lousy road trip. Being home always helps. Of course you wouldn't know about that since you don't really have a home base in auto racing."

"True. So I have to be good everywhere."

Drew laughed. "And humble, too."

"You know it, buddy."

They got up and headed into the living room to sip their beers and watch sports on television.

Gray's dad finally came out and Drew got up to shake his hand.

"Nice to see you, Mr. Vice President."

Mitchell Preston laughed. "You used to call me Mitchell, or Mr. Preston."

"That was before the election, sir."

"I'm not any different now, and I don't expect you to treat me any differently, Drew. You're a guest here for the holidays, so please relax."

"I'll try, sir."

Gray rolled his eyes and nudged his dad. "I'm just going to call you *Dad*."

"Funny. Is anyone hungry? Aideen said she was going to make chicken and fruit salad for lunch."

Drew's stomach grumbled. "That sounds great."

"I'm starving," Gray said.

They had lunch in the kitchen rather than the dining room. Drew couldn't get past the Secret Service hanging around, but the vice president said he was so used to them now he didn't even notice them anymore.

Still, having some dude with a gun looking over your shoulder while you were trying to eat your chicken was a little intimidating. Drew felt like if he gave the vice president the wrong look, he might be wrestled to the ground and carted off in one of those black SUVs.

Gray kept shooting him smirks, too, as if he knew exactly what Drew was thinking.

After lunch, Gray's dad excused himself, saying he had some calls to make and they'd catch up again later.

"Afraid you were going to get shot over lunch?" Gray asked as they headed outside with their iced teas.

"Hey. You might be used to it. I'm not. No wonder you and your sister declined the protection."

Gray shrugged as they took a seat by the pool. It was uncharacteristically warm for December, though there were outdoor heaters, so it was perfect to sit out on the patio.

"We're both adults and it's not like we're minor children of the president. We didn't need the protection, and they offered us the option. I think the Secret Service has better things to do with their time than babysit us."

"True. Though they might enjoy going to all your races."

Gray laughed. "I kind of doubt that. You know the nomadic lifestyle I live. They'd probably hate it. Not much action, and they told us both they didn't consider us to be under any threat of danger, so it's all good."

"Glad to hear it."

"So we've talked a lot about me and what's going on with my life. Tell me about yours. Are you dating?"

This is where Drew could come out and tell Gray about him and Carolina. Not that they were dating, per se. They weren't, really. Or maybe they were. They'd had sex a couple times, a fact that Drew was sure Gray wouldn't want to hear about.

"Not really. Kind of busy with the start of the season, so I haven't had any time."

"You know, you're not getting any younger. You might want to stop going through one woman after another and find one to settle down with."

Drew laughed. "Oh, come on. Just because you've found the love of your life, now you're going to try to get the rest of us to follow you along into a lifetime of happiness?"

Gray smiled and took a long swallow of his iced tea. "Something like that."

"I'll get around to it one of these days."

"You're only saying that because you haven't found the right woman yet."

Or maybe he had. He hadn't ever given much thought to what happily ever after might look like, because for the past years he'd focused only on his career.

But now, he was at a strong place in his career, and he felt settled, at least in that respect. It was his personal life that felt unsettled.

Carolina was the catalyst for that. When she'd popped back into his life, he'd started questioning everything having to do with the "personal" part of the equation. Suddenly, he was seeing how she fit into that part of his life.

Only he knew she would never see it that way. He knew she was only focused on her career, and not on having a relationship with him.

But were the two of them even compatible?

He liked having sex with her. And she was fun to be around.

They were just beginning to get to know each other.

It was too soon to start thinking about that happily ever after.

"You never know when that right woman will walk into your life," Drew said, staring out over the water.

"Spoken by someone who thinks they might have already found her?"

"I didn't say that."

"So far, you haven't said much of anything. We used to talk about women all the time."

Drew cocked a grin. "That was back when we thought of women as conquests. Something to brag about. I'd like to think we've grown up some."

"True. So if you have someone you're not talking about, she must be special."

"Maybe." He was treading treacherous waters here, and he should just shut the hell up before he drowned.

"Then I'll respect that. Let's go play some pool."

Relieved to take that subject off the table, Drew stood. "Now you're talking."

They went into the game room and immersed themselves in pool and darts and watching TV. Even the vice president joined them in a game of pool until Aideen called them for dinner.

They had steak and shrimp with a really damn fine wine. They talked the state of the country with the vice president, along with just about every sport on the map. They probably sat at the table

for a couple of hours. It was the most relaxing and fun dinner Drew
had had in a long time. It was good to catch up with Gray, and it
was great to see him connect and have fun with his dad.

Drew even forgot about the Secret Service guys hanging
around.

"When do your Secret Service guys eat?" he asked the vice
president.

Mitchell laughed. "I don't know. Hey, Paul, when do you eat?"

"We swap off, sir. Gage and I will have dinner when we switch
with Rogers and Bennington at eight p.m."

"Ah. I see. Looking forward to Aideen's steak and shrimp?" the
vice president asked.

"Very much so, sir."

Drew smiled. Very official. And the guy hadn't so much as
moved. He supposed that was a good thing, but he'd bet the guy
noticed every movement around them.

The only time the Secret Service moved was when Mitchell did.
When they finally got up and made their way into the game room
to watch TV, the agents followed. By then, they had swapped out
for another pair. Really, it was confusing. Just statues in black suits.

In fact, when Drew heard the front door, the agents still didn't
move. Though he assumed it was because they'd already been noti-
fied through their earpieces who was entering.

"We're back!" Loretta Preston's voice rang out from the
entryway.

"We're in here, Loretta," Mitchell said, rising to go greet his
wife.

Drew and Gray got up, too, and headed toward the living room,
where an obscene number of packages were being laid down on the
sofas.

"Holy shit, Evelyn. Did you buy out the mall?" Gray went over
and put his arms around his fiancée.

"Seems that way, doesn't it?" Evelyn kissed Gray. "My feet and back are killing me. Your mother is a world-class shopper."

Drew zeroed in on Carolina, who looked sexy in tight jeans, knee-skimming black boots, and a long sweater. She turned and saw him, then smiled. "It's much easier to shop when you have the Secret Service as an escort. It's like the parting of the Red Sea. We had no trouble getting into any of the stores."

Loretta laughed. "That's because the boys always have to clear out the store in advance. Kind of embarrassing, really. It's not like anyone knew we were coming."

"Protocol, ma'am," one of the men said.

Loretta waved her hand. "I know, but still, if I'd thought about it in advance, we could have shopped online. I hated inconveniencing all of those other shoppers."

"Mom, I think all those other shoppers enjoyed getting a glimpse of Phil and Leon's muscles. I don't think they minded at all." Carolina winked at her mother.

"If you say so. Either way, it was such a fun day. And now I'm utterly exhausted." She looped her arm through Mitchell's. "How was your day?"

"Good. Busy. Hung out with the boys for a while."

Loretta turned to Drew. "Oh, Drew, I'm so sorry to be rude." She came up and put her arms around him to give him a hug. "We're so glad you're here."

He hugged her back. "Thank you for having me, Mrs. Preston."

"Loretta. Stop being so formal. We want you to feel at home." She pulled back. "Carolina tells me your parents are off on a cruise for the holidays?"

"Yes, ma'am."

"How lovely for them. I'd love to take a cruise with Mitchell sometime. Please have your mother call me after she gets back. I want to hear all about it."

"I'll be sure to do that. She'd love to talk to you."

"Would you like me to help you carry these packages upstairs?" Mitchell asked.

"Yes, that would be great. My feet are sore and right now I'd love nothing more than to soak in a bubble bath. It's been a long and very taxing day."

Loretta turned to Carolina and Evelyn and hugged them both. "Thank you for spending the day with me. I enjoyed it so much."

"I did, too, Mom," Carolina said, kissing her mother on the cheek.

"Thanks, Mom. You helped me finish up my Christmas shopping," Evelyn said.

"Good night, all," Mitchell said, arms laden with bags as he followed Loretta up the stairs. The agents followed behind them.

Evelyn fell onto the sofa and propped her feet up. "Lord, what an exhausting day."

"I could rub your feet or give you a bubble bath," Gray said, waggling his brows.

Evelyn laughed and patted his leg. "Both are very enticing options. I'll reserve both for later. Right now I'm just enjoying not standing."

"I'm with you on that," Carolina said. She took off her boots and, with a loud groan, pulled her feet up on the sofa. Drew took a spot on the same sofa, but deliberately didn't sit too close to her.

"So shopping was fun?" he asked.

"For us, yes," Carolina said. "For you and Gray it would have been torture. Be thankful you weren't here."

"Hey, I was here, and I was spared," Gray said.

"You were. Your mother suggested I invite you. I said you wanted to spend time with your dad today. See how deeply I love you?" Evelyn batted her lashes at Gray.

"It's obviously true love. And you have my undying gratitude." Gray brushed his lips across Evelyn's.

"Ugh. You two should get a room," Carolina said.

"We have a room. Upstairs, as a matter of fact. And that hot bath your mother mentioned is sounding better and better. I can't believe it's ten thirty."

Drew arched a brow. "Shopping marathon."

"Well, to be fair, we did stop and eat breakfast. And lunch."

"And dinner," Evelyn added. "So we did get to sit down here and there. But still, my future mother-in-law can shop, and once she gets started, she goes and goes. And goes."

Evelyn yawned.

Gray stood and held out his hand. "Come on. Hot bath time for you. Then we'll cuddle up on the bed and watch movies."

"Sounds like a plan." She waved at Drew and Carolina. "Good night you two."

"Night," Carolina said.

"Good night."

Carolina turned to him. "I'm so tired. I should probably head upstairs."

"You probably should. From the looks of all those bags, you have a lot of wrapping to do."

She laughed. "Yes, there's that, too."

"You had a good day?"

"It was great. I don't get to spend a lot of time with my mom, so spending the day catching up with her was fun."

"Good."

"How was your day? What time did you get in?"

"A little before lunch. And my day was fine. I got to kick back with Gray and your dad. We played some pool and watched television. It was nice to relax, especially after a long stretch of games. Plus I got to catch up with Gray."

"I'm glad you had that time together."

"Speaking of your brother . . ."

She frowned. "What about Gray?"

"He doesn't know about you and me. At least I haven't said anything to him."

"Well, he hasn't heard about it from me. That would be . . . complicated."

"Yeah. That's what I was thinking."

"And really, what is there to tell? It's not like we're dating or anything. We're just—"

He gave her a look. "Just what? Fucking?"

Her gaze shot to the stairs. "Drew."

"I could take you out, you know. If you'd let me."

She shook her head. "I don't have time for a relationship."

He let out a short laugh. "Isn't that what we're having? A relationship?"

"No. We're doing exactly as you said." She paused, then whispered—"Fucking."

"Okay. Call it what you want. I just don't want to complicate things by letting Gray know we're doing whatever it is we're doing."

She nodded. "I agree. So you should probably keep your distance while you're here."

He didn't like the direction this conversation was going. "So you want me to just hang out with Gray and ignore you."

He could tell she didn't like it anymore than he did, which made him feel at least a little better.

"I guess that's probably a good idea."

He stood. "Done."

"Where are you going?"

"To bed. I'm tired."

"Oh. Okay."

"You want me to help you upstairs with your bags?"

"No. I've got them." She got up, grabbed her boots and shoved them under her arm, then started wrangling all the shopping bags.

No way was she going to make it in one trip.

He grabbed the majority of them.

"Lead the way. I'll follow."

"All right." She headed up the stairs, Drew a couple steps behind, which gave him a stellar view of her butt encased in those very tight jeans.

Ignore her, huh? Yeah, like that was going to be possible if she kept wearing jeans that looked like they'd been sewn on her ass. His dick twitched just thinking about the other night when he'd had her bent over, his cock sliding in and out of her hot, wet pussy.

And then he went fully hard.

Shit. He swallowed and counted the number of steps up to the second floor, hoping his erection would be gone by then.

No such luck, because Carolina had a natural sway to her hips that made him groan.

She gave him a look over her shoulder. "Are you okay back there?"

"Fine," he said through gritted teeth.

"It's just down the hall here." She'd dropped her voice to a whisper, no doubt not to disturb anyone.

She opened the door to her room and flipped on the lights. It was spacious, with a big bed he could already imagine seeing her naked on.

Which wasn't helping his pounding dick. He needed to erase those thoughts.

He laid the bags down. "Nice room. Has this one always been yours?"

"Yes. And thanks. Is your room okay?"

"It's fine. I don't need much, and my room here is plenty big enough."

"I'm glad. Which one did they put you in?"

He leaned against the wall. "Why? Thinking of paying me a midnight visit?"

She rushed over and pulled him inside, then shut the door. "Why don't you broadcast to the entire family? I thought we agreed we were going to be discreet?"

"Yeah, well, that was before you walked ahead of me up the stairs. He palmed his dick through his jeans, and Carolina's gaze went right there, which only made him rub his erection more.

"Drew." Her tone was a warning, but she looked torn herself.

"I can't help it, Lina. You make me hard."

She shuddered out a breath. "We can't do this."

But she didn't back away, and she didn't open the door for him to leave.

"Okay. We can't do this."

He waited. And she came closer.

"Drew."

He slid his fingers in her hair. "Yeah."

She rose up on her toes and brushed her lips across his. He swept his arm around her back and flipped her, pushing her back against the wall next to the door. Then he kissed her, taking what he'd wanted since she walked in tonight—a deep, soul-shattering kiss, pressing his body full-on against hers, letting her feel what she did to him.

She moaned against his lips and he wrapped his tongue around hers while letting his hand roam along her back and lower to cup her butt. He pulled her in, driving his shaft against her.

He wanted her naked, wanted to sink inside her, the need for her driving his desire to a primal level that left him mindless.

She reached for his shirt and pulled it up. He released her lips and tugged the shirt over his head, then grabbed her sweater, doing the same. He undid the clasp of her bra and removed it, her breasts spilling into his waiting hands. With relentless need, he bent and took each bud into his mouth, sucking until she whimpered, pulling at him, kissing him with the same fevered hunger that drove him.

He stepped back and undid the button on his jeans, kicking his shoes off at the same time he shucked his jeans and boxers to the floor. Carolina was already reaching for his cock, dropping to her knees and putting her mouth on him.

He groaned when she took him between her lips, and as he watched his shaft disappear into her hot, wet mouth, he propped a hand against the wall for support, because his legs shook. He pumped his cock into her mouth, then partly withdrew. She lifted her gaze to his and cupped his balls, gently squeezing as she propelled her lips forward and squeezed his cock between the roof of her mouth and her sweet tongue.

He was going to come if she kept doing that, and he wanted inside her pussy. He pulled out and lifted her, undoing her jeans and helping her as she wriggled out of them.

"I'm going to fuck you up against this wall," he said.

"I have condoms." She dashed over to her bedside and reached into the drawer, pulling one out and hurrying back.

He smiled at the thought of her bringing condoms. Maybe she'd wanted this as much as he had. "So did I." He took the condom from her and sheathed himself, then pushed her back against the wall, lifting her arms over her head and capturing her wrists. He took her mouth in a hot, sweet kiss as he spread her legs and buried himself inside her.

She bit down on his lip when he entered her. He tasted blood, and that fueled the fire that raged within him. He needed her, wanted her like he'd wanted no other woman before her. That need drove him as he pumped into her, hot and fiery as he ground against her, listening to her rapid breaths, feeling the way she arched against him and begged for more.

He released her hands and grabbed her butt as she slid her fingers into his hair and yanked on it, hard. The pain fired his pleasure and his lips slid across hers, both of them in a frenzied haze of passion and need as he rolled his hips across hers, giving her the friction she needed to come.

And when she moaned against his lips and her pussy tightened around his cock, he knew she was climaxing. He thrust hard and fast into her and his orgasm rocketed through him. He met her cries with groans of his own as he emptied into her, sweat pouring down his back as his lips stayed molded with hers and he rode out this incredible climax that left him spent and breathless.

He held on to Carolina, bracing her against the wall with the last ounce of strength he had left. They were glued together with sweat, Carolina's hands roaming over his back while he kissed her neck, both of them sawing out breaths as if they'd run a marathon.

"You okay?" he asked.

"Yes. God, Drew, what you do to me."

"Yeah." He pulled back and rested his forehead against hers. "So, anyway, I guess I'll ignore you while I'm here."

She let out a soft laugh. "That's a good plan."

They disentangled and he went into her bathroom to straighten up and get dressed. She followed him in, still naked, her skin marred from his kisses and the rough way he'd handled her.

He touched the marks on her butt and her shoulder. "I'm sorry. I was a little rough."

She sighed, then smiled and pressed a soft kiss to his neck. "I don't recall complaining."

He pulled her against him and kissed her, this time gently. His dick quivered to life again. "I'd better get out of here or I'll still be here in the morning."

She laid her hand on his chest. "Yes, you should."

"Good night, Lina."

She leaned against the sink and gave him a look he couldn't quite fathom. Regret, or wistfulness?

"Good night, Drew."

FIFTEEN

IT WAS A GOOD THING THAT TODAY WAS CHRISTMAS Eve, and Carolina was too busy wrapping and baking and doing a million other things, so she didn't have time to think about last night with Drew.

So much for maintaining their distance and keeping things impersonal between them.

She ached from last night. Parts of her were tender. And she wanted more.

How was she going to survive the next two days with him in the house? How was she going to keep her family—mainly Gray—from finding out about the two of them?

She wasn't certain how Gray would react if he knew there was something going on between her and Drew. Gray and Drew went way back, all the way to their wild partying days at college. Gray knew Drew as well as anyone, knew how Drew was with women. There was something about guys not wanting their best friends to date their little sisters, some unwritten code or honor or some ridiculous man-code bullshit like that.

"Is it safe for me to enter?"

She looked up from her spot in the family room, where she had a wide swath of wrapping paper and shopping bags. She smiled at Evelyn. "I wrapped your presents an hour ago. Come on in."

"Great. I've been wrapping for two hours straight and I needed a break."

"Ditto." Carolina stood and stretched. "Have you seen my mom?"

"Yes. She hightailed it out of here about an hour ago with your dad. They were going to a neighboring ranch—something about seeing some old friends?"

"Oh, right. The Nelsons. How about we hit the kitchen for some tea?"

"That sounds like a great idea. I don't know about you, but my back is killing me."

Carolina laughed as they crossed the foyer and went down the hall toward the kitchen. "Mine, too. And did you notice when the word 'wrapping' is mentioned, all the men are suddenly scarce?"

"Yes. Gray said something about them going to the lodge to play golf since the weather is so nice today. I think they were just trying to escape having to wrap presents."

"Or maybe they're doing last-minute shopping."

They entered the kitchen and Carolina poured two glasses of iced tea.

"God, I hope not. I'd like to think Gray had the presence of mind to have done his shopping weeks ago."

They took a seat at the table. "Seriously, Evelyn? He's a man. They never think ahead."

Evelyn sighed. "You're right. They're probably at the mall now, along with every other guy in town, with that deer in the headlights look they all get because they've waited until the last minute to do their shopping."

"Which means you'll get a toaster for Christmas. Or gloves."

"Or kitchen towels or something equally hideous. Ugh."

Carolina laughed. "Which makes me glad I don't have a man in my life. See? This way I'm not disappointed in gifts."

"What about Drew? Surely he'll give you something."

"Why would Drew get me anything?"

"Because the two of you are in a relationship?"

Uh-oh. "No we're not. He's only here because I found out his family wasn't going to be around for the holidays. And of course, because he's Gray's friend."

Evelyn gave her a look. "Honey, this is me you're talking to, not your brother. I see the way he looks at you, and the return looks you give him. You might be able to fool your mother and your brother, but I've had the hots for a guy before—your brother, as it was. I know when a woman is lusting after a man, and you are definitely in full-on lust mode."

Defeated, she leaned back in the chair. "And I was hoping not to be so blatantly obvious about it."

"Oh, it's not obvious. At least not to everyone. You and Drew did a fine job last night of appearing like you weren't even breathing the same air. But you smiled at him, and then he smiled at you, and I just so happened to be looking at both of you when that happened. Oh, the chemistry between the two of you is explosive."

She sighed. "It is, isn't it?"

"And you two share a history, if I recall. From back in college?"

"Yes. And not a good history, either."

"I remember that somewhat contentious reunion last year here at the ranch. So you've forgiven him for how he treated you back then?"

Carolina shared Drew's apology, and what had transpired between them since then.

"It sounds to me like he's been trying to make amends."

"It seems that way, but my career right now is vitally important to me. I don't really want to get involved with anyone, least of all Drew."

Evelyn nodded. "I understand. The timing of Gray and I getting involved couldn't have been worse. But love happens when you least expect it to."

"Love? We're not anywhere close to being in love. This is just lust and an incredibly hot sexual attraction. It'll burn itself out in due course."

Evelyn gave her a lopsided smile. "Sure it will, honey."

"Seriously, Evelyn. That's all it is. I wanted him for so long back in college. And now that he's reentered my stratosphere and seems genuinely interested in me, it just seems natural for me to want to take advantage, you know? There's nothing else to it. We're so cosmically different in every respect. He's a hotshot athlete, and my future is in fashion. We have nothing in common other than the sex."

"Right. And Gray and I were so well matched, what with me being in politics and him being in auto racing." Evelyn gave her a pointed look.

"That's totally different."

Evelyn arched a brow. "Is it? People have fallen in love and have found a forever together with much less than what they do for a living as a foundation, Carolina."

"I have zero intention of falling in love with Drew. So I'd appreciate it if you didn't tell your brother about this. I wouldn't want anything to come between Gray and Drew's friendship."

"Of course. Anything you tell me stays strictly between the two of us, as long as it doesn't directly harm Gray. And as far as I'm concerned, your relationship with Drew is none of his business."

Carolina laid her hand over Evelyn's. "Thank you."

"Just be careful of your heart, Carolina. You might be surprised what could happen between you and Drew."

"Honestly? I'd be very surprised if we're still seeing each other after Christmas. Other than him being involved in my fashion line, we're just using each other for sex."

Evelyn laughed. "Well, at least enjoy that part."

Carolina smiled. "I intend to."

DREW AND GRAY RETURNED SEVERAL HOURS LATER, their faces windburned. Obviously, they *had* been at the lodge playing golf.

"Was it cold?" Carolina asked as they grabbed a beer and took seats with her and Evelyn in the living room.

She'd finished up her wrapping and all the gifts now sat under the tree.

"Nah. Weather was in the sixties today. Just a little windy," Drew said.

Gray grinned as he pulled Evelyn in closer. "Perfect day for golf. There were surprisingly a lot of people there. You'd think the place would be deserted, since it's Christmas Eve."

"No doubt all those men trying to hide out from last-minute shopping or wrapping duties," Evelyn said with a nudge to Gray's side.

"Ouch. And hey, I did my shopping weeks ago. If you'd check under the tree, you'll see there are gifts for you."

"Hopefully none of those gifts are toasters."

Gray frowned. "Why the hell would I get you a toaster?"

Evelyn looked at Carolina, who laughed. "Why, indeed."

Carolina's mom and dad showed up about four. "Sorry we're late, but we had such a nice time catching up with the Nelsons. And they're coming over for the party tonight."

Carolina stood. "I guess that means we should go get dressed."

"Yes, we should, since the first guests will start arriving by six," her mother said.

Christmas Eve had always been a special event at the Preston Ranch. Aunts, uncles, and cousins were going to be in attendance. Neighbors were invited, too, and since this year her father was the vice president, local media and special guests of the state would also be allowed in, though only briefly, to catch up on what Mitchell and Loretta Preston were doing to celebrate the holidays in their home state.

Which meant everyone was required to dress up. The house had been exceptionally decorated, though that was the norm every year, anyway. Carolina went upstairs, took a shower and did her hair and makeup, then selected a dress she'd made herself, a black cap-sleeved cocktail dress with a curved neckline. She wore her grandmother's pearls and a pair of slinky silver heels. Conservative for a family party and for the daughter of the vice president, yet still fashionable.

The caterers had come in while Carolina had been upstairs getting ready. Hors d'oeuvres were set up, waiters and waitresses were milling about, and champagne was flowing.

She'd spent so much time immersing herself in work, that this was a nice interlude. Relaxing with her family and getting caught up on what everyone had been doing was a nice way to push work out of the way for a while.

And spending time with Drew wasn't a bad thing, either, though her talk with Evelyn earlier was worrisome.

She wasn't getting involved with Drew. She knew—and she was certain he felt the same way—that this was just fun and games. Just sex, and nothing more. They shared a mutual attraction that was going to burn itself out in a short period of time. Drew was the kind of guy who had a different woman every month. She'd read about him, had kept tabs on him over the years. He never had a serious relationship, and it seemed as if there were always reports about a new woman in his life, and never anything serious.

He didn't do relationships, which suited her just fine, because she didn't either. She focused solely on her career, and so did he. In that respect, they were perfect for each other.

She was already practicing in her head what she'd say to him after Christmas. He'd be on board. In fact, he likely had the same speech. After all, he was probably used to breaking up with women. He'd appreciate her practicality.

She turned and caught sight of a dark shape at the top of the stairs. Her breath caught as she recognized Drew, in a black suit that was most definitely not off-the-rack. It was cut too sharply, fit him too perfectly. His white shirt was crisp and tailored, the red tie a classic accompaniment for the season.

She inhaled and held her breath as he descended, not at all used to seeing him like this.

And she thought he wasn't right for a suit? Dear God, he looked amazing, especially with the slight scruff across his jaw. A little sexy and daring to go with the classiness of the attire.

One of the waiters came by bearing a tray of champagne. As Drew came up beside her, he scooped up two glasses and handed one to her, then smiled.

"You look stunning," he said. "One of your designs?"

"Yes."

"The way it fits you is sinful."

"Thank you. It's supposed to be family-appropriate and conservative."

"Babe, nothing that hugs your body like that could ever be considered conservative."

She couldn't help but be pleased that he noticed. "Thank you. Again. And you look amazing."

"Thanks."

"Where did you get the suit?"

"I've had it for a while. Occasionally I have to play dress up, and the New York media can be tough. Plus, I dated a model once and she told me off-the-rack was shit and I needed to have a suit made for me."

Carolina laughed. "It's good that you can be taught about fashion."

"I pick up things here and there."

She could tell from the way he dressed. Even in casual clothes, he always looked good. "You'll make a fine model for my line."

"Good to know I won't embarrass you."

She took a sip of champagne. "Not with that body you won't."

"I see how it is. You're just using me for my model physique. You don't appreciate my brain or my superior hockey talents."

"I do appreciate how smart you are."

He laughed. "Come on, gorgeous. Introduce me to all the bigwigs here."

She loved that he was comfortable in his own skin, that he wasn't intimidated by the large crowd that had started to gather, including a doubled Secret Service team.

By nine p.m. the house was packed with people, many of whom Carolina knew, some she didn't. But her parents, of course, knew everyone in attendance, and Carolina had no problem introducing herself to those she didn't know. There were television personalities who'd finagled an invitation, as well as throngs of media willing to give up their Christmas Eve to be in attendance at the vice president's personal residence.

She'd long ago lost sight of Drew as she was called away for family photographs and then an interview about her new fashion line, which she was glad to do. Anything to bring attention to her work was a good thing, even though she was asked the typical questions.

"Miss Preston, with your family money, connections, and of

course, now that your father is the vice president, do you think it will be difficult for your fashion line to be taken seriously?"

"Miss Preston, do you believe the fashion world will have a hard time believing someone of your background is all that serious about fashion, given that many will think you've bought your way into your own line?"

"Miss Preston, how much influence has the Preston name, money, and the vice president had on launching your line?"

She had to smile and grit her teeth through all the insulting questions, and explain that she went to college and majored in fashion design, that it was her dream to be a fashion designer long before her father ever became the vice president, and that she had worked for several designers as an apprentice, seamstress, and assistant designer before she ever decided to launch her own line, and that she may have the financial resources, but she believed she also had the talent to design. And that come Fashion Week, she hoped she'd be able to prove that.

What she wanted to tell them all was that she'd paid her dues, she'd worked hard, and she'd proven herself a capable designer. She also wanted to tell them all to shove it, but she had to be polite. The media could make or break a fashion designer, and being a rude bitch wouldn't gain her any favors.

When she finally managed to pull herself away, she found the nearest waiter and grabbed another glass of champagne. She headed down the hall into one of the private rooms off-limits to guests. After two rather large swallows and several deep breaths, she had managed to calm down, though not nearly enough.

"Wow, those were tough questions."

Drew.

She nodded. "Yes, but not the first time they've been asked, and probably not the last time, either."

"They were insulting."

"The media always feel they're entitled."

Drew nodded. "I get that a lot, especially after a loss. They shove a camera in your face after you've played what you think is the lousiest game of your life and then they ask you how you feel? How the hell do they think you're going to feel? You feel like shit. And then they either want you to talk about why your previously awesome game play has suddenly disappeared, or they want you to throw one of your teammates under the bus. It's a no-win scenario with the media. Even if you win and are on top of your game, they find something to criticize."

He led her over to one of the sofas and sat her down. She took another couple sips of champagne. "I have three strikes against me before I ever launch my line. One, I'm the daughter of the currently sitting vice president, which makes me high profile. Two, I'm a Preston, and I come from money, which will lead everyone to believe I staffed out the creation of this line to ghost designers and it will be anything but original. Three, because I worked for David Faber, everyone will be watching what I send down the runway to be sure I haven't stolen any of his designs. Which means I have to fight twice as hard to be taken half as seriously as other designers."

He swept his hand down her back. "It's a lot of pressure on you."

"Yes." She finished off the glass of champagne and laid it on the table in front of her.

"But you're smart, and I've seen your work. You're very talented. And because you've lived in the public eye so long, I think you handle the media very well."

She shifted her gaze to his. "Thank you for that. I appreciate your confidence in me."

Drew leaned back against the sofa. "When I was in college, I struggled. School was tough, the whole studying while playing a sport kicked my ass, and I wasn't the best player out there. I wanted to party with my friends who didn't have to work as hard as I did. For a while there, I wasn't sure that I could cut it. It was just too tough on me and I wanted to take the easy way out. But I got some really great advice from a mentor who reminded me that I'd been playing hockey since I was a little kid, and it's what I'd always loved. And that if I wanted to give up and quit, that was my choice to make. I was smart enough that I could become a teacher or an accountant or I could do any damn thing I wanted. But he told me he knew I'd never be happy unless I was playing hockey. And if I wanted to play, I'd have to suck it up and work hard at it.

"He was right. So I sucked it up and studied hard and played hard and got better at both. And I proved to my coach and to my teachers that I could focus. Not that I was a scholar or anything, but I got the grades I needed to get, and my hockey play improved enough that I got drafted right out of college by the Travelers."

"That's amazing."

His lips curved. "Not really. I still wasn't all that great. I was a passable player, but not as good as a lot of guys my age. The Travelers sent me down to minor league hockey for a while, where I kept trying to prove myself. And the media rode my ass. The press kept saying I'd never be good enough to get called up."

"That must have been difficult for you."

He shrugged. "All it did was piss me off and make me work harder so I could prove them wrong."

Carolina touched his arm. "Which you did."

"Yeah, I did. I hated all those assholes that didn't believe in me. I was determined to show them just how good I could be. It took me two damn years, but the Travelers called me up, and I've been there ever since. And I'm good, Lina. I'm very good at my job."

She loved seeing the fire in his eyes, the confident way he spoke about playing hockey. "You know, in college, I always thought of you as the hot jock all the girls chased. I never thought of you as having any substance. I never thought of you as someone who struggled."

He shrugged. "We didn't really know all that much about each other back then. I thought of you as the rich girl who had it easy."

She laughed. "I struggled so much in college. I was chubby the first year, then after I slimmed down, I was socially awkward. I didn't know how to deal with all the attention I was getting. And I was trying to focus on my studies, which were so important to me. That drove me. And then, of course, I had that monster-size crush on you. You were such a distraction."

"Uh . . . sorry?"

"It's not your fault. Totally mine. But typical for the age. And that's in the past, anyway. The thing is, I understand what you're saying. About then, and about now. There are some things I can control, and other things I can't. I can't control what the media says and thinks. I can only control what I do. How I create my line. That's my performance. And I'm working my ass off to design it the best way I know how."

He rubbed her back. "That's all you can do, Lina. You can't be anything other than what and who you are. You can't apologize for being a Preston, for having money, or for your dad being the VP. All you can do is say, 'Hey, I'm Carolina Preston, I'm a fucking brilliant designer, and here's my stuff. Like it or kiss my ass.'"

She burst out laughing. "Well, I don't know that I want to go that far in my advertising, but I like the sound of it."

"Okay, so you can modify it some, but babe, there's a lot of shit you can't control. The media is one of them. Just do what you do best, which is make clothes. And try to tune out the rest of it."

She looked at him, struck by how gorgeous he was. Beyond that, she was amazed at how perceptive and deep he was. And she'd always relegated him to the dumb jock category.

How very wrong she'd been. "You're very smart. And you possess a lot of common sense."

He leveled a wry smile at her. "I like to think of it as self-preservation."

She laughed, then stood. "I guess we should stop hiding out in here before someone comes looking for us."

"Too bad. I was just thinking we could make out on the sofa."

"Terrible idea, especially if the person who comes looking for us is my mother."

"Or your brother."

"Yes."

They made their way back to the party, where, thankfully, the media had gotten their photos and sound bites and had taken their leave. Which meant everyone was free to enjoy the rest of the evening. Drew led Carolina over to the buffet, where they enjoyed crab- and lobster-stuffed pastries, along with so many other delicacies that Carolina was so full she could barely suck in her stomach by the time Drew had filled two plates for her.

"This dress is going to burst," she said.

"Bull. You've hardly nibbled."

"You're comparing me to yourself, and you burn off a lot more calories than I do."

"Just do some of that yoga stuff that you women like to do and have another plate."

She laughed. "Yoga stuff? Maybe I should go ice skating. Then I'll end up with a sculpted body like yours."

He leaned in closer. "If your body looked like my body, I wouldn't want to have sex with you."

She heated from the inside out. "You need to kill the sex talk in this crowded room. And stop standing so close to me."

She took a step to the side and Drew grinned at her. She shook her head and went off to find Evelyn, who was at the other end of the buffet line.

"I can't stop eating," Evelyn said.

Evelyn looked gorgeous in a red dress that flared out at the waist into a wide skirt. She had pulled her hair up into a fashionably messy knot, and had diamond drop earrings on.

"Love this dress," Carolina said.

"Thanks. I can't wait to wear the Carolina Preston line. I'm excited to see what you're going to put out there."

"I'm equal parts excited and dreading the show."

"Worried about the critics?"

"Of course."

Evelyn put her arm around her. "Nothing you can do about them. They're going to think whatever they think. I already know you have amazing talent. And I have a feeling that the critics are going to love you."

"I hope so."

"Gray and I will be up after Christmas so you can test-dummy him for whatever clothes you want him to wear."

"Great. I'm sure he's just so thrilled."

Evelyn giggled. "Beyond belief. But he's your brother and he loves you and he's happy to help out. Have you fitted Drew?"

"For some of the clothes, yes. Not for the underwear, which of course won't go down the runway, but I have an advertising campaign I want to run, and I can already imagine how I want to structure it."

"You do? Care to share?"

Her mind was whirling, because the idea had just hit her. "Actually, not just yet. I have to finish formulating it in my head."

"Your eyes are sparkling." Evelyn inched closer. "Is it dirty?"

Carolina laughed. "Not exactly. But it's definitely sexy."

"Will Drew go for it?"

"I have no idea. I certainly hope so." Now that the idea was in her head, she wanted to do the shoot right away. She wondered how soon after the holidays she could arrange it. She'd have to discuss it with Drew. And with his team. And Madison Square Garden. If it worked out like she was hoping, it could be profoundly sexy. And an incredible draw for her line.

Gray came over and slipped an arm around her shoulder. "You look like you're lost in thought."

"Oh, yeah. Thinking about work, actually."

He gave her a playful squeeze. "It's Christmas. Stop thinking about work for five freaking minutes, would you?"

"Do you stop thinking about work from February through November?"

He lifted his gaze to the ceiling. "Uh, not really."

"Then shut up."

"Shutting up. And filling my plate with more food."

"Good. And Evelyn says you're coming up for fittings?"

He grimaced. "Only if I have to."

"You promised. And you have to."

"You're not going to make me wear anything stupid, are you?"

"You mean like a clown suit? No. Nothing stupid like that."

He gave her a dubious look. "Carolina. What exactly are you putting me in?"

She squeezed his arm. "Clothes that will make you look fabulous, obviously."

Evelyn slid her arm around Gray's side. "What? You don't trust your sister?"

"Not a bit."

Carolina laughed and moved off, finding her father and mother talking to an Oklahoma senator she knew well. She stopped and chatted with them for a few minutes, then excused herself, wandering around to make sure the guests were all taken care of. If there was one thing her mother had taught her, it was how to be a good hostess. And since her mother was occupied, it was up to her to see to the guests.

She mingled for about an hour, chatting up the guests and making sure to thank them for coming tonight. She crossed paths with Gray and Evelyn a few times, who were doing the same thing—playing good hosts.

But she hadn't seen Drew. She wondered if he was hiding out. Not that she'd blame him. Sometimes these parties could be excruciating, especially if you didn't know everyone.

She finally spotted him in a corner with their neighbor, Gil Nelson, and Senator Ed Langton, the three of them engrossed in some deep conversation. She had no idea what they could possibly be discussing, so she surreptitiously made her way in that direction, hoping to eavesdrop.

"You're out of your mind, Drew. St. Louis has the edge in the playoffs this year. Grant Cassidy, their quarterback, has the best stats in the NFL this year. He's taking them all the way."

Drew shook his head. "I think you're full of it, Senator. It's New York all the way this year."

Senator Langton let out a loud snort. "I don't know what's in that drink, son, but you're delusional."

"I'm afraid I'm going to have to agree with the senator, Drew. Cassidy has the talent at quarterback, and with Cole Riley at wide receiver, the two of them are unbeatable."

"I think you're both going to be disappointed when your team crashes and burns."

Sports. Of course. Carolina shook her head and started to wander off, but a few minutes later, a hand wrapped around her upper arm.

"Thought you'd escape, huh?"

She smiled at Drew. "Well, you were all tied up arguing about football."

"We're done. They don't know what they're talking about."

"And I suppose you do."

"You bet I do. New York will take it all this year."

Since she had zero investment in football, she nodded. "Okay. I'll take your word for it."

"Not a fan?"

"I don't watch a lot of football."

"But you know the teams. I mean, come on. You're a New Yorker. You have to be a die-hard fan."

She laughed. "No, I don't."

"I'm not sure I can continue to talk to you if you're not going to take a stand here."

"What are your thoughts about cashmere versus silk?"

He frowned. "What the hell are you talking about?"

"Exactly."

"Oh. I get it. You have about as much interest in football as I do in fabric."

"See? I knew you were smart."

"But you like hockey."

"I do like hockey. I also like baseball."

"But not football."

She shrugged. "Never got into the sport much."

He followed her as she wound her way through the rooms.

"And obviously, you like auto racing."

"Obviously."

"Do you ever go and watch Gray race?"

"Yes, when I can get away from work. I also go to watch baseball games. And of course, hockey games."

"But again, not football?"

"No."

"I'm taking you to a game."

She paused to look up at him. "Totally not necessary."

"I feel it's my duty to educate you. You don't know what you're missing. I'll get us play-off tickets. You can spare a few hours to go to the game. You can't work twenty-four hours a day."

"Can't I?" He was right, of course, but she was enjoying bantering with him.

"You probably would. But you shouldn't."

"What shouldn't my daughter be doing?"

Carolina cringed when her mother came up beside her.

"I'm trying to educate your daughter about the wonders of football, Mrs. Preston. It turns out she's not a fan."

Her mother looked at her. "You're not? How did I not know this?"

"I don't know, Mom. Surely this doesn't surprise you."

"I thought you liked all sports."

"Correction. I like a lot of sports. I've just never gotten into football."

"And I told her I could take her to see a New York play-off game. She's trying to tell me she has to work."

Mrs. Preston shook her head. "She's always working. Too hard, unfortunately. Drag her away from work for a few hours and make her go breathe in some fresh air, Drew."

"Yes ma'am."

"Oh, there's Felicia. I haven't had a minute to talk to her yet tonight. Please excuse me."

After Carolina's mother walked away, she turned to Drew. "You planned that."

Drew gave her a look. "You think I secretly met with your mother and concocted a plan with her to take you to a football game?"

"Okay, maybe not. But it sure was convenient."

"It was, wasn't it?"

She rolled her eyes. "I'm not going to a football game. I don't like football."

"Because you've never been to a game. Trust me, once you're there, you'll love it."

"I don't like being told what to do."

"Then I'll call you up and ask you out. You'll say yes, and we'll go to a football game."

"You're infuriating."

He grinned. "I know."

He was also gorgeous, and she wanted to slide her hand along the very crisp lapels of his suit. Keeping her hands to herself tonight was proving to be difficult.

"Have I mentioned how very gorgeous you are tonight?"

She snapped her gaze to his. "Yes. And I appreciate it very much. And you should stop looking at me like that."

"Like what?"

"Like you're hungry and I'm a midnight snack."

He leveled a predatory smile at her. "Is it midnight yet?"

She looked at her watch. "After midnight."

He leaned in closer. "I want to swipe my tongue across your neck, then take a bite."

Fighting the shudder, she stayed put and whispered, "Stop that."

"Stop what? Am I turning you on?"

"No."

"You're lying. You have goose bumps."

She ran her hands over her arms. "It's . . . cold in here."

He laughed. "No, it's not. In fact, I'd guess you were hot."

Why was she even having this conversation with him? "I'm going to see to the guests."

"Okay."

She walked away, but he was right. It wasn't cold in here. The staff made sure the temperature was comfortable. Not too hot, and definitely not too cool. It was Drew that gave her goose bumps, ones that still stood out on her skin because his words still lingered like a slow-moving picture playing in her head.

Her, reclining on the chaise in her room. Drew, coming up behind her to slide his tongue across her neck.

She rubbed her arms again as her nipples tingled.

Damn him. She was going to immerse herself in this party and forget all about him for the rest of the night.

No matter how difficult that was going to be.

SIXTEEN

IT WAS AFTER ONE IN THE MORNING BEFORE ALL THE guests had left. As was typical for her parents, they stayed up until the last guest was out the door.

Secret Service cleared the place out and did a double check. Her parents went up to bed, Gray and Evelyn following behind them. Carolina was exhausted, so she headed upstairs, too. Drew was talking to Arthur, one of the staff who apparently was a football fan.

She left him downstairs to his heated discussion. Yawning, she slipped out of her dress and went into her bathroom to brush her teeth. The quiet of the house was the best part of the night.

Okay, the best part of the night was seeing Drew in that suit. It made her rethink all of her options for dressing him.

She switched off the light in the bathroom, then laid down on the bed and stared up at the ceiling, mentally playing out each outfit in her head. She grabbed her notepad and jotted down a few things, wondering if Drew would be up for wearing one of her suits.

He likely wouldn't care. Then again, maybe he would.

She'd discuss it with him later. She laid her notepad to the side, her eyes drifting closed. But then another thought came to her so she grabbed the notebook again.

Thirty minutes later, she was staring at the wall, nowhere close to falling asleep.

This was ridiculous. She grabbed her phone to check her email.

Of course there was nothing pressing, because it was Christmas and everyone was home with their families, enjoying the holiday.

Releasing a frustrated sigh, she climbed off the bed and put on her robe, went to the door and opened it.

Not a sound. Everyone had gone to bed. Everyone was tired, including her.

Or at least she had been. Now she was wound up and for some reason her feet carried her down the hall, where she stood in front of Drew's door.

What was she doing here? She should go back to her room. This was ridiculous.

She gazed up and down the hall, grateful the rooms were spread out. But if someone came out . . .

You're already here, idiot. Just get this over with.

She knocked as lightly as she could, cringing at each rap of her knuckles.

Drew opened the door right away.

"Well, this is a nice surprise," he said with a smile. He stared down at her in her robe. "Is this my early Christmas present?"

Before she could utter a word he pulled her into his room and shut the door.

His lips covered hers before she could explain the reason for her middle-of–the-night visit.

Not that she had a good reason, anyway. She had no idea what she was doing there. And now that he was kissing her, his hand roaming over her back to draw her in close to his mostly naked body, she couldn't remember what had brought her to his room. Only that she was there, and he was happy to see her. And kissing her in the way she'd wanted him to kiss her all night long.

She moaned against his lips and he walked them backward, bringing her farther into his room. When they fell onto the bed, she landed on top of him, breaking their kiss.

Something about fashion, about her clothing line. That's what she'd wanted to talk to him about. But moonlight spilled over his magnificent chest, and damned if she wanted to talk about clothes right now. In fact, the only thing she wanted was to shed hers.

She untied the belt of her robe and slid it off her shoulders.

"So that's what you had on under your dress tonight," he said, snaking his fingers over the demi cups of her bra. Her nipples hardened. Such sweet, sweet pleasure.

"Yes." She removed her robe and tossed it to the floor.

"And these, too? Now it would have been a shame if I didn't get to see these tonight, Lina." His hands roamed down, over her belly, until he rested them at her hips, where she wore panties that matched her bra. Only the tiniest string held the two pieces of fabric together.

Decadent, yes, and she'd really had no idea Drew was going to see these tonight, but she'd be lying to herself if she didn't admit she'd worn them with him in mind. In fact, she hadn't taken them off, hadn't put on her pajamas. Maybe she'd subconsciously planned to come to his room all along.

Oh, that subconscious. Such a devious little devil.

She rolled her head back as he cupped her breasts, his thumbs brushing the fabric of her bra.

Such delicious torment, when all she wanted was his bare skin on hers. But this was good—so, so good, and when he released the clasp on her bra, she let it fall away.

Drew lifted up and put his lips over one bud, capturing it with his tongue and the roof of his mouth to suck it, gently. She ached with the pleasure of it, the way he tugged on her nipple, the sensation drawing down to her pussy, making her throb with need. When he released her nipple and took the other one, she could have died from the exquisite pleasure.

"Drew," she whispered, clutching his hair tight in her hands. "I love that."

He released her nipple, then cupped her breasts, giving them a gentle squeeze before lying back against the headboard.

"You looked so hot tonight," she said, running her hands over his chest.

"Is that why you're here? Because I was so irresistible tonight?"

She loved his sense of humor. "Partly. I also wanted to talk to you about . . . something."

He arched a brow. "Yeah? What is it?"

"It can wait. Right now I want you inside me."

"Let's get your panties off, then." He rolled her over onto the bed, then slipped her panties over her hips.

When he palmed her sex and rubbed his hand over her, she fell into a languid state, content to let him pleasure her, especially since he'd nestled up next to her and kissed her while he touched her.

She couldn't get enough of his mouth, the way he lazily brushed his lips across hers while he took his time caressing her with his fingers. There was no fast and furious rush to get her to the finish line. He rubbed his fingers over her sex, a tease that made her lift her hips to meet him and wrap her tongue around his.

She wanted this, needed him to make her come. And when he increased the pressure, giving her just a little more, she grabbed his wrist and held him right there, right at the point that would guarantee to sail her to oblivion.

But he pulled her wrist away and deepened the kiss, then tucked two fingers inside her while swirling his thumb over her clit.

She was going insane, needing that burst. She rolled to the side and lifted her leg over his hip, driving against him so he'd get her there. Unashamed, she thrust against his fingers, and he groaned against her mouth. And when she came, he soaked up her cries with his lips, taking every moan and whimper while he continued to pump his fingers into her and she rode the wave of one fantastic orgasm that left her shaken.

She was still trembling from the aftereffects when Drew pulled away only long enough to grab a condom. Then he was back, rolling her underneath him. She was still throbbing when he slid inside her, cupping her butt to raise her hips so he could push deeper.

He lifted his torso off her and held himself up with his hands, staring down at her. She smoothed her hands up his arms, feeling the strength in his muscles as he moved within her with slow, easy thrusts.

He kept his gaze trained on her face, his eyes intense, hot, and filled with a passion that equaled hers. She rubbed her hands over his arms, tightening her hold on him as he eased down on her and ground against her, heightening the sensation to peak level.

She brushed his hair away from his face, feeling the sweat across his forehead. She cupped the nape of his neck and drew his face closer. His lips took hers in a feverish kiss that made her tighten, made her nerve endings tingle. And when he groaned against her mouth, she wrapped her legs around him, urging him to give her more.

He pulled his lips from hers and looked down at her. "I love the way your pussy tightens around my cock, Lina. Do you know I can tell when you're about to come? You squeeze my cock and your pussy quivers."

He drew back, then slid back in, ever so slowly, rolling his hips against hers, giving her the friction that tore her apart. "Like now. You're ready to come, but you're holding back. Is it good?"

He was right. Every sensation was so delicious, she wanted to savor the moment. She could have come again already. He mastered her body, was so in tune to what gave her pleasure. But being with him like this, wrapped in this cocoon of heat and desire, was a never-ending source of sin and delight. She never wanted it to end.

"Yes," she said, lifting against him until he powered in deep. "It's so good. I want more. I want to come."

He rolled against her again, and this time, she knew she wouldn't be able to hold back. She dug her nails into Drew's arms, lost in the way he moved against her, the tidal wave of sensation that engulfed her as her climax hit.

He kissed her as she came, absorbing the cries she couldn't help but release as she rocked against him. And when Drew came with a hard groan and shuddered against her, she held tight to him, her lifeline in this wild, out-of-control storm of pleasure.

He held her, stroked her hair and brushed her lips with soft kisses as she came down from the high, out of breath but utterly content.

And then he got up and went to the bathroom and Carolina rolled over, exhausted. When Drew came back, he pulled the covers over them both and snuggled his body against hers.

She could barely keep her eyes open. "I need to go back to my room."

"Okay."

But his warm body against hers was her undoing. Her eyes drifted closed and she was out cold.

SEVENTEEN

DREW LISTENED TO THE SOUND OF CAROLINA'S DEEP breathing, and knew she'd fallen asleep.

He'd wake her in a little while. He usually slept light, so he'd make sure she was out of his room early enough, before everyone got up Christmas morning.

Though he had no idea how early everyone got up. He leaned over and reached for his phone.

Three a.m. That wasn't going to give them much time for sleeping.

He smiled. Worth it, though. He wrapped his arms around Carolina and breathed in the sweet scent of her hair.

He liked having her in his bed, liked the warmth of her naked body nestled against his. His cock twitched, but he forced those thoughts aside.

Yeah, he wanted her again. He wanted her all the time, but she needed at least a few hours of sleep.

Just an hour of her next to him in bed would be good enough. Then he'd wake her and she could sneak back to her room.

No one would know.

No one *could* know. That would be a disaster.

He yawned and closed his eyes.

THE RAP OF A COUPLE QUICK KNOCKS PENE-trated the thick fog of dead sleep that had sent Drew spiraling off into oblivion.

But the sound of Gray's voice shot him up in bed.

"Hey, Drew, I thought we'd get a head start on everyone else—"

Gray saw the body in bed next to Drew at the same time Drew threw the covers over Carolina's head.

"Oh, shit. I'm sorry, man. I had no idea." Gray started to back out, then paused as Carolina threw the covers off her head.

"Drew, what's going on?" she asked.

And then it was like a scene in a really bad movie.

Because Carolina woke enough to see her brother standing in the doorway, a horrified expression on her face.

And Gray realized it was his sister in bed with Drew.

"What the ever-loving *fuck* is going on here?" Gray asked.

"Gray. Get out so your sister can get dressed."

Carolina, eyes wide, said nothing.

Gray, however, looked pissed as he narrowed his gaze at Drew. "You and I need to talk as soon as you get dressed and come downstairs."

His lips clamped tight, Gray shut the door.

Shit.

Drew dragged his fingers through his hair and climbed out of bed.

"I'm sorry. I meant to wake you a couple of hours ago. I just passed out."

He expected panic on Carolina's face. Instead, she seemed . . . calm. She slid out of bed and grabbed her clothes. Drew couldn't help but admire the sleek lines of her naked body. "I'm a grown woman, Drew. My brother is going to have to get over it."

"Yeah, well, I don't think that's going to happen."

"I'll talk to him."

"No. I'll talk to him."

She shrugged. "Don't worry about it. He's just being overprotective. He'll realize that this is none of his business." She went over to him and pressed a kiss to his lips. "I'm going to take a shower, then I'll see you downstairs."

He wrapped his arm around her and tugged her close, prolonging the kiss until, despite the upcoming conversation with Carolina's brother that he was dreading, all he could think about was throwing Carolina back in bed and spending an hour or so with her.

But she pulled away. "I really need that shower, before the rest of the family wakes up."

"Yeah. Me, too." He swept his thumb over her bottom lip. "Too bad we can't take one together."

She sighed. "That would have been fun. The drawback to being surrounded by family—one that *doesn't* knock before entering a room."

He laughed. "I'll see you downstairs."

After Carolina left, Drew took a quick shower and got dressed. Not one to delay the inevitable, he found Gray downstairs, brooding over a cup of coffee.

"Where's everyone else?"

"My parents and their security went for an early morning walk. Evelyn's still asleep. What the hell are you doing in bed with my sister?"

Drew went to the coffeepot and poured a cup for himself, then faced Gray. "I don't really think that requires a detailed explanation, do you?"

"Come on, Drew. She's my sister."

"And well over twenty-one, and more than capable of making decisions about who she shares a bed with. It's not like she's a kid anymore, Gray. You need to let this one go."

"It's a rule, man. You never mess with a friend's little sister. You broke the cardinal rule of friendship."

"That was a rule set up when we were nineteen." Though no way was Drew going to mention he had, in fact, broken that rule back in college. Gray would never forgive him.

"It's one that still holds true."

Drew took a couple long swallows of coffee. After not enough sleep last night, he wasn't ready to fight this battle with his best friend. "Come on. Are you saying I'm not good enough for her?"

Gray paced. "No. That's not what I mean at all. But I know your lifestyle. I know you go through women as often as you change socks. I don't want Carolina to be hurt."

"And I don't want to hurt her. It's not like that."

Gray let out a short laugh. "Right. I'm sure you say that about all the women you sleep with, then dump."

"You need to stay clear of this one, buddy. My relationship with Carolina is my business, and hers. Not yours."

Drew knew right away it was the wrong thing to say. The look Gray leveled at him was not one of friend to friend. It was big brother looking out for little sister.

"My sister's happiness is always going to be my business. And if I think she's seeing the wrong guy, I'm going to step in."

Immediately defensive, Drew stepped forward. "Since when am I the wrong guy?"

"Okay, enough of this."

Drew looked over at the doorway where Carolina had walked

in. Instead of coming toward him, though, she went to Gray and put her arms around him for a hug.

"Merry Christmas."

Gray hugged her back. "Merry Christmas to you, too."

Then she came over to Drew, and gave him the same innocuous hug. "Merry Christmas."

"Merry Christmas, Lina."

Gray shot him another one of those looks that could kill. Tough.

Carolina grabbed a cup and the teapot and started to make tea. Then she turned to face her brother. "I'm an adult. This is my life, and I get to make the decisions about what—and who—is right for me. While I appreciate you being protective, Gray, you being irate about me sleeping with Drew is out-of-bounds. He's your friend, and I don't want your friendship with Drew strained over this. If this goes wrong and I get hurt, that's on me. I'm in this willingly and with my eyes open. Got that?"

Gray looked at Carolina for a long minute, then his shoulders finally relaxed. "I guess. But you know I'm always going to watch out for you."

"I understand and I appreciate it. And if Evelyn had had big brothers who would have been unhappy about you sleeping with her, what would you have said to them?"

Gray looked at her for a minute, then shrugged. "I'd have probably told them to fuck off, because my relationship with Evelyn was nobody's business but the two of us."

Carolina stared at him.

"Okay, point taken." Gray looked over at Drew. "Sorry for flying off the handle."

"It's okay," Drew said. "And Merry Christmas."

Gray laughed. "Back at you."

"And can we please not mention this to Mom and Dad? I've had enough drama this morning. I'd like to keep my relationship with Drew under wraps for the time being."

"Why?" Gray asked.

"Because it's new. And you know how Mom is about stuff like this. Just me seeing a guy will have her so excited she'll be picking out china patterns for us."

"Okay, you have a point. I won't say a word. How about Evelyn?"

"I'll . . . mention it to Evelyn," Carolina said, and then slid her glance to Drew, which gave Drew the impression that Evelyn probably already knew.

Given that women talked to each other about relationships all the time, that didn't surprise him. Or bother him.

"Now that that's settled, I'm going to make some tea and try to wake up the normal way."

It wasn't long before Gray and Carolina's parents came back from their walk, and Evelyn came downstairs. Then there was a flurry of activity and wishing everyone a Merry Christmas. They had breakfast, then everyone gathered in the family room to open gifts.

Drew settled back to watch the family open their gifts, then was surprised when Mrs. Preston handed one to him.

"For me?"

She smiled at him. "Of course."

He opened it up, and there was a framed photograph of him scoring a goal in a game against New Jersey. It was a great shot, too, with his stick in forward motion right at the net.

He stood and hugged her, then shook the vice president's hand. "Thank you for this. It means a lot to me."

"I'm so glad you like it," Mrs. Preston said.

Evelyn and Gray had given him something, too. A mug with a hockey stick that said, "I have a big, hard stick and I know what to do with it." He laughed out loud.

"This is perfect."

"Evelyn picked it out," Gray said.

Evelyn grinned. "It seemed appropriate for you."

When Gray gave her a look, her eyes widened and her cheeks flushed red with embarrassment. "That's not at all what I meant."

And then everyone laughed.

He'd brought gifts for all of them, too, though considering what went down this morning, he wasn't sure the gift he'd gotten for Carolina was going to go over all that well with Gray. But he'd found it and he thought it suited her, so he handed it to her.

She was sitting on the floor in front of the tree, so while everyone else was busy, he sat next to her and handed her the box.

She looked up at him. "You got me a gift?"

"Yeah. It's nothing special."

She opened the box. Inside, a single silver chain. He wasn't even sure she'd like it since she typically wore no jewelry.

He leaned in closer. "I know you don't wear jewelry, but I love your neck, and when I saw this, I pictured it around your throat."

Carolina took a deep breath and fingered the chain in the box. She lifted her gaze to his. "It's lovely. It's perfect. Thank you."

She pulled the chain out, then lifted her hair. "Would you mind?"

He undid the clasp, then fastened the chain around her neck. He leaned in and whispered to her. "Now, when you wear it, you can think about me."

She turned to face him. "I really want to kiss you right now."

But her gaze drifted, and Drew looked to see Gray staring at them. "Later."

She reached under the tree and handed him a box. "This is for you."

He opened the box and inside was a pair of boxer briefs with the Carolina Designs logo.

"My first pair. And a part of me that I want touching you," she said, her voice low and soft.

He smiled at her. "Believe me, I'll definitely be thinking about you when I'm wearing them. Thank you."

"And that's what I wanted to talk to you about. A photo shoot for the underwear line. On the ice."

He cocked a brow. "What? You want to make my balls shrivel up like walnuts?"

She laughed. "I haven't even mentioned making it look like you're sweating, so we'd have to pour water over you."

He rolled his eyes. "There are ways to make me actually sweat, you know."

"Obviously we're going to have to talk about this another time."

"Obviously."

After they finished opening gifts, everyone dressed for church. Drew wasn't much of a churchgoer, though he typically went with his parents on Christmas, so it was fine going with the Preston family.

The media was in attendance again today, and the church was packed. He sat next to Carolina, trying not to hold her hand as they listened to the minister talk about new beginnings.

A lot like Carolina and him. Their relationship had started out as a disaster, and she'd harbored a grudge for a long time. But the ice between them had slowly been melting. So maybe this was a new beginning for them. He'd enjoyed spending the holiday with her and her family, and, despite Gray's misgivings, he thought he was good for her. She worked too hard, and the one thing Drew liked to do was take some time to relax and play.

Even Gray had to see the benefit in that, and maybe before he left tonight he needed to have another conversation with Gray and talk about the good things he could bring to a relationship with Carolina.

After church and more media time, they headed back to the house, where the staff had cooked up an amazing turkey dinner.

Drew's eyes bugged out at all the food. Turkey, ham, and more side dishes than he could put on his plate.

And then there was wine.

"When's your next game, Drew?" the vice president asked.

"Monday. But I head back tomorrow for practice."

Mitchell Preston nodded. "As do I. Not for practice, of course, but there's a lot to be done and the time off is always brief."

"Unfortunately," Mrs. Preston said, laying her hand on her husband's arm.

"At least we'll have a little more time off for New Year's," Mr. Preston said.

"Will you be back here?" Drew asked.

The vice president shook his head. "No, we'll be taking in New Year's in D.C. Gray, will you and Evelyn be there?"

Gray shook his head. "We're heading to the house in Daytona for New Year's Eve. Some alone time for the two of us."

Evelyn smiled at Gray.

Mrs. Preston nodded. "Understandable. You two don't get nearly enough of that, and soon enough Gray will be gearing up for racing season to start again."

Evelyn sighed. "That's true. And it seems as if it just ended."

"But we still have time before that revs up in full, so we'll take advantage while we can."

"And speaking of those wedding plans . . ."

Evelyn looked at Mrs. Preston. "We're working on it."

"And yes, Mom, we're working on setting a date. Just haven't pinned one down yet," Gray said.

"As busy as both of you are, I want that to happen sooner rather than later. How will I ever get grandchildren?"

"We're practicing for that," Gray said.

The vice president laughed and Mrs. Preston shook her head.

"I promise, Mom. We're getting married next year."

She frowned. "That doesn't give me much time."

"Oh, please. Loretta Preston can put together a wedding in a month if she needs to. You're a woman who makes things happen."

Drew listened to all this back-and-forth with a smile on his face. He'd always liked Gray's mom, and having Gray and his dad get along so well had to be such a relief for Gray. All through college there had been such tension between them.

Now his life was settled. He had a woman he loved and his family was whole again. He was happy and in love and looking forward to a secure future.

In the meantime, Drew had spent a lot of years wandering aimlessly, dating women who definitely weren't the settling-down type.

Until . . . recently.

Though Carolina wasn't ready to settle down, not with what she had going on in her life right now.

He shifted his gaze toward her. She was smiling as she listened to Gray and Evelyn talk wedding plans. He wondered what she thought about that, about where her life was. Did she even compare them, or was she satisfied and thinking only about her fashion line?

He knew it was her priority, that her career was the number one thing in her life.

And where did he fit into all that?

Maybe he didn't fit in at all, and he was just someone she fucked to ease the tension.

He sure as hell had used women in his past to ease the tension from his job, and then thought nothing about letting them go.

Why did he even care? They were just having fun, right?

AFTER LUNCH, CAROLINA TOOK HER GIFTS UP TO HER room, needing a few minutes of quiet time. It had been nonstop motion after rocketing out of bed this morning.

She needed to pack. She'd head back to New York tomorrow morning, back to the frenetic pace of work and deadlines. This had been a relaxing interlude, and she was grateful to have been able to spend time with her family, because it would likely be the last bit of relaxation she'd have before Fashion Week.

She fingered the necklace Drew had given her. Such a surprise. He didn't seem the romantic type. She hadn't expected a gift from him at all, and if he had gotten her one, maybe a Travelers jersey or something. Nothing like this. She went into the bathroom and stared at herself in the mirror.

The necklace was simple. Nothing extravagant, and yet what she'd told him had been the truth.

It was perfect. She felt his touch burn into her skin even as she stared at the necklace.

Ridiculous. She no more belonged to him than he was hers. Drew saw a lot of women, and none of them on a long-term basis. And why would she even be interested in what he did? They were just having some fun. He was going to go back home, play hockey, and no doubt hit on other women, while she was going to head back to work and not have sex with anyone else. She'd gotten exactly what she wanted out of him—hot sex and tension relief.

But as she stared at the necklace, she wondered how Drew felt, if what was between them was more than just sex.

Right. Like it could ever be anything more than just sex.

"You're being such a girl, Carolina."

A soft knock at her bedroom door saved her from her ridiculous thoughts. She opened the door and smiled at Evelyn. "Hey, come on in."

"I thought you might be up here packing. Have you had enough of family time?"

She let Evelyn in, then shut the door behind her. "Actually, I've really enjoyed these past few days. I don't get to see Mom and Dad all that often, or you and Gray. Even less this past year since I decided to start working on creating a fashion line. So this has been nice. Really nice."

Evelyn took a seat in one of the chairs. "I'm glad. And I think so, too. Though Gray and I love to have time alone, he needed this time with his family, too."

"Until my mother brought up wedding planning?"

Evelyn drew her knees up to her chest, and wrapped her arms around her legs. "Well, that isn't without its own set of complications."

"What's holding you two back? Unless it's none of my business."

"It's not that we don't want to get married. God, we really do. If Gray had his way he'd haul me down to the nearest courthouse and marry me tomorrow. And I'd be just fine with that."

"But my parents—and I'm sure your parents, too—want a big formal wedding."

"My parents don't really care, as long as I'm happy. But your father is the vice president now, and with that comes a certain amount of responsibility."

"Meaning there has to be the pomp and circumstance of Vice President Preston's only son having a formal wedding, as opposed to hopping a flight to Vegas and getting married at the Elvis Chapel?"

Evelyn laughed. "Something like that. But your mother is right in that we do need to speed up the timeline."

"Why?" When Evelyn didn't answer, Carolina frowned. Then it dawned on her. "Oh, my God, you're pregnant."

Evelyn nodded. "Just a little."

Carolina wanted to scream and grab Evelyn into a huge hug. Instead, she ran over and grabbed her hands. "I'm so incredibly excited for you. And honey, you can't be just a little pregnant. How far along are you?"

"I have no idea. Probably not too far. I was due to have my period before Christmas, and it didn't happen, so I ran out and bought a pregnancy test. Hard to do in nosy small towns, too, so I had to do it surreptitiously."

"Secret's going to come out in a hurry."

"I know."

"How did Gray take it?"

"Are you kidding? He's over-the-moon excited. I cried, he cried, and then we hugged. It was sloppy romantic."

"Awww." Tears pricked Carolina's eyes and she sat on the edge of the bed. "You're going to make me cry now. I'm going to be an aunt."

Evelyn sniffled. "I know. I'm so thrilled. And terrified about what his parents are going to say. We're ruining everything."

"They aren't going to be angry. Are you kidding? Do you have any idea how long my mother has been waiting to be a grand-mother? She'll be thrilled."

"But your father—and his stature as vice president."

Carolina waved her hand. "So you'll be a little pregnant when you walk down the aisle. I think the country can weather that small scandal. There are bigger fish to fry, like the deficit and foreign relations and the economy and the price of oil and—"

"Okay, okay, I get your point," Evelyn said.

"When are you telling Mom and Dad?"

"Today. I'm nervous."

"Do you want me to come with you?"

"No, I think this is something Gray and I have to do alone. I wanted to tell you first, though."

"Okay. If you change your mind and you need me, let me know. I'm here for you."

"Thanks."

"And speaking of things that need to be revealed . . ."

Evelyn gave her a look. "You're not pregnant, too, are you?"

Carolina laughed. "Uh, no. But did Gray tell you he walked into Drew's room this morning and found Drew and I in bed together?"

Evelyn's eyes widened. She planted her feet on the floor and leaned forward. "Oh, my God. He so did not tell me this. Was this before I got up this morning?"

"Yes. I fell asleep in Drew's room, and I guess Gray must have just opened the door to ask Drew to have coffee with him first thing this morning . . . and there I was."

Evelyn put her hands over her cheeks. "Oh, God, Carolina. Was he mad?"

"At first. You know, the whole overprotective-brother thing that we talked about. But then Drew talked to him, and I reminded him I wasn't sixteen years old anymore. I think he's all right."

Evelyn nodded. "I'll talk to him, too."

"You don't have to do that. You have enough on your plate to deal with."

"It's a long flight back to D.C. We'll have time to talk about things besides the baby." Evelyn stood. "Oh, God, I'm going to have a baby. How am I going to fit that into my life?"

Carolina came over and hugged her. "This is the life you wanted, the one you dreamed about. A husband and a family. You and Gray will make it work."

"You're right. We will make it work. As long as your father doesn't fire me."

Carolina laughed. "He's not going to fire you. He thinks of you as another daughter. He loves you."

"Wish me luck, then."

"You won't need it, but good luck."

Carolina finished packing, then went downstairs. It was quiet. No doubt Evelyn and Gray were somewhere having a conversation with her parents. She found Drew watching a basketball game on television. She fixed herself a cup of tea, then sat down beside him.

"Hey," he said, muting the television. "Where did everyone go?"

"No idea. Are you all packed?"

"Yeah. Are we flying out together tomorrow?"

"My flight is at ten thirty."

"Mine, too."

She smiled at that. "I figured my mother's social secretary would put us on the same flight since we're going to the same place. Do you have a home game next?"

"Unfortunately, no. We have two road games in a row. Then we come back home."

"That's too bad."

"What about you?" he asked, tucking a strand of her hair behind her ear. "Is your staff coming back?"

She shook her head. "I gave them time off until after New Year's."

"That's generous of you. So you'll be toughing it out alone?"

"That's okay. It'll give me some quiet time to do some planning on advertising and take care of some of the myriad minor details I don't have time to mess with when the staff is in."

"A quiet way to settle back in after Christmas."

"Yes."

"Maybe you can even take New Year's Eve off."

She paused and looked at him. "Are you asking me out?"

"Maybe. If I was, would you say yes?"

"Maybe. You know, it's a little late in the game to be making New Year's Eve plans."

He grinned. "I have connections, you know."

"You wouldn't dare drag me out in the middle of Times Square, would you?"

"Where's your sense of adventure, Miss Preston?"

"My sense of adventure wants nothing to do with the middle of Times Square on New Year's Eve."

He shook his head. "So is that a yes?"

She smiled. "Yes."

The door to her father's study opened, and her father was laughing, his arm linked with Evelyn's as the four of them spilled out. Carolina wasn't sure she'd ever seen her mother grin so much. And it looked like she'd been crying.

"What's that about?" Drew asked.

"I think you're about to find out."

"Oh, good, Carolina, you're here," her mother said. "We have news."

"Is that right? What kind of news?"

"I'll let Gray and Evelyn tell you." Her mother and father stood back.

"We're pregnant," Gray blurted out.

"Well, *I'm* pregnant," Evelyn said with a wide grin. "But Gray helped get me that way."

"What? This is awesome," Drew said, going to Gray and giving him a big hug. "Congratulations, buddy."

"Thanks."

Carolina gave Evelyn a hug. Again. "I'm so thrilled for you both." Then she hugged her brother.

"So it looks like the kids have set a date. The wedding will be in May."

"I'll definitely have a belly by then, but hopefully I won't be grossly pregnant. The baby's due in August."

"And I don't care, because I'm going to be a grandpa," Mitchell said, beaming.

Champagne was uncorked, though Evelyn settled for juice, and toasts were made to the upcoming Preston baby. The family spent the rest of the afternoon celebrating and talking wedding plans. Carolina was shocked and humbled when Evelyn asked her to be her maid of honor. Of course she accepted immediately, and then she was doubly shocked when Evelyn asked if Carolina would make her wedding gown.

"Are you sure, Evelyn?"

"I can't think of a better designer to make my dress."

"Evelyn. There are a million designers who would love to make the wedding gown for the vice president's daughter-in-law."

"Yes, but I want you to do it. And you'll be working with an expanding waistline. No easy task."

Carolina laughed. "I can handle that, but I don't want you to feel like you're under any obligation. My feelings wouldn't be hurt at all if you have a favorite designer you want to use."

"I want you to do it. Unless you're too busy. Then I'd completely understand. You have so much going on right now with Fashion Week and launching your line." Evelyn sat back. "I didn't even think of the imposition."

Carolina took Evelyn's hands in hers. "I'd be honored to make your gown. I already have ideas. In fact, let me go get my sketch pad and we can talk about it if you'd like."

"Are you kidding? I'd love that."

Carolina dashed upstairs and grabbed her sketch pad, then came back and sat with Evelyn. She roughed out a few sketches, allowing for Carolina's expanding belly. With Evelyn's suggestions, they came up with some ideas. It wasn't yet refined but by the time they finished, they had at least a few options.

"I love these. They're unique and beautiful for a spring wedding."

"I'm so glad you like them. I'll work on them some more and send you something more detailed later."

"Take your time. You have other things to do—and now, so do I. In fact, I need to call my parents." Evelyn grinned. "They're going to be so thrilled."

They hugged, and Evelyn went off to find Gray so they could do a video call with her parents.

Carolina wandered off and found Drew in the living room with her father, talking politics of all things. She leaned against the doorway listening to them argue current events. It was fascinating to hear him hold his own. He didn't agree with everything her father stood for, in fact he deeply opposed some points. She knew her father would respect Drew's viewpoint. And to Drew's credit, he didn't get angry, just listened to her father speak about the things he believed in and why. It was a very civil discussion and Drew was polite, but passionate, just as her father was.

She was impressed. When her father looked up and saw her, he smiled.

"Care to jump into the fray?" he asked.

Carolina grinned. "Not on your life. I've had way too many political arguments with you over the years. I know how many hours those can last."

Her father laughed and stood. "Oh, come on. It was good practice in standing up for yourself and what you believe in. Unfortunately, I have a few calls to make, so I'll have to leave the two of you."

Her dad shook Drew's hand. "If you ever decide to leave hockey and join politics, I'd say you have a good future ahead of you."

Drew laughed. "I think I'm fine right where I am, sir, but I enjoyed the discussion."

Her dad walked by and gave her a kiss on the cheek, then left and headed down the hall to his office, leaving her with Drew.

"Eventful Christmas Day," he said.

"I'll say."

"So, it's a pretty big deal for you to design Evelyn's wedding dress, isn't it?"

"It is."

"Which means a lot for you to do with everything else you have going on. Can you handle it?"

"For family, I can handle it."

He slung an arm around her shoulder. "Well, aren't you just a superhero?"

She laughed. "Not quite. But I'm used to multitasking. And I work very well under pressure."

"Do you? You mean like the pressure of one of your family members possibly walking in at any moment and catching me running my fingers up your leg?" He laid his hand on her thigh. It had been such a busy day, and she'd missed his touch. Part of her wanted to move away, but she was enjoying it too much.

"I should finish packing, see what my Mom is up to." But she didn't move.

"Or . . . you could kiss me."

She leveled a warning glance at him. "Drew. We're hardly seventeen."

"I know. That's what makes this so much fun."

"And I think my parents have had enough shocks today."

He leaned back. "Would it be so shocking to find out you and I are seeing each other?"

"Is that what we're doing? Seeing each other?"

He tunneled his fingers in her hair and gave her that wickedly devastating smile that never failed to curl her toes. "I definitely see you. Do you see me?"

Her gaze darted down the hall, but she knew it would be a couple hours before her father resurfaced. She had no idea where her mother had disappeared to.

"Carolina." Drew cupped her chin and turned her to face him. "What are you so afraid of?"

She had no idea. But when he leaned in and brushed his lips across hers, she forgot all about everyone else in the house. He tugged her against him and, though he kept the kiss light and easy, she wanted more. She laid her hand on his chest and clutched his shirt, taking in his breath, the hard plane of his body, and how safe she always felt in his arms.

He pulled away before she did, leaving her dizzy and wanting more. His eyes had gone dark, filled with desire.

"I want so much more than that, you know," he said.

She swallowed, hard, and wondered if he meant the kiss, or something more.

EIGHTEEN

DREW'S TEAM HAD THREE GAMES IN BETWEEN CHRIST-
mas and New Year's Eve. The break had been great, but his head
was fully in game mode again. Winning at least one game on the
road had helped. Maybe the break had been good for them, because
he felt fired up and ready to kick some ass.

Tonight they were playing Colorado, they were back in the
Garden, and they were all confident this would be the push they
needed to start on a winning streak.

He loved being out on the home ice. Loved the smell of it, the
way he knew every corner of it, and the way the home crowd fans
got into the game with their noise.

When they took the ice for introductions, the home crowd went
crazy. Drew soaked in all the energy. It fueled him for game time.
He wished Carolina could be here, but he knew she was deep in her
work, just like him. He hadn't even asked her because he didn't
want to put her on the spot.

Besides, he had a date with her tomorrow night. He smiled as he skated around the ice for warm-ups. Tomorrow was his night with Carolina.

Tonight was his night to beat up on Colorado.

Trick took the face-off, and Drew waited, his body poised to go after the puck as soon as it dropped. Trick flipped it toward Colorado's side, and Drew skated after it, Colorado's defender shoving into him before he could get to the net. On the defensive, Drew hustled after him. Fortunately, the Travelers defense was right there to protect the net and Kozlow fought for the puck.

Drew had every confidence in Avery Mangino, the Travelers goalie, but he much preferred to be at the other end of the Garden, trying to shove the puck in Colorado's net. So when Kozlow slid the puck their way, he and Trick volleyed it back and forth, then Trick passed it to Litman while Drew skated down the ice, beating Colorado's defenders to get in position.

He took the pass from Litman and launched a shot at the net, deflected by the goalie.

Damn.

By the end of the first period, they were scoreless.

Unacceptable.

Colorado was good. But they were better.

In the second period, it was just as intense, with a lot of shots on goal by both teams and nothing to show for it. Time was ticking down and when Colorado got called for high-sticking, that gave the Travelers a power play.

This was their chance to make a charge at the goal. With Trick just past center, Drew and Litman drove down the ice with the puck, passing it to Trick, who volleyed it to Sayers. Drew got into position, shoving the defender out of the way just in time to receive the pass. He took a shot and swung it into the net.

They'd scored! Elated, they gathered to celebrate for a few seconds, and then it was back to work.

By the third period, they were up two to nothing, but Colorado was driving, holding them deep in their own end. Trick got a two-minute penalty, so that left them short on a power play.

It was time to dig deep and hold Colorado scoreless.

Sweat dripping down his face and back, Drew was determined to keep his focus on two of Colorado's players. He dug in his skates and worked them, moving double time as they worked the net trying to score. He slung the puck down to Colorado's side, but they quickly doubled up on him and forced it back down the ice. Kozlow pushed into the defender and wrestled for the puck. Kozlow won that battle, and shucked it to Drew. He skated away with the puck like he'd stolen it.

Fighting for breath, he moved as fast as he could to stay ahead of the Colorado players who were just as desperate to get hold of the puck as he was to keep it. At Colorado's net, they jumbled up, a tangle of bodies and sticks wrestling for the prize. Drew took a shot and Colorado's goalie swept it into his glove.

Damn. They went back toward the Travelers net. Drew took a quick look at the clock. Still too damn much time left on Trick's penalty and Colorado was hungry.

They surrounded the Travelers net and then it was a free-for-all, a mass of players shoving in sticks to grab the puck. Drew saw a shot on goal, and when Avery came up with the puck in his hand, Drew expelled a giant sigh of relief.

By then the power play was over, and time was ticking down to end the third period. Normal play resumed, and though Colorado fought hard to score, they ended the game without getting the puck in the net. The Travelers won, and the team celebrated by high-fiving at center ice.

Drew was exhilarated, exhausted, and ready to eat a twelve-ounce steak. So were the rest of the guys. They planned to shower, do their media interviews, and they were all going to meet at the steakhouse for dinner.

He dressed and grabbed his phone, surprised to find a text message from Carolina.

Amazing game. You kicked butt. Congratulations!

He dialed her number. She answered on the second ring.

"I thought you'd be out celebrating."

He grinned. "On my way. You saw the game?"

"Yes. I was doing some minor beadwork at home, so I had the game on while I worked. Though I have to admit for a while there, I was riveted to the television. Nice goal, by the way."

"Thanks. I would have invited you to the game. I wanted you to come, but I figured you were going to be busy."

"I am busy. Which doesn't mean I can't catch your games on TV. I just wanted to let you know I was cheering you on."

He took in a deep breath. "Thanks for that."

"You're welcome. Now go enjoy your celebration."

"Okay. I'll call you tomorrow. Don't work too hard."

"I'll try not to. Good night, Drew."

"Night, Lina."

He hung up, and grinned.

"What the hell, man? Get up and let's get going. I'm starving here."

"Yeah, yeah." He put on his shoes and followed Trick out the door.

NINETEEN

CAROLINA HATED NEW YEAR'S EVE IN NEW YORK CITY. Typically, she either hightailed it out of town, or hid in her apartment, content to let everyone else crowd the streets and celebrate.

She anticipated with dread whatever Drew had in store for her for tonight. Knowing him, he'd thrust some hideous party hat on her and drag her out to Times Square.

She was sipping her tea when her phone rang. Frowning, she looked at the time. It was only eight in the morning, and it was Drew calling.

"A little early for our date, don't you think?"

"Not really. Pack a bag. We're heading out."

"Staking out our place in Times Square already?"

He laughed. "Do you really think I'd do that to you?"

"I have no idea."

"Pack a bag. We're getting the hell out of here."

"Okay. And what should I pack?"

"Pack for the beach. I'll be there in an hour to pick you up. Can you be ready?"

What did he think she was, some diva who needed three hours to prep? "Yes. I'll see you in an hour."

Pack for the beach? Where were they going? As long as it was out of here, she was game.

She headed into her bedroom and grabbed her bag, threw in some capris, a sundress, and, though it was a ridiculous notion, her swimsuit. It was winter. Even if they hopped over to the Hamptons, which sounded like a delightful idea, it was still winter. She added a sweater and her yoga pants, too, just in case.

She took a shower and got dressed, then grabbed a bagel to eat while she waited.

Drew showed up exactly at the time he said he would. She liked that about him. He rang the bell, so she grabbed her bag and went downstairs.

When she opened the door, he smiled. "I love a woman who's on time."

"Hey, I even had time to eat breakfast."

"Well, aren't you efficient. Is this it?" he asked, grabbing her bag.

"You're not kidnapping me for a week, are you?"

He led her down the stairs toward the waiting taxi. "Nice thought, but we both have to work, so no. Just overnight."

They climbed into the taxi.

"Are you going to tell me where we're going?" she asked.

"It's a surprise."

"Seriously? You're not going to tell me?"

"We'll be there before you know it. Just sit back and enjoy the ride."

The ride ended up being to one of the smaller airports, where she was surprised to see the Preston jet.

They boarded, and buckled in.

"How did you arrange this?"

Drew settled in next to her. "I talked to Gray, who talked to your dad."

"Good morning, Miss Preston. Mr. Hogan."

Carolina smiled at Oren, the captain of the flight crew. "Good morning, Oren."

"We'll be taking off shortly. We'll have you into Daytona Beach in no time. Enjoy the flight."

After the captain went into the cockpit, Carolina turned to face Drew. "We're spending New Year's Eve with Gray and Evelyn?"

"Not exactly. They had a change in plans and decided to go to Virginia to be with Evelyn's parents. With the baby news, they wanted to spend some time with her parents and talk wedding plans. So I talked to Gray, and he's letting us use his house."

"Oh. This is fantastic." An overnight in Florida trumped a cold New Year's Eve in Times Square every time.

"I knew you didn't want to be in the city for New Year's Eve. I thought you might like to go someplace warmer. I actually was going to get us a hotel room there and asked Gray about the plane, but then he told me they were heading to Virginia and offered up the house. I didn't refuse."

"It's a great house on the beach. And someplace warmer is a wonderful idea. Thank you."

They took off, and Carolina busied herself with working on her line. She had models in place, and had pretty much decided on which clothes each of them would wear. There might be a few switches, but other than completing production, she was mostly finished. Now she just had to get advertising going, and she had to get Drew on board for that, along with one of her female models for the women's line. She'd already talked to the agency and had selected one of the female models to do the advertising shoot for the women's line.

She leaned back and closed her eyes, needing to rest and gather her thoughts.

The next thing she knew, Drew was shaking her shoulder.

"We're getting ready to land."

She blinked and opened her eyes. "Already? I must have fallen asleep."

He smiled at her. "Just how hard have you been working this week?"

"Oh, not too hard."

He gave her a look. "I don't think I believe you."

They landed and she and Drew both thanked the crew, who insisted they were thrilled to spend New Year's Eve hanging out on the beach. Her father was flying their families out to spend it with them, so they were all excited.

Drew had rented a car. They threw their bags in the backseat and headed toward the house.

Carolina loved Gray's house. She'd been out a few times, and he'd even let her stay there on vacation when he was away racing. She loved the expansiveness of it—right on the beach, no neighbors close by. It was gorgeous and peaceful, and as they pulled into the driveway, one of Gray's staff was there with the key.

"Thank you, Louisa," Carolina said, taking the key from her.

"The house is fully stocked for you. I'll be back tomorrow—at three o'clock, Mr. Preston said—to get the key back?"

"That's right," Drew said.

Louisa nodded and left. Drew took the key from Carolina and opened the front door.

Carolina could already smell the ocean breeze wafting in from the open terrace doors. She walked to the terrace and outside.

It was warm out, so much warmer than Manhattan. She wanted to immediately shed her clothes and take a walk on the beach.

Drew came up behind her and put his arms around her. "I

thought this might be more fun than the craziness at Times Square."

She leaned her head back against his chest. "It's absolutely perfect. There's nothing more calming than the ocean."

"Do you want to get changed and go take a walk?"

"Absolutely."

They went upstairs and headed into the guest room down the hall from the master bedroom. The guest room was amazing. Oversize, with a big bed, a deck overlooking the ocean, and its own bathroom. Carolina changed into her swimsuit and put on her capris and a tank top, then slid into her flip-flops.

"This feels so decadent for December," she said as she turned to Drew, who'd thrown on a pair of board shorts and a sleeveless top. She loved seeing all that muscle exposed.

They walked outside and Drew grasped her hand. She felt giddy, like she was on vacation, without a care in the world.

Of course, she had a lot of cares, a lot of tension, a lot of stress.

But not today. Today she wasn't going to think about all of that. One day off was all she needed to melt all of that away.

The warm sunshine bathed her skin as they kicked off their shoes and hit the sand. It wasn't summer by any means, but it was warm here, and it felt good. The salt in the air rejuvenated her as they walked parallel to the water. Carolina dug her toes into the sand, wishing it were summer already.

"We used to go to the shore a lot when we were kids," she said as they strolled along at an easy pace. "It's one of my fondest memories of my childhood. Playing in the water with Gray, splashing and dunking each other. Dad didn't come with us all that often because he was so busy when we were kids, but Mom was always there, and aunts and uncles and of course cousins would join in. We had such a blast."

Drew shifted his gaze toward hers and smiled. "That sounds like fun."

"It was. We'd spend a week at the shore every summer. I looked forward to it every year."

"I love the beach, too," Drew said. "Of course, growing up in Oklahoma we didn't have the beach, but there are a lot of lakes. We'd go camping. Everyone would go out on boats and water-ski."

"Did your parents have a boat?"

He shook his head. "We didn't, but my parents were friends with people who did, so we'd all camp together and we'd ski off their boat. Then when I was a teenager, I had a friend whose parents had a boat, and we'd head off on the weekends to go water-skiing."

She stopped and turned to face him. "So what you're saying is that you're an amazing water-skier."

He gave her an adorably boyish grin. "Hell, yeah. If the water out there wasn't so cold right now I'd show you."

"How unfortunate. Some other time, then."

He took her hand and continued to walk. "We'll come back in the summer. Then I'll impress you with my water-skiing prowess."

He assumed they'd still be together in the summer. She didn't know what to make of that.

Would they be? She had no idea. She'd never had a long-term relationship with a man, had never progressed beyond a few dates or a month at best before the whole thing fizzled out due to lack of interest or her just being too busy to care if the relationship went any further. Her focus had always been on her career, and never on a man.

Her career had to remain her number one priority, now more than ever.

But the idea of not having Drew in her life made her ache, and she didn't like that.

She'd never depended upon a man for her happiness. The thought of it had always seemed ludicrous to her. The only thing she had ever wanted, the only thought that had ever made her happy was launching her fashion line.

Something inside her was changing, some subtle shift in her priorities.

"Your shoulders are getting red. Did you put sunscreen on?" Drew asked.

"Oh, you know what? I was so excited about getting outside in the warmth that I completely forgot."

"We'd better head back then, and get some sunscreen on you before you fry up like a lobster."

She laughed. "Yes, that would be bad. Sunburnt is definitely not a good color on me."

They turned around and Drew walked them farther up the beach into the shade on the way back.

Once inside, she headed into the kitchen.

"How about something to drink?" she asked.

"A beer sounds good."

"Okay. Actually, that sounds pretty good to me, too." Normally she disliked beer, but it was warm outside and she was parched, and today it felt like summer. And summer meant beer. She grabbed two beers and handed them over to Drew, who opened them both and gave her one. They went out onto the terrace and took a seat.

There wasn't a soul out there, just the whitecaps billowing over the water. Carolina spotted a boat far off in the distance, but couldn't make out what kind it was. It disappeared along the horizon, so all she could see then was water. No one else could be seen along their private stretch of beach. She felt like they were the only people in the universe right now. Shipwrecked, alone, and utterly in their own world.

She kind of liked it.

"Tell me how work is going."

She shifted her gaze to Drew. "I don't want to talk about work today. I'm on vacation."

He cocked a brow. "I've never known you to not want to talk about your work."

"So you're saying I'm obsessed?"

He laughed. "No. I think you love your job. Nothing wrong with that. I talk about hockey a lot, because I love what I do. So do you. If you didn't, you probably shouldn't be doing it."

"True. And I do love it. I've also been a bit obsessed by it for the past several months."

"Rightly so, I imagine, since you have a lot riding on this being a success."

She drew her knees to her chest. "Don't remind me."

"Oh, right, because you're on vacation today and you want to obliterate it from your mind."

Her lips lifted. "Exactly."

"I can take your mind off work."

"You can, huh?"

"Yeah." He got up and grabbed his beer and hers. "Follow me."

He led her through the door and into the house, down the hall and into the side yard, an oasis of greenery and palm trees, where there was a pool and a hot tub surrounded by a tall fence. He sat them down at the edge of the pool.

She tucked her feet and legs in the water. "Ah yes. At least this one is heated, unlike the ocean."

Drew sat next to her and sank his legs in, too. "Yeah. And it's a lot more private here."

She laughed. "I didn't see anyone out there."

He clinked the tip of his beer bottle to hers before taking a long swallow. "But I have nefarious plans for you, and I wanted privacy."

"Really. What kind of nefarious plans?"

"First, we're going to take a swim, so get out of those clothes."

"I like the sound of that." She pulled off her top and her capris, then slid into the water, which felt warm and glorious. She swam a few laps side by side with Drew, who then scooped her into his arms and swung her around before dunking them both. She came up laughing, and then he took them under again, this time kissing her underwater. She wrapped her arms around his neck, loving the buoyant feel of the water and the way his lips felt on hers.

When they surfaced, she turned in his arms and wrapped her legs around him.

"This is a good start," he said, pushing through the water toward the cement stairs. He sat her on the edge, then untied her bikini top, letting it fall to her waist.

Undaunted, she untied the back and tossed the top to the side of the pool. "Part of your nefarious plans?"

"I'm only just beginning. But first, sunscreen for you."

"Oh, that's right. We're in the sun again."

Drew got out, water dripping from his body as he headed over to the supply cabinet on the covered veranda. There was such fluidity to his movements, the way he walked with such ease and confident masculinity.

It was the same as when he was on the ice. When he skated, whether he was coasting or zooming along at some crazed speed, it was a beautiful thing to behold. She was mesmerized by him, and she'd caught each of his games when they were apart this past week. Not just for the lines and watching the movements of his body, but also because she'd missed him.

Which was a dilemma she had decided not to think about today.

He came back with lotion, pouring some in his hands. "Lean forward," he said.

She did, pulling her hair out of the way so he could spread the lotion across her back and down her arms. His motions were thorough, and yet slow and sensual, heating up her body more than the sun had. Each touch was a caress, as if he was learning her body for the first time. He swirled the lotion down her spine and across her back, all the way to her bikini bottoms.

"Now, lean back."

She smiled up at him as he spread more lotion on his hands, then began at the front of her shoulders, moving his way inward, toward her collarbone, cupping her neck in his hands and using slight pressure of his thumbs as he caressed her throat. She watched his face when he did this, his expression so serious, as if he wanted to make sure to cover every inch of her skin. His brows knit tight in concentration, his lips compressed. She had to smile at how seriously he took this task.

She swallowed as he made his way down across her collarbone. He cupped her breasts, teasing her nipples until they tingled.

He lingered at her breasts, using his thumbs to brush across the aching buds until she arched against him. Then he looked up at her, and the heat and desire in his eyes made her breath catch.

"I like you touching me," she said, watching as he continued to tease and torment her nipples.

"You have the most beautiful breasts, Lina. I could play with them all day, watching your nipples harden. And from the way you move when I touch you, I know you like me lingering here." He proved it by swirling his thumbs over her tingling nipples. Her lips parted, her breaths coming out in fast pants.

"Yes, that feels so good."

"And there's more of you I want to touch."

He moved down to her stomach, putting more lotion in his hands and rolling across her abdomen, her hips, her lower belly, and then lifting each leg to rub and caress every part of her, all the way down to her calves. It was a soft, lingering sensual massage that awoke every nerve ending in her body.

She'd never felt more alive, or more ready to touch him in return.

"My turn," she said. "Lie down here next to the pool."

She grabbed a towel from the stack on the chaise and laid it next to the pool. Drew lay facedown on it, but instead of putting lotion on her hands, she slathered sunscreen on her body, then lay on top of him.

"Now this is interesting," he said.

She fit her body against his, and rubbed against him, her nipples aching as she slid against his back.

"Lina," he said, turning his head to the side to look at her.

She pressed her hands to his shoulders to keep him in position. "Just stay there and let me touch you."

"You're driving me crazy."

"That's the idea, isn't it?"

She continued to roll over him, the lotion making her body slick as she lifted, then slid down his body, touching him every-where with her breasts and sliding her still-bikini-clad pussy against his firm butt.

At this point she wasn't sure who was more tortured—him, or her.

She stood, planting her feet on either side of his hips. "Now, roll over on your back."

He turned over, smiling up at her as he did. "Now there's the most beautiful thing I've ever seen."

He made her feel bold and beautiful. She kneeled beside him and put sunscreen on his legs, massaging them the way he'd done hers. She wanted him to feel as good as he always made her feel. She straddled his hips and sat, then swept her palms over his chest and shoulders.

He grasped her wrists. "Your hands are so soft. Do you know how hard I get when you touch me?"

She shifted, sliding over his cock. "Yes."

"Take your bikini bottoms off and let me lick your pussy."

Shuddering at the prospect, she stood and untied the strings at her hips, then pulled away the material and tossed it to the side.

"Now come sit on my chest and let me suck your clit. I want you to scream for me."

Grabbing the smaller towel next to them, she tucked it under his head. She leaned forward, bracing her hands on the cement as she lowered her sex to his face. Drew grabbed her butt and buried his face in her pussy, his tongue snaking out to lick the length of her.

A rush of heat and pleasure engulfed her. That she was looking down at him, could watch his eyes as he explored every inch of her, was the most intimate thing she'd ever experienced. She rocked against his face, already close as he flicked his tongue around the sensitive bud and then closed his lips around it and sucked.

His mouth was pure heaven, his tongue a thing of the devil himself as he flicked it over her clit, then laid it flat against her and, oh, the things he did to her. He slid his tongue inside her, then pulled out, rolling his tongue over her clit again. Tingling vibrations shot through her.

She tilted her head back, letting the sensations surround her until she couldn't hold back. Her climax was like an explosion, setting her nerve endings on fire at the center of her core.

"Drew," she cried out as she came. He dug his fingers into her hips as her orgasm rocketed through her, leaving her sweating and breathless.

When the trembling subsided, she slid back, lying on top of him so she could catch her breath.

"Your heart is beating fast," he said as he stroked her back.

She smiled. "I might need some cold water to drink."

Drew wrapped his arm around her, then sat up. "I'll go get it."

She sat on the edge of the pool and dangled her legs in the water while Drew went inside. He came out with two glasses of water and a condom packet.

She took the glass of water he offered, grinning at his still very obvious erection.

"Yeah, I'm going to fuck you out here."

She got up and grabbed her water. "I certainly hope so." After she took a drink she laid her glass on the table. "How about a swim?"

"Good idea."

They jumped in the water, but as soon as she surfaced, Drew was right there, swooping his arm around her to tug her close. She wrapped her legs around him and kissed him. He cupped her neck to hold her there as he slid his tongue inside her mouth, backing her against the edge of the pool. His erection rubbed against her pussy, awakening her desire again. He grasped her breast, brushing his thumb against her nipples until the sensations made her moan against his lips.

He carried her out of the pool with her wrapped around him and deposited her on a smooth, wide stone ledge leading from the pool to the hot tub. Set several feet off the ground, it was a place to sunbathe or to dive into the pool. She looked up at him, the ends of his hair dripping water as he bent over to press a hot, lingering kiss on her. She shivered, but not from the cold. The sun warmed her body, and Drew's kiss set her on fire.

He left her only long enough to get the condom and put it on, then he was back, scooping her forward and spreading her legs. He eased inside her and she leaned back, closing her eyes to let the feel of his expanding cock wash over her.

"I love watching you," he said. "Watching us together. The way your pussy grabs onto me when I'm inside you. Can you see it, Lina?"

She lifted and leaned forward, watching his cock spear her. The visual combined with what she felt caused vibrations of pleasure to tumble within her. She lifted her gaze to Drew. "Yes."

"You rip me to shreds, Lina."

His words tore her apart, and then he thrust deeply, slid his hand under her butt and nearly lifted her off the stone as he plunged in and out of her so fast and hard she thought she'd die from the pleasure of it. And the entire time, his gaze remained locked with hers, as if there was something he was trying to tell her.

But there were no words between them, only gasps and groans as he furiously moved within her, and she rocked against him, giving him the only thing she had to give him.

Herself. Everything she had. She wound her arm around his neck and impaled her pussy on his cock, burying him deep within her. And when she came, tears filled her eyes. She squeezed her eyes shut, forcing them back as wave after wave of orgasm slammed into her.

"Lina," Drew said, his soft voice reaching her through the haze of her epic climax.

She opened her eyes and met his gaze, his features tightening as he came. She held on to him as he thrust and shuddered with his orgasm. She'd never seen anything so amazing as a man who gave her that much raw honesty.

She fell back against the stone and Drew went with her, taking her lips in a kiss as soft as the breeze flitting around them.

Drew rolled to her side. Carolina could barely take a breath, unable to fathom what had just happened between them.

Maybe it had just been really phenomenal sex, but she had felt so incredibly connected to Drew.

She closed her eyes and let herself relax, drawing deep, calming breaths.

Don't overthink this. It's not what you think it is.

And even if it was, she had no time for that in her life.

"Are you okay over there?"

She smiled, forcing those monumental thoughts out of her head. "Mmm hmmm."

"You know what?"

She tensed. "What?"

"I'm hungry."

She laughed and rolled over to face him. "We should probably take a shower and do something about that."

Drew sat up. "Good idea. I know they're doing a fireworks thing in town tonight. If you're up for that, we can go."

She laid her head in her hand. "Or?"

"We can barbecue here and just hang out."

"I love the sound of that. Unless you like big crowds and fireworks."

His gaze was pointed, and very warm. "I'm happy just to be here with you."

And there was that giant warning signal pinging in her head again.

She stood and reached for his hand. "Ditto. Let's go take a shower. Then you can get the grill started."

TWENTY

DREW GRILLED STEAK AND LOBSTER, AND CAROLINA
made rice and asparagus. They opened a bottle of wine to have
with dinner and ate outside on the terrace. The night was clear,
they were alone, and it had been a really damned good day.

He didn't want to leave tomorrow, but real life would intrude
soon enough.

He liked spending time with Carolina, and he wasn't the
kind of guy who thought much beyond what came after today.
But sitting across from her tonight, watching the ocean breeze
blow strands of her hair across her face, made him wonder
what made her so different from any other woman he'd ever been
with.

Because when he'd dated other women, he never thought about
them when he wasn't with them.

With Lina, he thought about her all the damn time. And that
was dangerous territory.

Was he ready for a long-term relationship? He was thirty years old. Maybe it was time to settle down with one woman.

"You're quiet tonight," Carolina said.

They had cleaned up the dishes and were sipping wine on the terrace.

He leveled at grin at her. "That's because you wiped me out today with your constant demands for sex."

She laughed. "Oh, right. I've seen you play hockey. I think you have an endless store of reserves."

He picked up his glass and took a sip before answering, studying how beautiful she looked in her sundress, her skin kissed with a little tan. "So what you're saying is that you'd like more sex?"

"I'm not sure there's an appropriate reply to that."

"How about yes?"

She gave him a look that made his cock tighten. "I can take it if you can."

He was sure she was probably sore. He'd given it to her pretty hard, especially this afternoon. She brought out his primal side, made him want to possess her. He'd never been like that with another woman.

"Maybe we'll just cuddle," he said.

"Now who's the wuss?"

"Are you throwing down the gauntlet, Miss Preston?"

He could see the fire in her eyes from across the table. "Maybe."

He pushed his chair back and came over to her, taking her hand in his. He pulled his phone out of his pocket, selected a song, then pressed Play.

Carolina looked up at him, a question in her eyes. "I can't believe you even have 'Unchained Melody' by the Righteous Brothers in your playlist."

"Why?"

"I don't know. It's . . . romantic, in an old-school kind of way. A classic love song."

He pulled her into his arms and began to dance with her. "What? And I'm not romantic?"

"You just strike me as a hard-driving-beat kind of guy. It goes with the hockey mystique."

"There's a hockey mystique?"

"Yes. Fast skating, hard partying, fights breaking out. Soft and romantic music doesn't fit."

He pulled her closer, turning her in rhythm to the song. "Then maybe you need to learn a little more about me, Lina."

She tilted her head back to look at him. He read the confusion on her face.

"You constantly surprise me."

"Just because I play hockey doesn't mean I listen to anger rock and go to the local bars looking for a fight. That's PR and I leave the fighting to the ice. If you really get to know me, you might find I'm a really nice guy, that one night in college notwithstanding."

"Okay, point taken. I might have had preconceived notions about you because of our past. And hockey does play up the bad-boy image."

"They do. And we play on that for our fans. But I'm not an asshole. Or maybe I was one in the past. But I'd never hurt you. Not intentionally."

He twirled her around, loving the feel of her in his arms. "Besides, I like this song. It's sweet."

She shook her head. "I would just never think of you as . . . sweet."

"When have I not been sweet to you?" At her look, he added, "Besides that giant mistake I made when we were in college that for some reason hangs like a black cloud over my head."

She didn't answer right away. "You're right. You've been very nice to me since we've rekindled our . . . whatever it is we're having."

He laughed and twirled her around. "I don't think we need to define it, do you?"

She laid her head on his chest. He liked having it there.

"I don't think we do, either. I like things the way they are, Drew. Right here, right now. Let's not mess with a good thing."

He didn't know what to make of that. Was she afraid of having a relationship, or just having a relationship with him? He knew he'd hurt her before. And he didn't know where he wanted things to go with them in the future.

Living for today always seemed like a good idea.

And that would have to do for now. For both of them.

The song ended, and Drew grabbed his phone to check the time.

"It's getting close to midnight," he said. "We should open up some champagne."

"I have a better idea." Carolina began to unbutton the front of her dress. She wasn't wearing a bra, so the visual had his cock twitching.

"I like where this is going."

"I want you inside me at midnight, making love to me at the end of this year and the start of the next." She grabbed his phone and backed inside, the swell of her breasts visible as her dress gaped open.

Under her spell, he followed, then took her hand as she led him upstairs and into the bedroom. He pulled a condom out of his bag and followed her out onto the deck.

"I thought we'd do it outside, under the moonlight." She dropped her dress to the ground.

Drew's dick pounded as he pulled off his shorts and tugged his shirt over his head. Carolina wriggled out of her panties, then walked into his arms. He kissed her, inhaling her sweet fragrance as his mouth covered hers.

He wanted to do this right, to make it good for her as they brought in the new year. There was a cushioned chaise lounge on the deck and he laid her down on it.

"I don't need foreplay," she said, spreading her legs and splaying her fingers over her sex. "I'm already wet and ready for you, Drew."

He sucked in a breath as he watched her touching herself. He took his cock in his hand and stroked as he watched her slide her fingers between the swollen folds of her pussy.

"Do you know what that does to me, watching you touch yourself like that?"

She looked up at him, giving him a hot, wicked smile. "Makes you hard?"

"Yeah. Makes me want to lick your pussy and make you scream."

"The clock is ticking, Drew. And I'm going to come with you inside me."

He pushed the button on his phone. "Five minutes until midnight."

He set an alarm on his phone, put on the condom, and climbed onto the chaise, using his knee to spread her legs wider. The fit on the chaise was tight, so they rolled to their sides, facing each other. Carolina raised her leg and placed it over his hip. He eased inside her, watching her face as he entered her.

God, she was beautiful, the way her lips parted when he seated himself fully inside her. And then she gasped when he withdrew and thrust. He went slow and easy, taking his time, feeling her pussy ripple as he made love to her with slow, gentle strokes.

She cupped his jaw, brought him forward to kiss her. He tasted wine on her lips, twined his tongue alongside hers, then brought it in deeper to suck even as he increased the thrusts of his cock. She moaned, and that sound gripped him, made his balls tighten.

He felt the pulses, knew she was close, and when the alarm sounded on his phone, he looked at her, saw the rapture on her face.

"Happy New Year, Lina."

"Happy New Year, Drew. Now make me come."

He ground against her, pulled out and thrust deep, and she shattered, letting go with a hoarse cry that splintered the quiet of the night. He groaned and released, going with her as they shuddered together, ringing in the new year in the best way he ever had.

He held her, stroked her back and kissed her.

"Can we sleep here tonight?" she asked.

"We could, but it might get cold."

"I could never get cold when your arms are wrapped around me."

He tightened his hold on her and stared up at the stars, listening to the sounds of the ocean waves.

A perfect night. A perfect woman.

Tomorrow, they'd go back to reality. But for now, it was the best night he'd ever had.

TWENTY-ONE

IT HAD BEEN MORE DIFFICULT TO GET BACK TO REAL-ity and the intense, frenetic pace of work than Carolina had thought it would be. The trip to Florida with Drew had been idyllic, a beautiful fantasy that had been equal parts relaxing and deeply disturbing.

She'd definitely had fun. She always had fun with Drew. And the sex, of course, had been phenomenal. But the underlying emotion of the day and night they'd spent together had been unexpected. She didn't know what to make of it, and had tried her best to push it aside, to concentrate only on the hot and fun aspects of her relationship with him.

And now her deadline loomed even closer, and she had spent a week buried with her team, finalizing clothes and making subtle changes to a few of the designs.

Gray had stopped by for a fitting during the week, so she at least had his clothing figured out now. All of the models had received final fittings, so everything was being settled.

She wanted to do a test shoot with Drew for the ad campaign, and she'd gotten permission from the Garden to do that with him after one of his practices this week. She wouldn't need the professional photographers until the day of the shoot. She just wanted to get positioning right, to make sure this idea in her head would actually work. That she could do with her own camera.

Drew had agreed to stay after practice and meet with her at the rink. She brought the clothes and met him outside the locker room after everyone had left. She hadn't seen him in two weeks. He'd had a few road games, his schedule had been packed tight, and she'd been over her head with post-holiday catch-up.

Though they had talked on the phone and texted every day.

She'd finally had to admit to herself that, like it or not, this was a relationship. Surprisingly, the idea of it hadn't panicked her as much as she thought it might.

She smiled as she saw him walking down the hallway toward her.

He pulled her into his arms and kissed her, thoroughly, until she went limp, content to let him work his magic on her mouth.

When he pulled back, his eyes had gone dark with desire, and every nerve ending in her body was zinging.

"It's been a long damn time since I held you in my arms. I missed you."

She smiled and looped her arm in his as they headed down the hall. "I missed you, too. How did practice go today?"

"Practice went good. It always does. If only we could figure out how to transfer those kick-ass practices into winning games."

"Your record isn't that bad."

"At home we're awesome. It's only on the road we're having problems."

"You'll figure it out, Drew."

"Yeah, we will."

He led her into the locker room. "Okay, what's the deal for this shoot?"

She laid her bag on the bench. "This is the underwear line I've created. I'd like to start with you in the briefs and T-shirt, and then just the briefs."

"And you want me on the ice in these?"

"Yeah. I know it's going to be uncomfortable, but I want you with your hockey stick in your hand, near the net. Did they leave the net up?"

"Yeah. I asked the crew to leave the net up. They're going to come back later and take it down and lock up."

"Okay, great."

He kicked off his boots. "I can't believe I'm going to freeze my ass off for you."

"I really appreciate this."

"Yeah, yeah."

He changed into the boxer briefs and T-shirt that Carolina had provided him.

"How do they feel?" she asked.

He looked down, then at her. "Like underwear."

She rolled her eyes.

"Why? Do they have superpowers? Or will my dick grow an extra inch when I'm wearing them? Because if so, you're going to make billions on these things."

"Never mind." She walked away.

He followed. "Babe. It's underwear. Men aren't picky about it. Besides, you're really advertising this to women, aren't you? Women buy a ton of underwear for their men, don't they?"

She stopped and turned to face him. "Yes."

"All right then. Let's make women want some men's underwear." He grabbed his hockey stick, and Carolina laughed.

Sometimes, Drew could turn the most complicated thing into something simple.

They headed toward the ice, where James had set up a carpet leading from the step off onto the ice and toward the net.

He owed James a case of beer.

"I'm pumped and feeling energized in these briefs. Like I could maybe even fly." He took a superhero stance.

She laughed. "Too late. Let's get you into position and take the pictures."

"Sounds good to me. I'm already cold."

Excitement fueled her. "Okay. Let's just do a few test shots of you standing next to the net."

Drew stood there holding his stick.

"Um, boring. Could you kind of get into a sexy position?"

He cocked a brow. "Define 'sexy position'."

"I don't know. Lean back."

He leaned back. And looked ridiculous. She laughed.

And Drew frowned. "So we're done now?"

"I'm sorry." She wasn't a professional photographer, the kind who could make a model feel sexy, who could draw out the vibes needed to get them in the mood.

But . . . she was a woman. And she knew what it took to get Drew in the mood.

She walked over to him. This visual had been in her head for so long, she just had to get it out, take the test shots, and see if this was even going to work.

"Put the stick in your left hand, then lean over this way, with your hand on the net. Yes. Just like that." She made sure to touch his body, to caress him the way she would if they were alone together.

She focused the lens on him. "I love seeing you in my clothes. Of course I love seeing you without any clothes."

His gaze hit hers, and she took the picture.

She smiled at him, then moved in closer, getting his face, the way he watched her whenever she touched him to realign his body.

"Spread your legs, just a little." She made sure to touch his butt, his thighs, to take deep breaths when she was near him.

"Carolina." His eyes looked dark and a little dangerous. Perfect.

She got the shot, and with every subsequent picture, she was certain she'd been right when she'd visualized this.

"Now, take off the shirt and let's get you in just the briefs."

He pulled the shirt off and she tossed it over her shoulder.

"Slide just the tips of your fingers inside the briefs, Drew. Let me see your hipbone."

"You asking me to do a striptease for you?"

She smiled, but kept her focus through the lens. "Maybe."

The look he gave her melted her. She clicked the camera, shot after shot, as he instinctively got into it. Now he knew what she wanted.

But then she lifted her gaze above the camera. "I don't think the erection is going to work."

"Then quit talking dirty to me."

She laughed, then came closer. Drew palmed his shaft, rubbing back and forth.

"I can't help myself. You bring out the best—or is it the worst—in me."

And now he wasn't the only one turned on. "This isn't productive."

He reached around to grab her butt. "Screw productive. I think you want to have sex on the ice. It's probably some long-held fantasy of yours."

"I'm thinking more likely it's yours."

"Nah. My fantasy has always been a blow job on the ice."

"Is that right? And just how alone are we here?"

"Everyone's gone. The crew didn't want to hang out, so I bought them lunch and told them I'd call them when we were finished here so they could clean this up and lock the place down."

"Is that right?" She dropped to her knees on the carpet, realizing he must be freezing in his bare feet. Even with the carpet down, it was really cold.

"Get up, Carolina."

Instead, she reached for his cock, sliding it between her palms. "We already know it's not too cold out here for you to get a hard-on. And like you said, we are alone here, right?"

His gaze had hardened, just like his cock. "Yeah."

She dragged the briefs over his hips, letting his cock spring free. She grasped it in her hand and stroked it, letting its heat warm her hands.

"You're hot."

He stared down at her. "So are you. You make my cock throb."

She licked her lips, then leaned forward, taking the soft head between her lips as she cradled his butt in her hands.

Drew couldn't believe Carolina had his cock in her mouth, right here on the ice. He hadn't wanted to do this test shoot, but he'd known it was important to her to get these initial shots to see if this advertising was going to work, and hell, it was only going to take a half hour, so why not?

He hadn't expected this, hadn't expected her touch and the way she talked to him to turn him on. He'd expected it to be uncomfortable and to freeze his ass off.

It was both, but he'd also gotten hard.

And now, watching her on her knees, taking his cock inch by inch into her hot, sweet mouth, it was pure heaven and hell. He swallowed, his throat desert dry as she cupped his balls and held them in the palm of her hand.

He laid his hand on the back of her head, giving her direction as she took him fully inside. And then she squeezed the base of his shaft with her hand, massaged his balls, and released his cock, mapping every vein and ridge with her tongue.

Christ.

When she worked the head with that amazing tongue of hers, lapping him up like she was going after her favorite chocolate marshmallow swirl ice cream cone, his legs trembled. He grabbed the net for support and grabbed a handful of her hair.

"Babe, that's going to make me come. Hard."

She tilted her head back and gifted him with the sexiest smile. "Tell me how you want it. Take control."

The best words a woman could ever give a man.

"Open."

She opened her mouth and he guided his cock between her lips, sliding it over her tongue. Between the cold around them and the heat of her mouth, he was about to explode.

"Now close your lips around me while I fuck your mouth."

Her lips compressed, and he tilted his hips forward, sliding his shaft in, then drawing it out, watching her cheeks hollow as she sucked him in.

Steam rose up on his body as sweat dripped down his face and neck while he pumped between Carolina's full lips.

He gripped the back of her head, then slid back and forth, his balls tightening as he fought the urge to come. Watching her take him in, giving in to him as he forced his cock into her mouth, easing it all the way back until he felt the tip hit her throat, was about the best damned thing he'd ever felt.

He knew she was uncomfortable, knew that ice had to be cold on her knees. But she wasn't complaining, just stared up at him, her sea-blue eyes giving him everything as he continued to thrust back and forth until his legs shook, until his orgasm had built up and he knew he couldn't hold back any longer.

"I'm going to come, Lina. I'm going to shoot my come into your mouth."

Her only response was a hum of acceptance, her gaze still focused on his face.

"Oh, yeah," he said, then pressed forward, shouting out as he jettisoned his orgasm deeply into her throat. She held on to his hips, taking him deep as he came. He grasped a handful of her hair as his climax shattered him, emptied him, leaving him shaking.

He pulled Carolina up off the ice and dragged her into his arms, something solid to hold on to while he recovered. She wrapped her arms around him, her body trembling.

She had to be freezing. He led her off the ice and into the locker room, grabbing a blanket to wrap around her.

"You're the one not wearing any clothes. You have to be cold."

He gave her a smile. "I'm sweating. You nearly blew the top of my head off."

She laughed. "Good. I enjoyed it. It turned me on."

She was an amazing woman. He threaded his fingers through her hair and massaged her scalp where he'd grabbed her hair so roughly. "Did I hurt you?"

"No. I told you. I liked it."

He let his hand drift down over her shoulder and arm, resting it on her hip. Touching any part of her body was always a turn-on for him. His cock twitched to life again, which surprised the hell out of him considering that she'd absolutely wrecked him not that long ago. "Yeah? So when you're watching my games, you're thinking about sex on the ice rink, huh?"

"Not particularly. Just sex with you. Location never matters much to me."

"Good to know. He reached for the button on her jeans. "Ever thought about the locker room?"

She looked around. "No. But it's an interesting idea."

He dropped down to his knees and pulled her boots off, then reached for her jeans, tugging them over her hips. "It would be a new experience for me, too."

Left in her panties, kneesocks, and a clingy top that covered her hips, she straddled the bench in front of his locker.

"You are just about the sexiest woman I've ever seen."

The look she gave him sizzled his nerve endings. "You say all the right things."

He pulled one of her legs over so she was facing him, then spread her legs. "I only say what's true, Lina. Now hold on to the bench while I take your panties off."

Carolina lifted her hips while Drew removed her underwear.

"Your knees are red," he said, kissing each one before smoothing his hands over her thighs. "Do they hurt?"

"They're fine." She'd been so tuned in to him on the ice she hadn't noticed the cold. Her gaze had been riveted on his face, the tightening of his jaw, the way his eyes narrowed when she'd sucked him in deep. Even now, remembering the way he'd arched his back as he filled her mouth, her clit quivered, her pussy aching to be filled.

Everything about Drew was a lesson in art, especially sexually. The two were intrinsically tied together. He was so honest sexually, and he loved exploring and pushing boundaries. He had no hang-ups that she was aware of, and being with him was so refreshing. Every time she was with him, she didn't know what was going to happen.

Like now, as he spread her legs and put his mouth on her sex. Here, in the locker room. She knew they were alone, but the thought of someone coming in, of being caught, added an element of danger, just as it had when she'd sucked his cock on the ice.

She arched into him as he rolled her clit with his tongue, then added his fingers to increase her pleasure.

She was already on the edge, so ready to come, especially in this danger zone. And yet, she resisted, mesmerized by Drew's dark head between her legs, his broad shoulders, and his oh-so-magical tongue doing incredible things to her. She gripped the bench and spread her legs wider, giving him better access, hoping beyond hope that he'd continue to do . . .

"Yes, right there. Don't stop, Drew. That's going to make me come."

And he did. She grabbed a handful of his hair and pulled it as she yelled out with her orgasm, all that pent-up energy releasing when she came. Drew grabbed a condom, sheathed himself and sat on the bench, pulling her on top of him while she was still spasming with aftereffects of her amazing orgasm.

She sat on his lap, sliding down over his shaft, every glorious inch of him filling her. Sensations were heightened from her climax, rippling through every nerve ending as Drew grasped her hips and thrust, burying himself deep.

She pulled off her top and unhooked her bra, giving Drew access to her breasts. When she leaned forward and slid her nipple between his lips, he sucked, and she thought she might die from the extreme sensation shooting straight to her pussy.

He cupped her breasts and fed from her nipple, sucking it deep, then moved to the other breast, kneading it and flicking the nipple with his tongue.

She moaned, sliding her fingers in his hair. "I really like that."

He popped the nipple out of his mouth and looked up at her. "I know you do. I can feel your pussy gripping me when I suck your nipples."

She dug her knees firmly to his hips and rode him, lifting and then dropping down on his cock, rubbing her clit against him so she'd go off again.

Drew cradled her face in his hands and kissed her, making her dizzy with the way his lips brushed against hers, softly at first, then deeper, a sensuous dance of tongues and lips that never failed to take her to emotional depths that turned her world upside down.

She pulled back and lifted, watching as his cock pulled partway out. She eased down over him again, taking him all the way in, teasing both of them until she thought she might explode.

She was close. Oh, so close.

"Take us both there, Lina," he said, holding tight to her while she rocked back and forth, getting the friction she needed.

She gripped his shoulders, rolling her hips over him, quickening her pace.

"I'm there," she said. "I'm going to come."

She let go, digging her nails into him as her orgasm washed over her, taking both of them as Drew let out a guttural groan. She ground against him as she shuddered out her release, holding his gaze as they both went over at the same time.

It was intense, shattering, and left her breathless, as it always did when she connected this way with Drew.

And when it was over, both of them heaving breaths and gasping for air, he still held her gaze, sweeping her hair away from her face.

"Carolina," was all he said, his voice a hoarse whisper.

She bent forward and kissed him, then climbed off and went into the bathroom to clean up. He followed, then they got dressed and went back out on the ice to retrieve their things. She packed her camera into the bag she'd brought, then turned to Drew and smiled.

"Thank you for tonight."

He grinned at her. "Which part? And I should be thanking you. From now on, every time I'm on the ice, or at my locker, I'll be thinking about you. About us."

She couldn't help but smile about that.

TWENTY-TWO

THEY WERE TIED THREE TO THREE WITH PITTSBURGH in the third period. On home ice, this was a critical game.

So when Trick passed the puck to Sayers and he took a shot that sliced in past Pittsburgh's goalie, the Garden lit up like crazy. Drew skated over and celebrated with the guys, then they concentrated on helping out the defense by keeping the puck away from Pittsburgh while the clock ticked down.

Not an easy task, because their forwards were formidable, but they managed to hold on and win.

They'd lost two on the road, but they'd won two at home, so at least they were still managing to kick butt on home ice.

As Drew made his way to the locker room, he couldn't help the grin as he looked down at his bench, remembering the hot night he'd spent here with Carolina last week.

And again, he missed her. She was back to being busy as hell, and he'd been on the road and came home to play two games this week.

"Good game, man," Trick said, slapping him on the back as he walked by.

"Back at ya."

"Yeah, we're good here. We've figured out how to master the home games so far. But we suck on the road."

Trick was right about that. They were in trouble on the road so far this season, and none of them had a handle on what was going wrong with their road games.

"We'll figure it out, Trick."

His friend nodded. "Sure. We will."

They had to stay upbeat and Drew felt it was his responsibility to keep his team morale positive. Even the coach was baffled by their lack of road wins so far, but the coach had said the same thing Drew had just said to Trick.

They would figure it out.

And when they did, they'd fix it.

Drew showered and got dressed, then packed up his bag.

"Hey, Drew."

He looked up as one of the assistant coaches called his name. "Yeah?"

"Some guy waiting outside the locker room for you. Claims he's a good friend. Name Trevor Shay mean anything to you?"

Drew grinned. "Yeah, it does. He's one of my college roommates, Leon. Tell him I'll be right out."

"Okay."

Drew finished putting all his gear away, then headed out the door. Trevor was leaning against the wall, talking to some of the other guys, who Drew was sure recognized Trevor.

Hell, everyone recognized Trevor Shay, since he was one of the few guys in sports who straddled the line between football and baseball. Or at least one of the few guys who'd tried it and was successful at it.

Trevor spotted him, pushed off the wall and came over to Drew. They shook hands. "Managed to pull that one out, didn't you?"

"I didn't know you were here. I could have gotten you a suite."

"Dude. I wanted front row on the boards, where all the action was. Good game."

"Thanks. What are you doing in town?" Drew asked as they headed toward the exit.

"I'm here for meetings with some PR people for advertising shit. Saw you had a game so I got my press people to get me a ticket. Are you busy?"

"No. But I'm hungry. Have you eaten yet?"

"No. Let's go get a big fucking steak."

Drew grinned. "Man, I'm glad you're here."

They took a taxi to the restaurant, ordered beers and their steaks, and settled in for what Drew knew was going to be a long rest of the night. Once he and Trevor got to talking, they'd never stop.

"So tell me what's been going on? It's been awhile since I've seen you."

"Football ended, baseball's gearing up. The usual shit." Trevor took a long pull of his beer.

"I don't know how you do it. Don't you want time off?"

"Why? What else have I got to do with my time?"

"I don't know. Take a vacation? Relax. Maybe grab a woman and get married and pop out a couple of kids?"

Trevor laughed. "Oh, right. Like I see you all domesticated with a wife, a couple rugrats, and a dog."

"Okay, maybe not, but at least if that's what I wanted, I'd have the time to do it. Football and baseball seasons overlap. Hell, how do you even find the time to get laid?"

Trevor leveled a smug smile at him. "Oh, there's plenty of time for that."

With Trevor's popularity, Drew didn't doubt women lined up just to climb into his bed. He shook his head. "Still, why not just pick one sport and stick to it?"

"If I only had a dollar for every time I've been asked that question."

Drew smiled. "Sorry, man. You're right. Not my business. I guess I'm just curious. And maybe a little jealous."

"No, it's okay. You're a friend, so it's different. I don't really have an answer for you, though, other than the reason I play both is because I love them both. It's pretty simple."

"Still, focusing on one would make you better at it, don't you think?"

"No. I think I'm pretty damn good at both of them."

Drew laughed. "Still as humble and modest as ever, aren't you?"

"You know it." Trevor grinned and tipped his beer toward Drew.

"Have you heard anything new about Bill Briscoe?"

Trevor's smile faded. "No. He's still at MD Anderson in Houston. I talked to Ginger last week and she said he's hanging in there."

Drew nodded. "I was down there about a month ago to see him, but there was no change. I was hoping . . ."

"Yeah, we all are, man."

"Have you seen Haven?"

"I saw her last time I stopped in to see Bill."

"How's she handling all this?"

"It's her dad, you know? But she's tough, and she's trying to hold it together for Bill. But I can tell this is tearing her up. Not that she'll talk to me about it."

Drew shook his head. Bill and Ginger Briscoe had been their dorm parents in college. Bill had been their rock, their shoulder to lean on, and the one person Drew had relied on to get him through the rough patches. To see him slowly fading away was so hard. He took a deep breath. "I hate losing him."

"Me, too. But there's nothing more any of us can do for him. This liver cancer is going to take him from us, and we can't stop it."

They both went silent for a few minutes, no doubt Trevor as lost in thought about Bill as Drew was.

"So tell me about you," Trevor said, obviously looking for a change of subject. "What have you been up to, other than scoring your ass off? I've caught a few of your games on TV. Impressive."

"Yeah, the home games. We're shit on the road so far this season."

"That happens sometimes. Road games are tough. It's still early in the season, though, so don't be so hard on yourself. You're working the kinks out. You pulled in some new players, and it takes awhile for the new guys to mesh in with the seasoned ones."

"You should be a coach."

"I'm better as a player. All these impressive skills of mine, you know."

Drew rolled his eyes. "Uh-huh. Plus, all the women you attract." Drew got his fair share of women's attention, but even here at the restaurant, Trevor was recognized. Not just by the women, either. Any guy who played dual sports, especially if he did it well, became an instant celebrity.

Throughout their meal they were watched. Drew was used to it, mainly in New York where he was recognized. But tonight, there were even more people taking pictures with their camera phones. He knew it was because Trevor was there with him.

"So, any special woman—or maybe women—in your life?" Trevor asked.

Sufficiently full after downing his steak, Drew pushed his plate to the side and took a couple of swallows from his glass of water. "I've been seeing Carolina Preston."

Trevor's eyes widened. "Gray's little sister? No shit. When did that happen?"

"A few months ago. She's launching her own fashion line and wants me to model for it."

Trevor snorted. "You're going to model clothes? I can't see that."

"Hey, I can walk in a straight line. And it's just once. I'm doing it as a favor."

"Good luck with that."

"Gray's doing it, too."

Trevor laughed. "I'm going to have to come and watch the two of you. Maybe heckle from the audience."

"Yeah, Carolina would just love that."

"So . . . you and Carolina. Is it serious?"

"I don't know. I've never gotten serious with anyone before. She's pretty focused on launching this line of clothes. And I've got the season to concentrate on."

"Which means it's just sex for both of you. Right?"

Drew disagreed, but he wasn't about to dissect his relationship with Trevor, who didn't really know Carolina all that well.

"I don't know. Maybe."

"How does Gray feel about that? Or does he even know you two are seeing each other?"

"Oh, he knows. I spent Christmas at the Preston Ranch with the family."

"Bet that was fun. You two sneaking around trying to cop a feel of each other. Oh, and her dad's the vice president now, so you had to avoid the Secret Service, too. That must have been a fucking nightmare."

"The Secret Service followed her dad. They mostly stayed out of our business."

Trevor took a drink of his beer and studied him. "So what aren't you telling me? Something happened while you were there, didn't it?"

"Gray walked into my room one morning, and Carolina was in my bed."

Trevor grinned. "Bet that was awkward."

"Understatement."

"And he didn't know about you and Carolina before that, did he?"

"No."

"He must have been pissed to find out that way."

"Just a little. But I talked to him. I mean she's not a kid anymore. She can make her own choices about who she sees."

"Yeah, but he knows your rep with women. You have one walking in the door while another is walking out."

"That sounds a lot more like your rep."

Trevor leaned back and signaled the waitress for another beer. "Okay, maybe. But it's not like you've been known for long-term relationships with women. Or any relationships for that matter."

"You're right. But this is Carolina, and she's different." She'd always been different. Not that he could explain that to Trevor. Or to Gray.

"So she does mean something to you beyond just the sex."

"Yeah, I guess she does."

"Does she feel the same way?"

"I don't know."

The waitress brought another round of beers. Trevor took a couple swallows, his gaze intent on Drew.

"What?" Drew shot Trevor a look.

"Why don't you just ask her?"

"Ask her what?"

"How she feels? Or tell her how you feel about her?"

Drew shook his head. "It's not the right time. For either of us. There's too much going on right now to talk serious shit."

Trevor laughed. "I've never known you to be a coward, Drew.

But it sounds to me like you might be afraid to take that step with her. Or maybe you're afraid of what she'll say."

"Oh, this coming from a guy who has never had a serious relationship in his life?"

"You have a point. But I know you. You're a good friend and always have been. I want you to be happy. Does Carolina make you happy?"

He thought about it, and realized that over the past few months, he'd never been happier. He loved spending time with Carolina. She made him laugh, she challenged him, and of course, the sex was off the charts. They had similar goals—their careers were their number one priorities right now. But there were a lot of other things they still needed to talk about, which had nothing to do with happiness.

"Yeah, she does."

"Then follow through. Talk to her about how you feel and see what happens."

"Maybe. When the time is right, I'll do that."

"That's the right move. You shouldn't let a good woman slip through your fingers."

"Sounds to me like you might be ready to take that step with someone."

Trevor let out a laugh. "Yeah, right. When? Like you said, I'm too busy, and having the time of my life right now. Long-term relationships just don't fit into my career plan right now."

"You never know, Trev. The right woman might just blindside you when you least expect it."

TWENTY-THREE

FASHION WEEK WAS BARRELING DOWN ON CAROLINA like a meteor hurtling through the atmosphere.

She barely had time to breathe. Her to-do list was a nightmare and every day she felt like pulling her hair out, because either beading had to be replaced on her signature dress or one of the suits wasn't fitting the model just right and had to be altered—again. She was sure a certain model was changing his physique in some way, because it fit him just damn perfectly a week ago and if she found out he was using performance enhancing drugs or pumping too much iron or something that was making her have to refit this coat one more damn time she was going to explode.

Or maybe replace the model, though she was out of time, and most definitely out of patience.

She sat in her office going through the lineup of the walk-through, numbering and renumbering everyone on her lineup card, when there was a knock on her door.

"Carolina, Esme is here for her final fitting."

She didn't even look away from her desk. "Get her dressed, Tierra, then call me."

"Okay."

She needed to schedule Drew in here for final fittings, too. She and Drew had traded phone calls, but hadn't yet connected. She picked up her phone and sent him a text message.

I need you to come in to my office for a final fitting. What does your schedule look like for this week?

She laid her phone down on the desk, hoping he'd text back today.

"Esme's in the dress."

Carolina left her office and checked the fitting on Esme's dress. Esme was a very sought-after model, so to get her for the show was a big deal. She'd put Esme into the beaded gown. It fit her perfectly. Esme walked for her, and of course she did it beautifully.

"What do you think?" she asked.

"I think it's a knockout dress," Esme said. "I want it."

Carolina grinned. "Thank you."

At least something had gone right today. Esme was going to be the hit of the runway. And she hoped the dress would be, too. She'd spent hours designing it, crafting it to absolute perfection. Esme was gorgeous, with her tawny skin, tall frame, amazing body with her curves in all the right places, and those golden brown eyes of hers that were incredibly mesmerizing. The dress, with its copper and orange beading, set off Esme's coloring perfectly. Carolina couldn't have found a better marriage between outfit and model.

"Thank you so much for agreeing to model this for me."

"Thank you for asking. I'm excited to wear it for you. Tierra gave me a peek at your line. I think you're going to go big."

Hearing those words from Esme, from a supermodel who wore the latest fashions from the biggest designers, made her heart race. "Thank you. I really hope so."

After Esme tried on the other two outfits, she left, and Carolina huddled with her staff, making some notes and adjustments. A few other models showed up, so they spent several hours doing final fittings and discussing alterations. She and her staff grabbed lunch and ate in the main sewing room together. She didn't get back to her office until dark. That's when she realized she'd left her phone on her desk. She'd missed several calls, and a return text from Drew.

I have an hour or so right now. After that I'm headed out of town. Want me to come over now?

That had been seven hours ago. She scrolled through her missed calls and saw that Drew had called, too.

She tried calling him, but got his voice mail. He was likely already on a plane headed for . . . somewhere. She left him a message apologizing for missing his call, and told him to call her when he got back to town.

Dammit. She couldn't believe she'd missed him. And now that she knew he was going to be out of town for at least a couple of days . . . she missed him already. Not just because she had deadlines to meet, but because she missed being with him. Work separated them so frequently that she could have at least spent an hour with him today.

She went home, disgusted, and warmed up a can of soup, eating in front of the television as she worked on her schedule.

There wasn't even any decent hockey on tonight.

When her phone rang, she grabbed it, smiling when she saw it was Drew.

"Hi," she said after she clicked the button.

"Hi yourself. Busy day?"

"Insanely. I apologize for missing your text and your phone call. I was in the workshop and left my phone on my desk. I'm clearly in idiot mode this week."

He laughed. "That's okay. I figured you were buried."

"No excuse, since I'm the one who bugged you. Are you settled in wherever you are?"

"I'm in Toronto, and yeah. Cold here."

"I'm sure it is. How long is the out-of-town trip?"

"I'll be back Friday. Can we arrange something then?"

"Let me take a look at my schedule. Hang on."

Her staff wasn't due to work over the weekend, but she could handle it. She pulled up her phone. "How about Saturday? Do you have a game?"

"I do Saturday night, but we could do it in the morning."

She chewed on her lip. She didn't want to be pressed for time. "How about Monday?"

"That'll work."

"Great. Thanks for making time for this."

"No problem. We'll get it done."

"I'm really sorry I didn't get to see you today. I was sad that I missed you and would have been happy to see you for that hour." The words tumbled out of her mouth before she'd thought about them. Now they were out there, a confession of sorts. It was the first time she'd said anything even close to her feelings. She cringed, even as she said them, wondering how he'd react.

"Yeah? I miss you too, Lina. I know we haven't been able to spend a lot of time together. Our schedules kind of suck right now, so I was looking forward to getting an hour of your time this morning before I had to fly out."

She palmed her stomach, rubbing the ache of loss. "I'm sorry. Again. I seem to be saying those words a lot lately. My head is going in a million directions right now. Normally my phone is on me at all times. I tossed it on my desk and promptly forgot about it."

"Babe. It's okay," he said, and she heard the laughter in his voice. "It's not like we're never going to see each other again. Monday, right?"

"Yes. Monday. But that's five days away. Right now it seems like an eternity."

She knew she was being foolish. She'd be swamped between now and Monday and wouldn't even think about Drew.

Much.

"We could always have hot phone sex every night. Then you wouldn't miss me as much."

Her body coiled with need, desire driving a pulsing sensation deep in her core. "I've never had phone sex before."

"Neither have I."

She settled onto the sofa. "Somehow I find that hard to believe."

"Why's that?"

"I don't know. It seems to me you've done just about everything."

"I'd never had sex at the Garden. Definitely never had a blow job on the ice before. That was a first. You've given me some mind-numbing firsts, Miss Preston."

She loved when he got formal with her. "We've had some firsts together, then."

"It's too bad it's not spring or summer. I'd like to take you out-side on your garden patio and make love to you out there."

She took a deep breath, imagining him pushing her up against the wall, sliding his cock inside her as a warm summer breeze blew over both of them. The flowers would be in bloom and the scent of jasmine would waft over her as Drew thrust into her, slow and easy.

She leaned back on her sofa and closed her eyes, her hand drift-ing down to cover her pussy. She ached with need for Drew, wanted him here with her right now.

"What are you thinking about?" Drew asked.

"You and me, up against the wall on my terrace in the summer. I'd wear a dress—no panties, of course—so all you'd have to do is unzip your pants and you could be inside me."

"You're making me hard, Lina."

"Are you touching yourself?"

"Yes."

This was thrilling, talking about sex over the phone. Not nearly as good as having him here with her, but her nipples were hard and her pussy wet. She slid her hand inside her panties, her fingers cool against her heated flesh.

"What are you doing, Lina?"

"I have my hand inside my panties and I'm rubbing my clit."

"Christ."

"And you?"

"I've got a stranglehold on my dick. Just listening to you breathe hard could make me come. Not to mention visualizing you touching your pussy."

She smiled at that, loved that she could push him right to the edge without him even seeing her. "I can't help it. You make me hot."

"Get hotter. Tell me what you do to get yourself off when I'm not around."

She pushed her sweats and panties down. "I rub my clit, and put two fingers inside me, pumping as if your cock is in me."

Now it was her turn to feel as if she was ready to come, because the sounds she heard over the phone were driving her crazy. It was almost as if she could hear him stroking his shaft. And his deep, harsh breaths were the most powerful aphrodisiac she'd ever heard.

"Sometime when we're together, I'm going to show you how I jack off. At the same time, you're going to rub your pussy and make yourself come for me."

She widened her legs and slid her fingers deeper inside her pussy, felt it tighten around her fingers as she hurried her strokes. "Yes. I want to watch you stroke yourself, want to see the come spurt out of you."

"Fuck. Fuck. I'm going to come, Lina."

"Yes. Oh, yes, Drew. I'm coming." She couldn't hold back her climax, and came, letting Drew hear it as she cried out. He returned the favor, increasing her pleasure as he groaned into the phone with his own orgasm.

For a while after that, all she heard was both of them breathing heavily.

"I'm going to need a minute here. Don't go away," he said.

"Okay."

Every part of her trembled as she stood and went into the bathroom. When she came back, she grabbed her tea and took a sip to coat her dry throat.

Wow. She felt dizzy, but she smiled.

"Still there?" he asked.

"Yes."

"That was fun."

"It was."

"Not as much fun as it would have been if I was there with you. But it'll do until I see you again."

"I'll definitely sleep tonight now. I thought for sure I'd pace all night long. Thank you, Drew."

"I'll talk to you again tomorrow night after my game, if you're up for it."

She smiled. "I'm definitely up for it."

"Night, Lina."

"Good night, Drew."

She hung up and laid her phone down, staring at all the paperwork she'd carelessly tossed onto the floor. Her most important work, cast aside in favor of phone sex.

She giggled and kneeled to pick it all up and re-sort it.

Sometimes even important work had to be put aside for really great sex.

TWENTY-FOUR

CAROLINA COULDN'T HELP THE SURGE OF PRIDE AND absolute awe as she watched her brother modeling her clothes. Gray had the perfect form for modeling, and as much as he hated it, he could walk a runway. The fit was excellent and wouldn't need much in the way of changes at all.

"God, that guy is hot," Evelyn said as she sat in the chair next to Carolina.

Carolina grinned. "And your hormones must be surging."

"That they are. But I'd think he was hot even if I wasn't pregnant." After the staff hustled Gray into the dressing room for a change, Evelyn turned to her. "You've done an amazing job, Carolina. I'm going to want to order all those clothes for Gray. He looks hot as hell in them. I would say, like they were made for him, but really, they were."

Carolina laughed. "They do look good on him, don't they? I'm really pleased with how everything turned out."

"You should be. How's your stress level right now?"

"Actually, not as bad as I thought it would be. Things are running pretty smoothly and I'm more or less on schedule." Carolina glanced at the dressing room, and not seeing Gray, she pulled out her notebook. "Since Gray's no doubt being stuck with pins at the moment, I have a few wedding dress concepts I'd like you to look at."

Evelyn's eyes widened. "Seriously? Already? I didn't think you'd have any time to work on or even think about my wedding dress until after the launch of your line."

Carolina shrugged. "It's a stress reliever and takes my mind off this whole Fashion Week thing. And when an idea pops into my head, I can't help but work on it."

She showed the drawings to Evelyn. "These are only concepts. Not fully fleshed out yet, just a few ideas."

Carolina held her breath, watching as Evelyn flipped through the three dress concepts she'd created. Evelyn looked at each one, studying them carefully, then going over them all again, which Carolina appreciated.

Evelyn laid her hand over the notebook and lifted her gaze to Carolina. The excitement on her face was evident. "These are gorgeous, Carolina. But how am I supposed to choose just one? Is it possible to wear three wedding dresses?"

Carolina exhaled, then laughed. "I'm so glad you like them."

"Like them? I love them. All of them. Oh, my God, they're amazing. I can't believe you designed these in the short time since Christmas."

Carolina flipped through each one, discussing how they could make subtle changes. "Anything you want, however you want it, we can alter. We can even take portions of one dress and add it to the other. And each one can be easily altered for your expanding waistline."

Evelyn grinned. "That'll be helpful, since I have no idea how big I'll be by May."

"How are you feeling, by the way?"

"Surprisingly good so far. No morning sickness. A little tired, but your father is giving me a lot of leeway in that regard. He's already told me to hire an assistant to help me out because he doesn't want me to work so hard."

"Well, that is his grandchild you're carrying. I don't think he wants you working twelve-hour days right now."

"I've been to see the doctor, who assures me I'm perfectly healthy and can carry on my normal duties for as long as I feel like it, so I'm thrilled about that. But I have a feeling your father is going to be watching me like a hawk the entire time. Along with Gray."

Carolina nodded. "And my mother."

"Yes."

"How did your parents take the news?"

"They were elated," Evelyn said with a wide grin. "They're so excited about the baby and the wedding. We're all getting together next weekend in D.C. along with Gray's parents to talk wedding planning. I'll be sure to take a lot of notes since I know you'll be too busy to attend."

"Thanks. I'll get up to speed on the whole wedding-planning thing with you as soon as I get Fashion Week out of the way."

"Honestly, Carolina, there's no hurry. I think with your mother in charge, neither you nor I will have to do much of anything, anyway. Which gives me a huge sense of relief."

Carolina laughed. "You're probably right."

"So back to the dresses. Can I get copies of these to look at?"

"Of course. I'll email them to you."

"And you won't give these to anyone else until I choose one?"

"Absolutely not. You're my first—and so far my only—wedding dress client."

Evelyn laid her hand over her heart. "I'm so honored by this, Carolina. And I love these dresses so much. But I think I already know which one I'm in love with."

"Which one?"

Evelyn scrolled to the second one. "This one. The scalloped edges and the sweetheart neckline. It's so modern, yet classic and traditional at the same time. And with the empire waist, I think it'll fit the expanding baby belly perfectly. It's the one that's in my head right now."

"I'm so glad. I think a dress like that will look beautiful on you."

"So do I. But I want to look at all of them again, just to be sure."

"I'll email them to you, and you can show the moms and get their opinions."

"Oh, good idea. Thank you, I'll do that."

Gray emerged from the dressing room and Carolina quickly closed the file. "But not the groom-to-be."

"Definitely not."

"What are you two talking about?" Gray asked.

"Wedding dresses," Evelyn said. "Which you can't see."

"Okay. But you know, I'm a pretty good judge of fashion."

Evelyn stood. "Not in this case. You'll just have to remain in the dark."

Carolina stood, too. "Thanks for coming up to play dress-up."

He kissed her on the cheek. "Don't you know? It's my favorite thing."

She laughed. "Yeah, I'll just bet it is. Which is why I appreciate it so much. But now you're good to go until the day of the show."

"Have you got time to have lunch with us?"

She didn't, but she would, for her brother and for Evelyn. "Absolutely."

She told her staff she'd be back in an hour. They acted like it was no big deal, which to them, it probably wasn't. They all had their assigned tasks and didn't need to be watched over. That's why they were all awesome. To her, she felt like she had to stay on top of everything, which was probably her own OCD nature coming out.

"Come on, Carolina. The world of your fashion line won't stop turning just because you grab a sandwich with us," Gray said, dragging her out the door.

He was right, of course.

They went down the street and ordered sandwiches from one of her favorite delis, which made Gray ecstatic, since they were huge sandwiches. Carolina and Evelyn split a sandwich, since the deli loaded about a half pound of turkey on each one. They split a fruit salad as a side dish, too.

"How are things going with you and Drew?" Gray asked.

"Oh, just fine." She had no idea how to have this conversation with her brother.

"So he treats you good?"

"He does."

Gray shook his head. "I still can't believe the two of you are a couple."

Carolina looked at Evelyn, who just gave her a helpless look in response.

"Well, we are. Sort of. I don't know. We're seeing each other. For now."

She cringed, even as the words came out of her mouth.

Gray frowned. "What the hell does that even mean?"

Evelyn laid her hand over Gray's. "I think it means your sister would like for you to mind your own business."

Gray's gaze shifted from Evelyn back to Carolina. "What did I do? I just asked how things were going. It wasn't like I was asking how good he was in bed."

Carolina laid her head in her hands. "And it goes from bad to worse."

"Okay, fine. I give up. I won't ask anymore."

"I'm sorry," Carolina said. "It's just . . . awkward, because the two of you are such good friends."

"So that means there are problems between the two of you, and you think if you complain about him to me that I'll get pissed off and go punch him out."

Carolina laughed. "No. Well, I mean yes. That could happen. Or maybe it wouldn't. God, I hope you wouldn't do that. That would be so juvenile."

Gray slanted her a look across the table.

"Okay, fine. No, there are no problems between us at the moment. We get along great. We have fun together. I can't define what it is that's happening between us, Gray, because, honestly, I just don't know. We enjoy being with each other, but we're both so heavily invested in our careers, I don't know where it's going. Or if it'll last."

"And if it doesn't, and you two break up, you think it'll come between Drew and me."

"Yes. And I'd rather that doesn't happen. I didn't want you to know about Drew and me at all."

Gray leaned back in his chair. "Cutting me out of that part of your life just because you think it will affect how I feel about my best friend kind of sucks, Carolina."

She blew out a frustrated breath. "For me, too. You and I have always been really close. There wasn't anything I couldn't tell you."

"Until now."

She nodded. "Because I also know how close you and Drew have always been. My relationship with him will affect your relationship with him. And it shouldn't."

"You can't change that. He's been one of my best friends for a lot of years. But you will always and forever be my sister. Family. Nothing trumps that bond. Not even friendship."

Gray's words shouldn't have made tears fill her eyes. But they did. He was right. The bond they shared had always been strong. And it always would be. How foolish of her to think anything, or anyone, would come between them.

She reached across the table and grasped his hand. "Thank you for that. But I'm a grown woman now. And if it doesn't work out between Drew and me, just know my eyes are wide open. And I can handle it, okay?"

Gray nodded. "Okay."

TWENTY-FIVE

TRICK PASSED THE PUCK TO SAYERS. DREW WAS IN position, and despite the elbow from the defender trying desperately to shove him out of the way, he was determined to stay in front of the defender's goal.

So when Sayers shot the puck to him, Drew turned and took the shot.

And the goalie scooped it up in his glove.

Shit.

Sawing breath until his lungs ached, Drew skated down the ice toward his own goal. They were only down one goal and there was still time left in the third period. They could pull this game out against Philadelphia, at least tie it up and then make a comeback. All they had to do was score. They were so damn close Drew could taste it.

But in order to do that, they needed the puck at the other end of the ice. Kozlow, their best defender, shifted and went after it, slamming the Philadelphia forward against the boards. Drew wanted, needed desperately, to be in the middle of that, but he stayed in position, moving fast when Kozlow wrestled the puck away and shot it down the ice.

Trick was there to take it and make the turn and dashed, time moving too fast for Drew's liking. He knew they were no more than a minute or two from the end of the game. If they tied, they'd go to overtime.

Drew took the pass from Trick and got an elbow to the neck from the defender. He fought for it, but another defender swooped it up and took it.

Shit. He dug in his skates and went after him, but Kozlow and Ebers were there.

It went back and forth like this for what seemed like an eternity, with the defense holding on, keeping Philadelphia from scoring, while the offense couldn't get the damned puck into the net.

And when the buzzer sounded signaling the end of the game, it was the worst damned sound Drew had ever heard.

They'd lost by one fucking goal. He'd have rather gotten his ass kicked by a blowout than to lose by one goal. They'd been close so many times, but they just hadn't been able to muster up enough offense to get the job done.

Again.

They had another road game before heading home, and he hoped to God they could pull out a win on that one, because things weren't looking good for the team otherwise.

Fuck. Fuck, fuck, fuck.

He'd gone out with the guys after the game, but none of them were in the mood to do much talking or partying. They all headed back to their rooms early.

Drew grabbed the remote to watch television, but there was really nothing on he wanted to watch.

He grabbed his phone to call Carolina, but it was late, and he didn't want to keep her up. The clock was ticking on Fashion Week, and he knew she was probably putting in a lot of long hours.

Instead, he sent her a text message saying he was going to bed early and he'd talk to her when he got to Chicago tomorrow.

Where he had another road game.

Another opportunity.

Or another chance to lose on the road.

No. He pulled his fingers through his hair and got up off the bed, determined to think positively. He stared out the window at the snowy Philadelphia night, feeling the chill all the way through to his bones.

They couldn't lose every fucking road game this season. At some point, they'd figure out what the cause was and turn it around, win on the road, and this would all be a distant memory.

An unpleasant, distant memory.

Shivering, he climbed back into bed and found some lame old movie on TV. Anything with sound so he wouldn't feel so alone right now. He stared over at his phone. No return text from Carolina, which meant she was either busy working, or already asleep.

He wanted to call her, to hear the warmth of her voice in his ear. He wanted her to tell him it was all going to be all right.

But she couldn't tell him that, could she? Because she didn't control his destiny. Only he did. Only he—and his team—could pull this shit hole of a season out of the crapper, and make it right.

He just wished he knew how they were going to do that, what the magic secret was to taking a team that kicked ass at home and sucked on the road, and turning them into absolute winners.

He closed his eyes and willed it to happen.

Because at this point, skill didn't seem to matter. And will, hope, and prayer were the only things he had left.

TWENTY-SIX

CAROLINA COULDN'T BELIEVE FASHION WEEK WAS just around the corner.

She felt ill-prepared, but it was here. The final touches had been put on everything, so ready or not, it was here, and there was nothing she could do about it now.

The one major item left was getting her print advertising moving along, and for that she needed Drew.

He'd texted her from the road, and called her a few times. She'd been working nonstop, twelve hour days, so their phone calls had been short, but she had to admit she'd enjoyed hearing from him. He'd seemed down since they had a couple losses on the road, and she was so in her own head she wasn't sure she was much good at cheering him up, but she did try to send him some messages about his games, which, surprisingly, she'd found time to watch.

She was hooked, and couldn't seem to not watch his games, no matter how busy she told herself she was. Even Stella came over one night for takeout and they watched together, since Stella and Trick were still bed buddies, though Stella insisted that's all that was going on between them.

"No emotional attachment?" Carolina had asked.

Stella laughed. "I'm too busy to be emotionally attached, and I'm pretty sure Trick is one of those girl-in-every-port kind of guys. Which suits me just fine, because my first love is dance, not men. And clingers aren't my type."

"Trick doesn't strike me as a clinger."

"He's not," Stella had said, opening up her fortune cookie. "Which is why I'm still sleeping with him."

Carolina wished she could be so laissez-faire about her ... thing with Drew. But it seemed so much deeper, so complicated between them. And maybe that was all in her head, and because Drew was tied into her fashion line. Maybe she was deliberately keeping him closer to her because of that.

She paused as she perused lighting and music for the show. Was that what she was doing? Was she keeping Drew interested because she needed him so desperately for her fashion show? Surely she wasn't that superficial. Besides, Drew had agreed to do it before the two of them had ever slept together. And he had been the one to pursue her—rather diligently, as she recalled. She could have said no, firmly, and he still would have agreed to participate.

Wouldn't he have?

She worried her bottom lip with her teeth and pondered.

No, that wasn't it at all. She thought about him all the time. There was more to it than that. Though her thoughts about him were often jumbled up between hot sex, how he made her feel, an ache in the pit of her stomach, and how hot he was going to look in her clothes.

She laid her head in her hands. What a mess. She'd hate to think she was using him. Then again, hadn't he done the same thing to her all those years ago?

Oh, please. She was so past over that now. He'd apologized, she'd forgiven. That was done and she wasn't going to think about it anymore.

Her phone rang and she picked it up with a smile on her face. "Hey, Stella."

"I'm starving. Are you finished working for the night?"

"No, but I'm tired. And hungry, so I need to shut it down."

"Great. How about pizza? There's a hockey game tonight, the Travelers last away game before they head back to town. Want to watch with me?"

"Sure."

"Great. I'll bring the pizza. Say a half hour?"

"Sounds good. See you at my place."

She wrapped up and headed home, stopping at the store down the street for a few things before going up to her apartment. She made it with five minutes to spare before Stella rang the bell. She opened the door to the smell of some very tantalizing pizza.

"My stomach is growling," Carolina said as Stella came in.

"Mine, too. You're lucky there's any pizza. I almost ate it on the way."

They grabbed plates and drinks, then sat in front of the television. The game was just getting under way. Carolina zeroed in on Drew, that tingle in her stomach prominent as always as he skated down the ice.

They ate and talked, mostly about the game.

"No wonder they're losing," Stella said. "There's something wrong with Mangino. Does he have an injury?"

Carolina gave her a blank look. "Like I would know anything about the Travelers goalie?"

"Well, you have the relationship with Drew. I thought maybe you'd have some insider intel."

"And you're sleeping with Trick."

Stella shrugged. "We're just having sex. You and Drew have something else."

Carolina blinked. "What do you mean, we have something else?"

"Oh, please. You brought him home with you for Christmas, and then he whisked you away for New Year's. That's a relationship, honey, not fuck buddies."

"He's also Gray's best friend."

"So? What does that have to do with your relationship with him?"

"That's why I invited him to come to the ranch for Christmas."

Stella took a big bite of pizza, chewed, and said, "Uh-huh."

"Seriously. My relationship with Drew is the same as yours is with Trick."

"Bullshit. It's totally different. Your eyes light up when you talk about him. Even when you watch him on TV. It's like you're in love with him."

And there was the word, the one she'd avoided even thinking about. "I am not in love with him."

"If you say so. But you are in love with him."

"Don't tell me how I feel, Stella. We're just having some fun. And we're together a lot because of the fashion line."

Stella waved her hand back and forth. "Denial, denial, denial. What are you so afraid of? He's not a bad guy. He's damn fine looking, seems to treat you well, you two have fun together, and obviously the sex is off the charts because you spend a lot of time in bed together. So what's the problem?"

Carolina frowned. "The problem is, my career is just about to take off. The very last thing I need is a relationship. And yes, he is all those things. But love doesn't fit into the picture for me right now."

"Oh, how sad that falling in love is so inconvenient for you. Should I open a bottle of wine and we can have a pity party?"

Carolina stood. "What the hell is wrong with you, Stella? Why are you pushing this?"

Seemingly unconcerned, Stella just sat there. "I'm not the one getting all pissed off and shouting in denial over something that's so clearly obvious. The question is, why are *you* getting so mad at *me*?"

Stella was right. She was being a total bitch. She took a deep breath and let it out. "I'm sorry."

"Don't worry about it. I know you, and I know the whole love thing scares you."

"I'm not in love with him." She kept her voice purposely low to avoid screaming it.

"Okay. I believe you. Now sit down and finish your pizza and let's watch the game."

Carolina ate another piece of pizza, but her stomach was twisted in knots and the pizza tasted like cardboard now. As she watched Drew tangle with the Chicago player, her heart climbed into her throat. It was a tough, physical game. Elbows were thrown, lots of penalties, and in the end, the Travelers lost.

Again.

She felt awful for Drew. That was four road losses in a row.

"Well, that sucked," Stella said.

Carolina continued to watch after the game as the media interviewed the players. Drew was one of them, and she caught the misery on his face. She ached for him, wanted to be there with him, to put her arms around him and tell him to keep pushing, that the team would get through this road game loss issue.

She wanted to tell him that she believed in him.

She turned to Stella, who had been watching her. "It's obvious I care about him."

"I know you do, honey."

"That loss tonight—" She glanced over at the television. "Watching the interviews, the look on his face. God, Stel, it just kills me inside to see him hurting like that."

"It means you feel something for him. I understand."

"But I don't know exactly how I feel, or how deep it runs. I've never taken the time to analyze. I don't want to think about it. All I have room to think about is the launch of my line. Anything else and I might just implode."

"Okay. I get that. So maybe after the launch of your line, you can figure out whether you're in love with him or not."

She smiled at Stella. "Maybe."

If he was still around then.

THAT HAD TO HAVE BEEN THE WORST FUCKING GAME Drew had ever played. And he knew the rest of the guys felt the same way. He'd gotten two penalties, including a five-minute for fighting, which had been total bullshit. It had been a physical game and they'd played tough, with everything they had. It hadn't been enough.

Avery was playing hurt, and it showed. He'd given up four goals, and that just wasn't like him. But their other goalie just wasn't as good. It was their job to make Avery's work easier while his thigh muscle was healing, and they'd failed.

Shit.

They had to find a way to win on the road. They all knew it, and the coach kept ramming it into their heads at the end of every period and after the games.

They were a much better team than they were showing, and they had to figure this out.

His head just hadn't been in the game lately. He knew part of this was his fault, and it was time he started taking responsibility.

He'd lost focus, and he knew why.

Carolina. He'd been chasing her since preseason, had put all his focus and attention on her instead of the game, and it was costing him, and his team.

It was time he started concentrating more on hockey, and less on Carolina. Though the thought of seeing her less made his gut clench.

Some guys felt that dating women during the season was bad luck. He wasn't one of those guys. Then again, when he played with his concentration fully on the game, he was an ass-kicker. He had to admit, he'd focused more on Carolina and less on the game so far this season, and it was clearly hurting his game.

Time to change that. As painful as it was, his career was his life, and he wasn't going to let anything jeopardize that, no matter what—or who—that was.

He showered and dressed, then packed his bag.

There was a text message from Carolina.

Watched your game. Rough loss. I know you can come back from this. I believe in you.

He smiled at the message, then checked the next one.

We need to set a time for you to come in for your final fittings, talk about the advertising campaign, and decide on the date for the photo shoot. Can we get together when you get back?

He stared at it for a long few minutes, then typed a message back to her.

Have a lot of work to do, game-wise. We're kind of a mess right now so coach wants extra practices. I'll get back to you and let you know.

He knew Carolina needed him. But so did his team.

And he had to prioritize. As of right now, his priority was his team. His career.

Carolina would have to wait.

TWENTY-SEVEN

CAROLINA HAD SENT DREW MULTIPLE TEXT MESSAGES, and had even called him a few times, but he kept saying he was busy with hockey stuff and couldn't find the time to work on her advertising campaign.

He'd actually popped in for the final fittings on a day she hadn't been here. She'd been at the event center, taking some photos and talking to the event coordinator. Her staff had handled the fitting, and he'd been gone by the time she'd come back.

He hadn't said a word to her. He hadn't called her or told her he was coming by, so they hadn't had a chance to talk about the advertising campaign.

She had the photographer ready to go. All she needed now was her model. A model who was being really goddamned uncooperative right now.

The test photos they'd taken had turned out phenomenally well. With a professional photographer on hand, she knew the real product would be spectacular. Half a day. A few hours. That's all she needed from him to get this finished.

She paced in her workshop, everyone else having left for the day. She'd known Drew was going to let her down. She should have gone with someone else. Not that it wasn't too late to do that. But dammit, the whole campaign was lined out perfectly in her head, and the only face and body she saw on there was Drew.

Maybe that was because she was personally involved with him, because she'd slept with him. There were many great-looking models who'd fit the advertising perfectly.

She tapped her pencil on her sketchbook, staring at it and getting nowhere. She pulled up the Travelers schedule. No game today, and yet her phone remained strangely silent, at least as far as Drew. Everyone else was texting and calling her about every last-minute detail, including wanting invitations to the show which was in three goddamn days. As if that wasn't enough to tighten her chest and make it hard to breathe. But the one person she needed to hear from had gone silent.

She dialed his number, the phone rang several times and then she got his voice mail, which sent her blood pressure through the roof. She knew from looking at his schedule that he had a stretch of home games, which meant he was in town and was going to be here for a while, including for the show, thank God.

If he even planned to show up for that.

She grabbed her coat and shut down the studio, then grabbed a taxi, giving the driver Drew's address.

She paid the driver, but asked him to wait while she went up to the door and pressed the buzzer. When Drew answered, she waved the driver off.

"It's Carolina."

"Oh. Sure. Hang on while I buzz you in."

She rolled her eyes when he hit the buzzer. She went inside and headed to his door. He'd already opened it and was leaning against the doorway. He didn't have a shirt on, only a pair of low-slung sweats. His hair was wet, the ends curling around his neck. Despite her profound irritation with him, she couldn't fight the surge of desire that kicked in as her gaze instinctively followed the droplets of water sliding down his chest.

Forcing her attention to his face, she saw him smiling.

"This is a nice surprise."

"You didn't answer your phone."

He frowned. "I must have been in the shower. Or maybe at practice. I just got home about twenty minutes ago and jumped in the shower right away. Sorry. Come on in."

She took off her coat while Drew went into the bedroom and came back with a shirt on.

"Do you want something to drink? A beer or a soda or water?"

"Water would be good, thanks."

He was being formal. He hadn't hugged her or kissed her. She didn't like it. It was like they had taken ten steps back in their relationship and she didn't know what was going on.

He handed her water and grabbed one for himself.

"Take a seat," he said, motioning to his sofa.

She sat and took a sip of water. "What's going on, Drew?"

"What do you mean?"

"I mean you're ignoring my calls and texts. You're ignoring me. You came in for your final fitting, and you didn't even tell me."

"Oh, yeah, that. I only had a few minutes and you weren't there. Your staff took care of it, and I had to hurry out of there. I told you I've been busy with games and practice."

"We have the photo shoot to schedule and I'm running out of time."

He didn't say anything. She studied him, saw the tension on his face and the way he held his body.

"Tell me what's bothering you," she said. "Is it the road games?"

"You're not really here to talk about hockey, are you?"

"I'm here to talk about you, about what's been going on since we were last together. You've been avoiding me."

"No, I haven't."

She cocked her head to the side and leveled a serious look at him. "Come on, Drew. Let's be honest here. If you've changed your mind about doing the ad shoot, at least tell me."

He stood and paced, spending more time looking out the window than at her. A bad sign. Carolina stayed on the sofa, because it was obvious Drew didn't want her close. The thought stabbed through her, the hurt palpable.

"I don't know. Work's been tough, you know? We've lost some games and we're all trying to figure out what's not working for the team. It's all I've been able to think about lately."

"Understandable. When things don't go right at work, it consumes you."

He stopped and looked down at her. "You're not mad."

"How could I be? All I needed was an explanation of where your head was at. And I do know how you feel. But the bottom line is, I'm at deadline for the print advertising. You're either in or out. My preference is you being in. It'll only take a few hours for the shoot, Drew, and I really need you."

She was laying it all on the line for him, telling him how much she was relying on him for this.

He looked at her, and she waited.

"I just . . . can't right now, Carolina. I have to give everything to the team."

"But you're still going to do the show, aren't you?"

He didn't answer her.

"Drew. You have to do the show. You're fitted. It's too late to get someone else."

"Yeah. Sure. I did the fittings, right? I'll do the show."

She'd never seen such a lack of enthusiasm. Not that she expected him to be thrilled about it, but . . . God, she had spent a year getting ready for this. And now it was three days away and he wanted to bail on her?

"You could have said no at the beginning, you know. It wasn't even my idea to have you in the show. It was Gray's."

He gave her a wry smile. "So you didn't want me."

She let out a frustrated sigh. "I'm not saying that. But it's too late now. I need you to say you're going to be there."

He shrugged. "I'll be there. For the show part, anyway, because I promised you I would."

He'd also promised her he'd do the advertising. Which meant he was giving her nothing. There was no emotion in his voice. He was walking away from her yet again. Somehow, it hurt more now than it had all those years ago when he'd dumped her. Maybe because she cared more now than she had then.

She stood, tamping down the hurt that wrapped around her like a pin-pricking blanket. She refused to take this personally. He'd made a business decision, and nothing more. "Okay. I get that your schedule is full regarding the print ad. I'll just go in another direction."

"Wait."

She stopped, hoping he'd changed his mind.

"Look, I was going to have something to eat. Maybe run out and grab a cheeseburger. Do you want to join me?"

She couldn't even force a smile. "I hate burgers. Thanks, but no. I have a lot of work to do, so I'll just grab a taxi and head out."

She put on her coat and went to the door.

"Carolina, I'm sorry."

She didn't want to see him anymore, couldn't even form words, hating that there was a catch in her throat, that she wanted to cry.

She had to be a professional about this, not act as if he'd just broken her heart.

But he'd just broken her heart, dammit. He'd let her down, and she couldn't help the way she felt.

This was what happened when she allowed herself to get close. She should have known better. If she'd have kept things business-only between them, she wouldn't feel as if he'd jerked her world out from under her right now.

She finally took a deep breath and turned around. "Don't say anything. It's all right."

She opened the door and shut it behind her before she did something incredibly stupid, like bursting into tears or asking him why he didn't care enough about her to do this one thing that meant the world to her.

A taxi was just pulling around the corner, so she hailed it and it stopped. She'd gotten lucky, was hoping she wasn't going to have to stand there under the windows of his apartment for twenty minutes waiting for an available cab. She climbed in and gave the driver her address, then sat back and thought about which of her models she was going to use for the print advertising.

There was no time to wallow in her misery, no time to think about herself. She had to get moving on the advertising campaign. Work had to take precedence.

When she got back to her apartment, she went to her model portfolios and brought them up on her computer, searching through each face, studying each body, imagining them wearing the briefs.

She'd have to scrap the shoot the way she'd envisioned it. Without Drew, it would no longer make sense. She'd have to come up with something else, something equally enticing.

Reaching into her bag for her sketchbook, she propped her feet up on the table and closed her eyes, letting her imagination have free rein.

The only problem was, her mind had gone completely blank.

DREW LEANED AGAINST THE WINDOW LEDGE AND WATched Carolina get into the taxi and drive away.

He was such a dick. It would have cost him nothing but a few hours of his time to go ahead and do the advertising campaign. They'd already run through it once. He knew what to expect. And then it would be over, she'd have what she wanted, and he could go on and do his thing.

But hell, what would he promote for her? Certainly not a damn winning image. He wasn't a winner. Not this season, anyway. She should go in another direction, get some famous model whose face would sell millions for her.

He sat on his sofa and dropped his chin to his chest. He felt washed-up and finished, like a loser. And it had been a long damn time since he'd felt that way. In college, when he'd struggled it had taken a kick in the ass from Bill Briscoe to remind him why he was there in the first place, and all the things that were worth fighting for.

Bill would kick his ass right now if he could see him sitting here in the dark feeling sorry for himself, when he should be trying to figure out what the problem was with his play, or with his team's play.

Instead, he was blaming the woman he cared about. But hell, he was grasping here, and what else did he have to grab on to other than Carolina as an excuse for everything that was fucked up so far about this season?

Something else Bill would likely kick his ass over.

His stomach tightened at the thought of not having Bill around to seek advice from.

He grabbed his phone and dialed Ginger Briscoe's cell. She answered on the third ring.

"Well, hello, Drew. How are you?"

"I'm doing fine, Miss Ginger. And you?"

"Hanging in there."

He didn't want to ask the question, but he had to know. "How's Bill doing?"

"Hang on just a second, Drew."

He heard rustling, then a door closing.

"He's sleeping right now, so I didn't want my talkin' to wake him up. It's not good, Drew. Doctors think the next week or two at most."

Drew took a deep breath. "I'm sorry, Miss Ginger."

"Nothin' for you to be sorry about. It's just his time. The nice doctors down here have done all they could but there's nothin' left to be done. It's in God's hands now."

"Is he in any pain?"

"No, honey. They've got him medicated. He sleeps a lot, smiles at me a lot, and he and Haven and I are just sittin' around laughin' about all the good times we had with all you boys."

Drew swallowed past the lump in his throat. "I'm going to head down there tomorrow."

"You do that. I know he'd love to see you before . . . well, he'd love to see you."

"I'll talk to you soon, Miss Ginger."

Drew hung up and got online, booked a flight to Houston, then called his coach, letting him know he'd miss practice tomorrow for family business. He explained the situation, which his coach said was fine with him. Drew promised he'd be back the next day.

It was important to see Bill, to be able to say good-bye while Bill was still around.

The next morning he hopped a flight to Houston and rented a

car, then drove to MD Anderson. He sat in the parking lot for fifteen minutes before he gathered up the courage to get out of the damn car.

He needed to see Bill. He wanted to see him, but he didn't know if he could handle this.

He loved his parents, loved his dad, but Bill had always been like a second father to him. He'd told all his deepest, darkest fears to Bill Briscoe. Bill had seen him at his absolute worst, and had pushed him along when he thought he couldn't become the man—the athlete—that he needed to be.

And as he stood in the lobby in front of the elevators, Drew needed to be that man right now.

He sucked in a breath and pushed the elevator button, taking it up to the floor where Bill's room was. He walked down the long hallway, the smell of medicine, illness, and utter hopelessness surrounding him like a dark cloud. By the time he got to Bill's room, he knew if he didn't shake this off, he was going to crumble when he walked in.

Fortunately, Haven opened the door, her gorgeous face a sweet balm to his tortured senses. Her eyes widened and she threw her arms around him.

"Drew. I'm so glad to see you."

He put his arms around her and hugged her tight. "Haven. I'm glad to see you, too."

She shut the door behind her. "Dad will be really happy you came. Gray came by last week. So did Garrett. Trevor was here the other day. I swear a day doesn't go by that one of the college boys doesn't show up. So many of you stopping by has meant so much to him."

"He means everything to all of us. I hope he knows that."

She squeezed his hand. "He knows."

"Is he awake or is this a bad time?"

"He's in and out a lot because he's heavily medicated. But come on in." She pushed the door open and led him inside.

"Look who I found loitering outside in the hall."

Ginger was sitting in a chair next to the bed, reading a book. "Drew." With a wide smile on her face, she got up and gave him a tight hug.

He hugged her back, closing his eyes as he held on to her. "Miss Ginger."

"Thank you for coming," she whispered before letting go of him. "Bill, are you awake? Drew's here."

Drew turned his attention to Bill, who had lost even more weight since the last time Drew had seen him. He looked frail lying there on the bed, his skin sallow and seemingly hanging over his bones. Bill had always been so vital, so robust and full of life. To see him lying there like that was like a knife in his stomach. Drew had to force a smile on his face as Ginger moved aside so he could get closer to Bill.

Bill's eyes were closed, so he grasped his hand. "Hey, Bill."

Bill opened his eyes partway, looking confused.

"It's me. Drew."

He blinked a few times. "Drew? Hey, Drew." Then he smiled. "Hey . . . it's Drew Hogan."

"Mom, how about you and me head downstairs for a quick bite to eat," Haven said. "Do you mind, Drew?"

"Not at all. I'll be here awhile."

After Haven and Ginger left the room, Drew turned back to Bill. "How are you feeling?"

Bill was a little more alert now and pressed the button to lift up the head of his bed. "Eh. I'm dying. It sucks."

Drew laughed. He'd always loved Bill's sense of humor. "Yeah, man. It does. I'm sorry."

"Nothing we can do about it. But they're giving me great drugs,

I'm not in any pain, and hell, I feel like a celebrity. People are popping in here all the time. Before long the paparazzi will be showing up thinking George Clooney is staying here."

"Then you'll end up on the cover of the *Enquirer*."

"Wouldn't that be some shit? I hope Ginger combs my hair before they do the cover shoot."

Drew hadn't expected this. He didn't know what he had expected, but not the old Bill. He was glad he'd made the trip. He pulled up the chair and took a seat.

"How's the season going?" Bill asked, obviously wanting to talk about anything but his health.

"It's shit. We're great at home, but can't win a game on the road."

"So . . . why is that?"

"Hell if I know, Bill. We're trying to figure it out. Our goalie is working with an injury, but we're not laying all the blame on him. We can't put decent offense together on the road, either. Our road statistics are terrible. It's like we're on vacation."

Bill laced his hands over his stomach. "Maybe you're just trying too hard. Lose a couple games on the road, you get a mental block, and the first thing you all think is that you can't win an away game. Then it becomes a self-fulfilling prophecy." Bill paused, letting the oxygen he was attached to fuel his lungs. "You tense up and make a lot of mistakes you wouldn't normally make. Especially if you're still good at home. That means the mechanics of your game are sound. Other than your goalie injury, it's obvious your team is solid, right?"

"Yeah."

"No trauma or drama otherwise, with coaching or teammates?"

"None at all."

"Then just play the same game you play at home. You'll win eventually. Stop acting as if it's the last game of the season and it all comes down to that one game. Just . . . play."

"You make it sound so simple."

"Because it is. It's not life and death, you know."

Drew cringed and gently squeezed Bill's frail hand. "You're right. It's not."

"Hey, I wasn't looking for sympathy here, kid."

"I know. But you're right. We're stuck in our heads in the worst way."

"Then get out of your heads and just play every game like it's just a game. Because that's all it is—just a game. The one you love. I think you forgot how to love it."

"Right again."

Bill offered up a grin. "I'm always right, kid."

Drew clasped Bill's hands in both of his. "I love you, old man."

"I know. Love you, too. And don't think that after I'm gone I won't still be watching over you, because I will. Be happy."

Drew's eyes filled with tears. "I hope you will."

He didn't want to think about how much he was going to miss Bill. They'd talked on the phone often. Bill would call him after his games and either congratulate him or chew him out when he screwed something up. In college, he'd kept him on the straight and narrow. After, they'd become lifelong friends. But he'd always counted on Bill to give him the best advice.

What was he going to do without him?

Bill drifted off to sleep and Drew sat there with him until Ginger and Haven came back in.

"Did you two get a chance to visit?" Ginger asked.

"Yeah, we did. A nice long chat."

Ginger put her arm around him. "I'm glad."

"I guess I should go."

"I'll walk you out."

Haven gave him a hug and Ginger stepped outside with him to walk him to the elevator.

"He's so strong, Miss Ginger."

She nodded. "He has his moments. He's fightin' it to the very end. But he's very aware that this is the end. He's accepted it."

"Well, he has you by his side, and I've never known a stronger woman."

Tears glimmered in her eyes. "We'll be fine. Now you go home and don't worry about us."

He hugged her. "I love you."

"I love you, too, honey."

When he pulled back, he took her hands. "If you need anything, call me."

"I will."

He started to leave, but then found himself unable to. He ended up sitting in a chair by the lobby. That's where Haven found him a half hour later.

"Hey. I didn't know you were still here."

He lifted his gaze to hers. "I can't go yet."

She nodded and took a seat next to him. "I know the feeling. I should get back to work. Mom said she'd call me when—well when it gets closer. But these are his last days. I can't not be here."

He took her hand and squeezed it between his. "I'm sorry, Haven."

"Me, too. Thanks for coming. It's meant a lot to my mom and me having you and all the guys come by. And it's been wonderful for Dad to know that he's that important to all of you that you'd take the time out of what I know are busy lives for all of you."

"None of us are too busy for your dad. He's important to all of us and always was."

She tilted her head and smiled up at him. "We all had good times together in college, didn't we?"

"Yeah, we did."

"Though all of you gave me a hard time."

"What? I never gave you a hard time. That was Trevor."

"Please. You teased me mercilessly. And especially Trevor, who tried to bribe me to do his schoolwork for him."

"Yeah, well, school definitely wasn't his thing."

She laughed. "Clearly. And look at him now. The superstud superstar."

"A legend in his own mind."

She laughed at that. "My hope is to someday be in a position to shove a microphone in his face and make him as uncomfortable as humanly possible."

"Well, you are in broadcasting. And he's in sports. It could happen."

"If things go well with this new national job I'm in line for, it could definitely happen."

"Oh, yeah? What new job?"

"National sportscaster."

"No shit?"

She grinned. "No shit. I don't want to talk too much about it in case it doesn't happen, but my fingers are crossed."

Haven was gorgeous. Tall, curvy in all the right places, short raven hair, the most amazing blue eyes he'd ever seen, and just about the smartest and savviest woman he'd ever known. She was on-topic on any subject, and she knew sports as well as any guy. "You'd be perfect for the job, Haven. I hope you get it."

"Thanks. Me, too."

"Have you told your dad about the opportunity?"

"Yes. He's very excited for me, but also sad he won't get to see me make the big time as a sportscaster."

He squeezed her hand again. "He'll be there watching over you, honey."

Her eyes filled with tears. "I know he will."

Not wanting to monopolize her time, and knowing he had a plane to catch, Drew finally stood. "I guess I should head out."

Haven hugged him. "Thanks again for coming today."

"Stay in touch, okay?" he asked as he hugged her back.

"I will."

He went down to the parking lot and climbed into his rental, but found himself staring up at the hospital, still unable to leave, to make that final break from Bill. He finally just dropped the keys in his lap and released the tears he'd held in check.

TWENTY-EIGHT

"I CAN'T BELIEVE IT'S HERE, CAROLINA. YOUR DAY HAS finally arrived."

Carolina took in a deep breath, knowing it was probably the last time today she'd be able to breathe. She turned to her assistants and nodded. "It is. I couldn't have done this without your help."

Edward pushed his glasses up the bridge of his nose. "You made this happen, but I'd be lying if I said I wasn't excited as hell to be here."

"You're going to knock them dead out there, Carolina," Tierra said. "And like Edward, I'm thrilled to be a part of it."

"Thank you. Both of you. Now let's go get everyone dressed. Is makeup here?"

Tierra nodded. "Just arrived. Hair people are here, too. And Jessica is checking in the models."

At least something was going right.

"Hey, gorgeous."

She turned and gave a quick hug to her brother. "You made it."

"Of course I did."

"Are Mom and Evelyn here?"

"Yes. Mom's so excited she couldn't stop talking."

Carolina grinned. "That's great. I'll go check on her."

"Don't worry about her. You have enough to do. Between Evelyn and everyone else fawning over her, she's in heaven. She gets to meet big designers and magazine people today. And watch her daughter's big debut."

Just the thought of who would be out in the audience today made her stomach do somersaults. Other designers, along with the editors of some major fashion magazines.

She grabbed Gray's arm. "I think I need to go lie down."

He laughed. "You're going to kill it. Now, where do you need me?"

"See that cute brunette over there? Just tell her who you are and she'll tell you what to do and where to go."

"Okay." He kissed her cheek and wandered off.

Carolina took a moment to center herself before dashing off to see to the rack of clothes currently being guarded by one of her staffers. She and a few of her staff removed the clothes from the bags and began steaming any wrinkles while the models were busy in makeup and hair.

"All the models are checked in," Jessica said. "Except for Drew Hogan."

Carolina squeezed her eyes closed and counted to ten. She tossed Jessica her phone. "His number's in there. Call him and ask him where the hell he is."

This fashion show would be a nightmare without Drew. He was supposed to wear three of her menswear outfits. He'd promised her he'd be here. He'd already bailed on the print ad—surely he wouldn't drop the ball on this, too, would he?

"No answer," Jessica said, handing her phone back. "I called twice."

Dammit. "Okay. Thanks, Jessica."

Dread dropped a lead ball into the pit of her stomach. What was she going to do if he didn't show up? She looked at the time on her phone. An hour until the show started. There was hair and makeup and coordinating the models into the lineups.

She wanted to tear her hair out from the roots, but her panicking wasn't going to solve the problem. She had backup models ready to go in case of illness or no-shows.

She found Tierra. "Get Gerard into hair and makeup and prep him for Drew's outfits."

Tierra nodded and ran off.

Though Carolina had a million things to do, her thoughts drifted to Drew.

He'd let her down.

Again.

But there was nothing she could do about that. She checked on her models, who were mostly prepped and getting into their outfits. The stage manager gave her instructions, and she sidestepped security to finish up last-minute details. With her mother in the audience, security was extra tight today, Secret Service being doubled because of the expected crowd. Even she and Gray had Secret Service protection today, though she mostly ignored them. It was enough to know they were there, extra bodies in an already tight space.

When there was a rush of crowd noise, she turned around to see Drew running toward her. Sweat poured down his red face.

"I'm so sorry."

"What happened?"

"Goddamned taxi rear-ended the car in front of us three blocks away. Traffic is a fucking nightmare. I finally got out and just ran the whole way."

"Oh, Drew. I'm sorry. You didn't have to do that."

"Sure I did. I promised I'd be here, didn't I?" He looked around at the models getting dressed around him. "Am I too late?"

He was sweaty, his hair wet from his run. Actually, he looked perfect. "No." She grabbed his arm and took him into hair and makeup. "Gel his hair, give him a rough edge. He doesn't need much in the way of makeup other than to tone down the redness from running. Otherwise, he's good to go."

"Probably a little deodorant would help, too," he said with a smile.

She laughed. "Whatever. I'll see you on the runway."

He'd made it. He hadn't blown this off. Her heart swelled with joy. One less thing to worry about.

In short order the models were lined up, Drew was in that fantastic outfit, and everyone was ready.

Carolina took in a deep cleansing breath, let it out, and when given her cue, stepped onto the runway.

"Good evening. My name is Carolina Preston, and I'm so thrilled to be here today to showcase Carolina Designs. This has been a long-held dream of mine, and I'm happy to set it free today. I hope you enjoy the show."

She turned and headed back behind the curtains, listening to the polite applause. She knew it wouldn't be wild clapping. She hadn't earned that yet. But she hoped her fashions would show that she was a capable designer.

The music queued up, and she sent her first model down the runway. As she watched them on the monitor, it felt a lot like giving birth.

The men were going first, and they looked spectacular from casual slacks and button-up shirts to Drew taking the runway in a weekend outfit of drawstring pants and a fitted Henley. He grinned at the end of the runway, turned, and oh, God, the way he walked.

Confident arrogance. No one could have done that outfit justice better than Drew. And Gray in a suit was something to behold.

The guys dashed back and changed, then went out again, everyone moving with precision. So far, so good. Gray came out next in a weekend casual piece, still very elegant, but oh, he looked so good. And Drew in jeans and a button-down shirt made her salivate. Every piece of her men's line had turned out perfectly. She could tell the audience was captivated. She hoped it was the same when it came time for the women, who were up next.

First down the runway was her camel leather jacket and beaded mini. She felt such a sense of pride seeing something she'd created walk the runway at Lincoln Center. Then came the flirty dark print skirt and body-hugging sweater, followed by the low-slung pants and matching knee-length coat.

Outfit after outfit walked, and with each one Carolina wrapped her arms around herself, her eyes shimmering with tears. She hoped—oh, she hoped so much they were well received.

And when Esme walked out in her gown, she heard the collective gasps, and knew she had the audience by the throat. The applause as Esme disappeared was loud, and as the men came back out, followed by the women, people were on their feet, the applause deafening.

She'd done it. It was over. And it had been damn good, so she no longer cared what anyone thought.

"This is your moment," Edward said, squeezing her arms. "Go take it."

She nodded, turned to her assistants who had been right there by her side since the beginning. "Thank you. For everything."

"Go," Tierra said, laughing.

She walked out behind Esme. All the models clapped for Carolina. When she reached the end of the runway, she took a bow, then clasped Esme's hand and mouthed "thank you" to her. Esme grinned and they walked hand in hand down the runway toward the curtain.

After, her staff surprised her with champagne. It was nonstop media and interviews and her mother and Evelyn came backstage, too.

"Oh, Carolina. You took my breath away," Evelyn said.

"It was more than even I hoped for you," her mother said, pulling her in for a tight hug. "Your designs are stunning. I'm so very proud of what you've accomplished."

"Thanks, Mom."

She did a few interviews and talked to some fashion editors, who gave her very favorable reviews. One, a very prominent editor with one of her favorite magazines, said she'd love to do an interview and article about her. She had to keep from squealing, so she did it on the inside.

"So . . . you did good."

She turned to her brother and Evelyn. "Thank you for doing this. You looked amazing today."

Evelyn laid her hand on Gray's chest. "He did, didn't he? You know I'm going to want a suit like that for him."

"And I'll be happy to make one for him. On the house, of course."

"Now how are you going to make money for Carolina Designs when you do it gratis."

"Only for my fantastic brother."

"I'm really proud of you, Carolina. I think you're fantastic."

That was high praise coming from Gray.

"Thank you."

"I have to agree with Gray. You are a top-notch designer."

Drew came to stand beside her.

"Thanks," Carolina said. "And thank you for running three blocks to get here in time. You didn't have to do that."

He shrugged. "I'm sorry I was late."

Gray frowned. "What happened?"

"Taxi rammed the car in front of us and then I got stuck in traffic, couldn't find another taxi. It's ridiculous out there. Who knew clothes were so popular?"

Evelyn laughed as she looked over at Carolina. "Men. They know nothing."

"Nothing about Fashion Week, anyway. But I do appreciate it. Were you hurt?"

"Nah. I'm fine. Just pissed off at the taxi driver, who was mad at me for wanting to leave. And he wanted me to pay him the fare."

"Seriously?" Evelyn asked, her eyes wide.

"Yeah. I cussed him out and told him he could chase after me if he wanted to, but I was already late and if he hadn't been zigzagging in and out of traffic, he wouldn't have clipped the car in front of him. Asshole."

"Man, you need a drink," Gray said.

Drew laughed. "In the worst way."

"Come on. Let's go get one. Carolina, can you get out of here yet?"

She looked around. The place was still filled with media, her assistants, and models. "I'm sorry. I can't. But you go on."

"Okay. We'll catch up later. Maybe for dinner?"

"Definitely. I'll text you when I'm free."

They left, with her mother and Drew and the Secret Service, which gave her a little breathing room. She and her crew wrapped up the clothing and took care of clearing everything out. Tierra and Edward were going to follow the truck back to the studio with the clothes.

"I'll finish up here and then I'll meet you back at the studio," she told them.

"No, you won't. Go take some time off," Tierra said. "You've earned it. Today is a day to celebrate. We'll take care of the inventory."

"And then Tierra and I are going to go pop a bottle of champagne and have a very expensive dinner. On you."

Carolina laughed. "You two both deserve it. Enjoy. And thank you again."

After she finished up, she texted Gray, who informed her they were all still at the restaurant. She managed to finagle a taxi despite the crowd and made her way over.

She was instantly handed a glass of champagne by Evelyn.

"I wish I could drink with you, but unfortunately, it's sparkling water for me today."

"Raise your glasses everyone," her mother said. "To Carolina Designs. May today be only the beginning of many wonderful years of beautiful clothes."

Carolina blushed as glasses were lifted toward her. "Thank you, Mom." She took a sip of the wonderful champagne, and for the first time that day, sighed in relief.

"Glad it's over?" Drew asked.

"Absolutely, deliriously glad it's over."

"But it's just beginning, honey," her mother said. "Now the real work begins."

Judging from the texts and emails she skimmed on her way over, that could be true. She had requests for interviews and orders from some very prominent celebrities who wanted to wear her designs, including an Oscar-nominated actress or two who insisted they come by to discuss wearing her for the awards. One wanted to wear the dress Esme had worn today.

Holy. Shit.

"I'm going to be busy, I think. Which is a wonderful, incredible, mind-blowing thing."

"I think the first thing you should do is call that former designer you worked for and tell him to suck it," Drew said.

Carolina laughed. "That would be very unprofessional." But she grinned just thinking about it.

"Drew is right about that, though of course you shouldn't call him. He didn't appreciate your talent. And look at you now." Her mother was beaming.

"Thank you. All of you. I couldn't have done this without you."

"You did it on your talent, Carolina. Nothing more."

Her gaze shifted to Drew. "Thank you."

They had all eaten already, and her mother had a plane to catch.

"We have to get going, too, unfortunately," Evelyn said. "Some race car business something-or-other that my fiancé claims to need to do in Florida." She rolled her eyes, then winked.

"Thank you all so much for being here today. It meant everything to me."

She hugged her mother and brother and Evelyn, and they left, Secret Service making a path for them.

"A lot quieter now," Drew said.

"Yes."

He signaled for their waiter. "And you should eat something. Have you even eaten today?"

"I don't remember."

"That probably means no."

The waiter stood by while Carolina perused the menu. She was suddenly starving, so she chose a baked chicken breast with asparagus and rice.

"You don't have to sit here with me while I eat."

He cocked a brow. "Trying to get rid of me?"

"Not at all. I just know you've all eaten already. I'm sure you're busy, too."

"No game today. I'm all yours."

She leveled a smile at him. "Thank you."

"About that. I have to apologize to you."

"For what?"

"For bailing on you."

Confused, she frowned at him. "You showed up today. Even with a car accident. My God, Drew, you ran three blocks."

"Not that. The advertising campaign."

"Oh."

"I was in my own head about the road games, trying to figure out what was going on and looking for something, anything—anyone—to blame." He lifted his gaze to hers. "I blamed you."

"Me? Why?"

He shrugged. "Because you were as convenient an excuse as anything else. Sometimes, in sports, they say dating a woman during the season is bad luck."

"Oh. And you think I'm your bad luck charm."

"Something like that."

"Okay." So this was his breakup conversation. At least she was getting honesty from him, a reason behind his recent behavior. It didn't make a whole lot of sense to her, but it was better than a disappearing act with no explanation.

"The problem was, it wasn't you. It was all me." He pointed to his temple. "It was all in my head. Still is. Whatever problem the team is having winning road games, it isn't you causing it."

"Good to know."

He grasped her hand. "I'm sorry I let you down, Lina. I'm sorry I wasn't there for you when you needed me. I acted like a selfish jackass and I hope you can forgive me."

Oh. So it wasn't a breakup conversation. It was an apology, and one she hadn't expected from Drew.

"There's nothing to forgive."

"I know you had to scramble to find someone else to do the photo shoot."

"Drew, I—"

"I know it came in the middle of you preparing for the biggest debut of your life."

"Drew, really, I—"

"And that makes me the shittiest boyfriend in the world."

Boyfriend? He'd called himself her boyfriend? They'd never once defined their relationship.

"You're my boyfriend?"

"I don't know. Lover? The guy who's in love with you. Whatever you want to call me, I suck at it."

She shuddered in a breath. He loved her? "You love me?"

"Shit. I told you I suck at this." He took her hand. "Yes. I love you. I should have told you sooner, Lina. Not that I deserve to have your love after what I did to you. I wasn't there for you when you needed me. And I promised you I wouldn't let you down again. I'm not a guy who goes back on his promises. Can you ever forgive me for that?"

She was so overcome by his words that all she could do was stare at him.

"This isn't going like I thought it would. You could say something. Kick me to the curb, tell me to go fuck myself. Or tell me you forgive me. Something."

She laughed. "I'm sorry. I was just stunned there for a moment. Of course I forgive you. We all go through things that are tough and emotional, and sometimes we take them out on the people we care about the most. First, I haven't done the photo shoot yet."

"You haven't?"

"No. I decided to delay it until after Fashion Week. I did find someone else to do the shoot, but Drew, no one could replace you. Not in my head. I could only see you in those shots. You're my perfect model for the print ad. I kept hoping you'd come around and maybe that's why I delayed it until after the show. I kept hoping you'd change your mind."

He lifted her hands and kissed them. "I'm a jerk."

She laughed. "No, you're not. Okay, sometimes you are. Sometimes I am, too. I can be self-absorbed and too into my own work. But the one thing that has consumed me for the past several months, sometimes to the detriment of my own work, has been you. I'm in love with you, Drew. I think about you all the time."

He got up and came around to her side of the table, then pulled her into his arms and laid a kiss on her that left her breathless and dizzy. And despite being in a public restaurant, he continued to kiss her, framing her face with his hands, until she was certain that he was most definitely in love with her, because no man would kiss a woman like that in public unless he had genuine feelings for her. Because there was suddenly applause and catcalls and whistles, and when he pulled away, he ignored them all, focusing only on her as he smiled.

"I love you, Lina."

She licked her lips, feeling as if this day couldn't possibly get any better. "I love you, too, Drew."

The waiter brought her food. Funnily enough, her near starvation of a few minutes ago had dissipated. But she ate anyway, while Drew watched her.

"You're watching me eat," she said.

"Yeah. So?"

"It's a little disconcerting."

He picked up the fork and scooped rice onto it. "Now I'm feeding you. Better?"

He slid the fork between her lips. She closed her mouth over it, but then found him watching her mouth.

"Now it just looks dirty."

"Stop, or you'll make me hard."

She laughed, pushed him away, and finished her meal. They left the restaurant and went back to her apartment.

"When is your next game?" she asked as he opened the door for her.

"Tomorrow night."

"Road game or home game?"

"Road game. New Jersey."

He helped her with her coat. She turned to face him. "At least we have tonight together."

He slipped his arms around her. "Yeah, we do, and it's been too damn long since we were together. I've missed you."

"I missed you, too. Now kiss me, undress me, and make love to me."

"I'm all over that." He gave her a wickedly sexy half smile she'd also missed—the one that tugged at her insides and turned her into mush.

He brushed his lips over hers, then pressed harder, opening her mouth and sliding his tongue over hers. She wound her hand around the nape of his neck to draw him closer, needing his hands, his mouth on hers, that connection they always forged that was emotional as well as physical.

The way he touched her, moving his hands over her body as if he were exploring her for the first time, never failed to send her nerve endings into overdrive. Her nipples peaked hard and tingled as he wound his hands down her sides and over her butt.

He dragged his lips over her jaw and across her neck, his hand roaming up her back to reach for the zipper on her dress. She shivered as he pulled the zipper down.

"Cold?" he asked.

"A little."

"Come on. Let's go to your bedroom."

He took her hand and led her into the bedroom, stopping next to her bed. He turned her around and pulled the dress from her shoulders, kissing the top of her spine. Goose bumps pricked her skin, but this time it wasn't from the cold. She pulled the long sleeves of her dress from her arms, then let the dress pool to the floor.

"Now there's an outfit," he said.

She looked down at her peach and cream lace and satin bra and panties, and the heels she still wore. She sat on the bed and lifted her foot for him to remove her shoe. He took one shoe off, then massaged her foot.

"Oh, God, that feels so good."

"You were on your feet all day." He took the other shoe off, holding the stiletto heel in his hand. "How do you women walk in these things?"

"We make sacrifices for the sake of beauty and to make our legs look good."

He tossed the shoe to the floor and rubbed her foot. "You could wear bunny slippers and your legs would look smokin' hot."

He moved from one foot to the other, and the combined pain and pleasure was so good it was better than any foreplay.

"You could do that for an hour or so and I won't complain."

"You need a hot bath. You're probably exhausted."

"What about the sex?"

He grinned. "We'll get to it."

He started into the bathroom.

"Drew. Wait."

"What?"

"I'll agree to the hot bath, but only if you take it with me."

"I'll take it with you, but only if there are no bubbles in there."

She laughed. "Deal."

She followed him into the bathroom. She loved her oversize tub with the jets. She sat on the side and turned it on.

"You'll probably enjoy the bath, too."

"I'll like being in there with you. Naked."

She shook her head. "Men and their one-track minds."

"Blame the penis."

He got undressed, and Carolina shed her underwear and put her hair up. By then the tub was mostly filled, so Drew held her hand while she climbed in. He got in behind her. The water was hot and enticing, and Drew was right. This was exactly what she needed after a long, stress-filled day. Warm water, the jets billowing around her aching body, and the man she loved giving her a magnificent shoulder rub.

"So how does it feel?" he asked.

"Mmm," she said. "It feels fabulous."

Drew laughed. "No, not the shoulder massage, though I'm glad that feels good. I meant how does it feel to be a success?"

"Oh. Well, I'm not a success yet. But I feel like I could get there." She turned around to face him, wrapping her legs around him. "For the first time, I have a confidence I've never had before, a belief in myself I've never felt before. I mean, I always thought I could do this. I believed in my designs, otherwise I would have never put my reputation on the line like that. But to have the reception that I had today. I don't know, Drew. That, I didn't expect."

He kissed the tip of her nose. "You need to believe in yourself more. You're a fucking rock star, Miss Preston."

Her lips curved. "I like the sound of that. Maybe I should put that on my business cards."

He leaned back in the tub. "Would look good on there."

She followed him, climbing onto his lap, then grabbed the

sponge, dipping it into the water. She wrung it out over his chest, then smoothed it over his shoulders.

His cock began to grow hard underneath her, which made her smile.

"You're just way too easy."

"And you're naked and slippery, and your pussy is moving back and forth on my dick. What did you expect?"

She let the sponge drop into the water, then lifted her fingers up, letting droplets fall over the top of his head. He laughed, shook his head back and forth, water spraying her.

Then he pulled her against him, kissing her until everything on her was throbbing. She rubbed her breasts against his chest, her nipples tightening to hard, aching peaks.

And when she dipped her hand in the water and reached for his cock, fitting it at her pussy, he grasped her wrist.

"Lina. I don't have a condom on."

"And I love you. You love me. I assume that means we're committed to each other. I'm on the pill and I never have sex with anyone without them wearing protection."

He stared at her, his gaze clear and dead serious. "Neither do I. I don't want to be with anyone else but you. I haven't been with anyone else but you since that night I walked in here when Gray invited me over."

That made her stomach tumble. "Drew."

"I just want you to be sure."

"Very sure. I want you inside me right now." She lifted, then slid over his cock, watching his expression change, the way his gaze turned to molten desire as he looked at her.

"Christ, Lina, you feel good. This feels so good."

She moved against him, feeling every inch of him expanding inside her.

"Fuck. Not like this," he said, grabbing her and pulling her out of the water.

He stepped out of the tub, her legs wrapped around him, and laid her down on the thick carpet on the floor next to the tub.

"I want to feel you. Just you. Your heat and the wetness of your pussy." He plunged inside her, and she arched against him.

"Yes. Like this, Drew. More."

His mouth met hers in a tangle of lips and tongues as he thrust harder, then stilled. "Feel me, Lina. Feel my cock twitch inside you. You make me want to come."

She did feel him, more than she'd ever felt him before. Expanding, moving, and taking her right to the edge of reason. His gaze met hers, his hair and body wet, droplets falling on her as he surged against her.

She arched to meet him, needing that contact to come. She tightened and quivered even as he ground against her. And when she splintered, he kissed her, his groan against her lips sending her spiraling out of control as he released inside her.

It was unlike anything she'd ever experienced, a joining of the two of them that was as emotionally fulfilling as it was physically. Drew tightened his hold on her, swept his hand underneath her to pull her closer as she cried out, the waves of her orgasm catapulting her over the edge again and again.

Out of energy and completely spent, she lay there underneath him, nipping at his bottom lip, drawing her hand over the sleek line of his shoulder while he buried his face in her neck.

"I'm sweaty," he finally said. "We should probably get back in the tub."

She smiled at that. "Probably. But I think I'd rather have a shower this time."

He lifted her up and they stepped into the shower.

"You are so sexy when you're wet."

She had submerged her head under the water, and opened her eyes to find him giving her that look, the one that enveloped her in heat and made her sex swell with desire.

He pushed her against the wall of the shower and kissed her until steam rose over them both. He slipped his hand between her legs, rubbing back and forth until she whimpered.

"I want to fuck you again."

"Yes," she said, nearly out of breath as he spread her legs and slid inside her.

She was ready, quivering and needy as he lifted her arms over her head and thrust into her, grinding against her clit.

God, she could come already, the way he rolled his hips over her, his body so close to hers. But then he pulled out and dropped to his knees, covering her sex with his mouth.

She looked down to see water sluicing over her body and dripping over him as he licked and sucked the sensitive nub.

"Drew. Yes, like that." She rested her head against the shower wall as he rolled his tongue over her and shattered her, making her cry out and shudder through another amazing orgasm.

When he rose, he took her mouth in a devastating kiss that kept the sensations rolling.

He lifted her leg and eased inside her.

"Your pussy is still quaking," he said. "It tightens around me and makes me want to come hard inside you."

She loved the way he talked to her during sex, the open, honest way he shared what he felt. "You make me crazy. The things you do to my body."

He gripped her butt and held her while he made love to her achingly slow, easing his cock in, only to slide it partway out until she was on the ragged edge, gripping his shoulder and propelling herself forward to impale herself on his shaft. She wanted more, needed all of him inside her. And when he thrust deeply, she growled, taking his lower lip between her teeth to nip.

He growled back at her, as lost as she was in the animal passion that drove them. He pushed her back against the wall and increased his thrusts, pummeling her until she cried out as sweet release seared her. Drew let go, too, pumping furiously into her and shuddering his release, his fingers digging into her flesh as he poured into her.

Her legs were shaking. Drew palmed the wall next to her and held on to them both.

"Good thing we're in the shower," he said, "because you made me sweat again."

She laughed. "How convenient."

She dipped her head back under the water to wet her hair, then grabbed for the shampoo.

"Let me," Drew said, taking the bottle to pour some shampoo in his hand.

"Oooh, this is a treat." She turned around and Drew lathered the shampoo in her hair. She felt decadent, her scalp tingling when he gave her a slow, delicious massage as he shampooed her hair. "Could you come over every day and do this for me?"

He paused. "Yes."

She rinsed, then opened her eyes to find him staring at her, an unfathomable expression on his face.

There were things they needed to talk about. But everything was so new between them, this declaration of love. It was still so tenuous, and she didn't want to do anything to break that bond. So instead, she leaned forward and kissed him, then laughed. "My own personal shampoo slave. I like that."

He laughed, breaking that tension. They finished cleaning up, dried off, and got dressed, then cuddled together on the sofa.

She could get used to having him here with her whenever he was in town.

But that was a topic for another time. Right now, it was enough that they loved each other.

One step at a time.

TWENTY-NINE

THE DREAD IN THE PIT OF DREW'S STOMACH WOULDN'T go away. Despite he and his team having had one hell of a pep talk in the locker room before the game about this being just another game, they all knew what kind of game this was.

Another goddamn road game.

And as soon as they took the ice, it was as if New Jersey already knew they could take this game away from them.

There was nothing like having the hometown crowd in your corner cheering you on. Typically he ignored the boos from the fans of his opponents. It was only natural for them to want their team to win, and the Travelers stood in their way. Fortunately, because New Jersey was so close, a lot of the die-hard Travelers fans often came to watch them, so he soaked in the cheers of their fans as they were introduced.

They'd need every ounce of fan energy tonight for this game.

It's just a game, just like any other game. He tried to remember

Bill's advice, tucked it inside him so he'd just focus on the game, not the location.

He lined up against New Jersey's defender and when the puck dropped, that was it. It was game time and everything else got shoved into the back of his head. He could no longer hear the crowd noise, whether they were cheering or booing. The only thing that mattered was getting to the puck and lighting up the net.

He and Trick were in sync tonight, their passes were on the mark, and when Drew scored the first goal, he was pumped, every part of him feeling as if they could turn this around.

At least until New Jersey scored three minutes after his goal.

Shit.

But they battled back, Trick forcing the puck on a breakaway. Sweat pouring down his back, Drew skated like his life depended on it, the defender right on his skates as he made his way to the New Jersey goal. He got the puck, passed it to Trick, who shot it between the goalie's legs.

Another goal, and Drew felt the momentum building. No one was going to take it away from them tonight. They were going to win this game.

At the end of the second period, they were tied. The coach told them they looked outstanding, and they were better than New Jersey. There was no reason they couldn't take the win.

Drew felt the same way. Avery's thigh had mostly healed and despite having two goals scored against him tonight, his reflexes were better than they'd been in weeks. His save percentage was off the charts tonight, especially with New Jersey being so aggressive at the net. The defenders were fierce, and the Travelers offense was determined. They were meshing like never before. This was their night.

When Drew and Trick came off the ice for a breather, Sayers and Litman came on, skating like they were on fire. They shot a goal right into the net between two defenders and the whole team lit up.

Drew and Trick did the same when they came back onto the ice, and suddenly they were up two goals with a minute and a half left. All they had to do was avoid penalties and keep the defense strong. There was no way they could lose this game.

Now Drew tuned into the Travelers fans who'd made the trip. Despite being in the minority at the stadium, they were pumped. And loud. He tuned into that noise and he and Trick went on the attack, double-teaming a defender. They fought against the boards for the puck, Trick coming up with it and heading toward the goal. Drew stayed in position while Trick, surrounded by defenders, sailed the puck across the ice to him.

Drew took the shot but the goalie deflected it. New Jersey's defender took it and handed it off, which meant, with the clock ticking down, they had to rely on their defense.

New Jersey took a couple shots on goal, but missed.

The buzzer sounded.

And goddamn if the Travelers hadn't won a road game.

The team took center ice and celebrated as if they'd won the championship. But it was a big win, and one they'd worked hard for. A giant monkey off their back, and Drew hoped now they could move past it and play every game—at home or away—like he knew they could.

There was a lot of chatter in the locker room, as well as the inevitable media, who had to give them shit about winning their first road game of the season and what it all meant. Drew, as well as the rest of the players, downplayed it, saying it was just another win. But all the guys knew what a big deal this had been, and what it had meant for the team. It was a huge confidence booster, and Drew was convinced this win was going to turn things around.

"Hogan," one of the assistants hollered from across the locker room. "You have a visitor."

Drew frowned. "Who is it?"

"Some hot-looking chick. Carolina, she said her name was."

Lots of ooohs and whistles. Drew rolled his eyes.

Carolina was here? In New Jersey? "I'll be right out."

"Carolina came to your road game?" Trick asked. "It must be serious."

Drew looked down at Trick, who was getting ready to take a shower. "It is serious. I'm in love with her."

Trick just stared up at him, then grinned. "Well fuck me. Congratulations, buddy."

"Thanks."

He got dressed and went outside the locker room. Carolina was wearing tight jeans, knee-skimming boots, and a long red coat. He'd never seen a more beautiful sight.

He dragged her into his arms and planted a big kiss on her, much to the happiness of the lingering media, who took pictures. He didn't care.

She smiled up at him. "Great game tonight."

Moving them away from the photographers and video crews, he led her down a side hallway. "I can't believe you're here. In New Jersey."

"A relationship goes both ways, Drew. It can't just be you being there for me. It also means I'll be there for you whenever I can. I told you I believed in you, and, win or lose, I was going to be in the stands cheering for you tonight."

An ache formed in the pit of his stomach, an even bigger one swelling his heart. "Thank you. That means a lot to me."

"You were there for me when I needed you. And even if I'm not physically here, I'll always be your biggest cheerleader."

He brushed his lips across hers. "I love you, Carolina."

"I love you, too. Now when do you get back to the city?"

"Bus leaves in about thirty."

"Good. So when you get back, unless you're planning to go out and celebrate with the team, I know this great cheeseburger place."

He cocked a brow. "You hate cheeseburgers. And eggs, as I recall."

"I do. They also have chicken. But you like burgers, and that's the sacrifice a girlfriend makes when her guy has just had a great game."

"Sounds good to me."

A couple hours later they were seated together in a cozy, understated burger joint. Drew was wolfing down a cheeseburger while Carolina had a chicken sandwich.

"So this is what it's going to be like, huh?" he asked.

"What what's going to be like?"

"A relationship. You making sacrifices."

She laughed. "Hey, I didn't say I was going to eat a cheeseburger or anything. But yes. We'll both make sacrifices."

He reached out and grasped her hand. "And we'll both probably make mistakes."

"Likely."

"But I'll never hurt you. And you know, you can say whatever's on your mind, even if you think it's uncomfortable."

She frowned. "What do you mean?"

"Last night. When I made a comment about being there every day to wash your hair. You looked uncomfortable."

"Oh. That. I didn't want to make you uncomfortable, or jump the gun on what was a very new thing for both of us. We'd just said we loved each other. I didn't want to invite you to move in or anything."

He wiped the corner of his mouth with a napkin. "I get that. You want us to get to know each other better."

She laughed. "Okay, this does seem stupid, doesn't it? We've known each other for what seems like forever. It's not like we need to . . . date or anything."

"But maybe you want to take things slow."

She paused, like she was thinking, then looked up at him. "I miss you when you're not with me. I think about you all the time. I want to sleep with you next to me at night, wake up with you snuggled up against me in the morning."

"That sounds good to me, too."

"We both have such busy careers and it'll be hard enough to see each other as it is. If you moved in with me . . . not that you have to or anything. I mean, if you want your own space, I'd totally understand."

He pushed back his chair and stood, then came over and hauled her up and kissed her until she was out of breath.

"I want you in my life. When I told you I loved you, I didn't mean, 'Hey, baby, let's go out a few times a month.' It meant commitment to me."

Carolina blinked as Drew wrapped his arms around her. "That's what it means to me, too."

"Then I'll move in with you. And we'll cohabitate. My toothbrush next to yours. And you'll learn to take some downtime, so when I'm in the off-season, I can take you to my place in Oklahoma."

"What is this downtime thing you speak of?"

He laughed. "It's that thing where you aren't working seven days a week."

"Oh, that." She leaned into him. "Yes. It'll be hard for me because I'm such a workaholic. But I do love you, and lately, being with you is the most important thing to me."

"I like hearing that. I don't want you to feel any pressure, Lina. We'll figure it all out together and we'll make it work. Because we love each other."

Drew had always turned her world upside down. From the time

she was a teenager and hopelessly infatuated with him, to the one night of passion that had made her a woman, to him walking back into her life several months ago, he was her one and only constant passion. He had melted the ice around her cold, cold heart, and she wanted to share the warmth with him forever.

"Yes, we do love each other. So let's make a home together, and figure out this living together thing."

He gave her that lopsided grin that never failed to make her heart turn over. "I like the way you think, Miss Preston."

Dear Reader,

I hope you enjoyed *Melting the Ice*. The next book in the Play-by-Play series is *Straddling the Line*, Trevor and Haven's story, coming out in July 2014.

We've all lost people we love in our lives, people we relied on, those we thought would be with us longer. For Haven Briscoe, losing her father has left a deep hole in her heart. Her father was her rock, the man she went to for guidance and advice. Now, her career seems empty, and she isn't sure her job as a sports reporter has the thrill and excitement it once held.

But when she's assigned to do an exposé on her college-crush-turned-pro-athlete, Trevor Shay, it brings them close again. Trevor knows Haven is grieving over her father, and he's determined to do whatever it takes to help her while still competing in professional baseball and football.

Trevor and Haven's story is deeply emotional, but also fun, exciting, and sexy. Please keep reading for a sneak peak at the first chapter.

In addition, I'm also including the first chapter of *Hope Ignites*, book two of the Hope Novels, my contemporary romance series, releasing in April 2014. This series focuses on the people who inhabit a small town in Oklahoma.

Logan McCormack is a busy rancher and doesn't have time for frivolous pursuits. He agrees to let a movie crew film on his land because the money is too good to pass up. However, when he meets Desiree Jenkins, the actress starring in the movie, he doesn't know what to make of the fiery, outspoken young woman. Nearly ten years younger than him, Logan thinks Des is off-limits. But Des is attracted to Logan and isn't afraid to state her intentions. She's in love with the wide-open spaces of the ranch, so different from where she lives in Los Angeles. She's also taken with Logan's quiet strength and work ethic, and the two of them embark on a very unusual romance.

But is theirs a forever type of romance, or a movie-set fling?

I hope you enjoy the first chapter of *Hope Ignites*, and fall in love with the town of Hope and all its characters, just as I have.

Happy reading!
Jaci

STRADDLING THE LINE

"HAVEN'S IN TROUBLE."

Those were words Trevor Shay never wanted to hear, especially not less than a year after the death of Haven's dad, Bill.

Bill Briscoe had been more than just a dorm parent back in Trevor's college days. He and his wife, Ginger, had been like substitute parents, especially to Trevor, who'd needed guidance more than the rest.

And now he sat in Ginger's living room, in a house he'd once thought of as his second home.

Trevor had always counted on Ginger's confidence, that smile and optimism that had assured him everything was going to be all right.

Now she just looked worried.

He picked up her hand. "What's wrong?"

"She hasn't been herself since Bill died. You know Haven. She's always been upbeat, and we thought she'd come to grips with the eventuality of Bill's death." Ginger took a deep breath. "As we all did."

Trevor squeezed her hand.

"It wasn't like we didn't know it was comin'. Bill prepared us all for it, made sure we were ready. Never thinking of himself."

He saw the tears welling in her eyes and wished he could take them away.

"I know, Miss Ginger. I know. I miss him, too."

She grabbed a tissue. "He'd kick my butt if he saw me crying over him. But Haven, she has a great life and an amazing future. She got a job with the network as a sports journalist."

Trevor smiled. "I heard about that."

"It's a great opportunity for her. One she should be seizing. I told her that her father would be so proud of her."

"He would."

"Instead, what is she doing? She's thinking about quitting the job and coming back here to live with me."

Trevor leaned back and frowned. "Coming back here? Why?"

"I don't know. She said something about getting a job at the local TV station instead."

"Is that what she really wants?"

"I don't think so." Ginger leaned forward. "Trevor, I don't know what to do. She hasn't even given this new job a shot. I think she's scared, and without her dad, she feels alone for the first time in her life."

"She's not alone, Miss Ginger. She has you."

"I know that. And believe me, I don't feel slighted in the least. I know Haven loves me. I also know she's worried about me being here all alone. I don't want her to make a mistake and screw up the best job she might ever have because of me, and because of her fear."

She paused, took a breath. "I was hoping you could offer me

some advice, tell me what I could say to her to make her stay in her job."

Trevor thought about it a minute. "Let me see what I can do about that."

"Thank you. I know you're big in the sports world, and I don't know if there really is anything you can do for her, but gosh, I'd sure appreciate anything. Anything at all."

An idea formed in his head. He had the pull. He could get this done. And he'd do anything for Ginger, and to honor Bill's memory. Haven needed help, and he sure as hell was in a position to help her.

Hours later, as he sat on the plane on his way back to St. Louis, Trevor had the plan formulated. The media were constantly hounding him for an exposé on his life and career. After all, there weren't many athletes who played multiple sports. At least not many who played them well. He'd been closed off to the idea of it for a lot of reasons.

He leaned back in his seat and smiled.

Now, it was Haven's turn to shine. And he was just the person to make it happen.

HAVEN TRIED TO MUSTER UP ENOUGH SALIVA TO SWAL-low as she pressed the button to return the phone call she'd missed from her boss.

She knew what was on the other end of that phone call.

Her ass was going to be fired, less than six weeks after she'd gotten the job of a lifetime.

It would have been better if she could have resigned. It would have looked better on her resumé, but then again, what did she care? Her career in journalism was over anyway, right?

Never quit. Whatever you do, Haven, never give up on anything until you're sure you've given it everything you have.

Her father's words rang in her ears, guilt squeezing her stomach until nausea caused her fingers to pause on the call button of her phone.

It was too late to beg to keep her job. She'd already passed up multiple travel assignments, content to do the local ones, then sit in her apartment in New York, dwelling on how much she missed home, her mom.

Her dad.

This wasn't the right career for her. She'd made a mistake accepting this job. She wasn't cut out for the rigors of sports news—the travel, the insane schedule, the arrogant athletes.

What was she thinking? Her father hadn't even been gone a year yet.

She couldn't do it.

Be brave, Haven. You can do anything, be anything you want to be. Just be happy.

Tears pricked her eyes and she swiped them away as she replayed every conversation they'd had those last few weeks over and over in her head.

Be happy.

She didn't know how to be happy without hearing her father's laugh, seeing his smiling face, being able to pick up the phone and talk to him every day.

Who was she going to go to when she needed advice?

She loved her mother, and in the ways of relationships and men and things like that, she had always gone to her mom.

But her dad—he'd been her buddy. She'd learned about sports from her father, had sat next to him and watched football, baseball, hockey, and every other sport imaginable. He'd taught her balls and strikes in baseball and the difference between a post pattern and a shovel pass in football. They'd driven up to St. Louis together and taken in hockey games, and she'd never been more thrilled than to see the players blasting that puck across the ice.

She'd learned to love sports because of her dad.

She'd gone after this job because of him.

And now she was going to be fired because after his death she hadn't had the energy to do this job she'd wanted for years. For that, she had only herself to blame.

"I'm sorry, Dad," she said, then pushed the call button on her phone.

"Haven. I've been waiting for you to call."

She cringed as the loud and very no-nonsense voice of her boss, Chandler Adams, came on the line.

"Hi, Chandler. Sorry. I got tied up."

"Well, untie yourself. I have a job for you."

"A . . . job?" He wasn't firing her?

"Yeah. You know Trevor Shay, right?"

"Trevor . . . yes, I know him."

"Great. We're going to do his bio. A whole feature on the life of Trevor Shay. Personal and professional. We've been after him for years to do this, and he's finally agreed. And he's asked for you."

"For me?"

"Yeah. Says you two go way back, to college."

"Uh . . . yes. I knew him in college."

"Then it's a damn good thing we hired you, Haven. Pack a bag. You'll meet him at his place in St. Louis to get everything set up. Narrative and background first, then we'll get camera work involved later."

Was she in some alternate universe? She hadn't been fired. In fact, she'd just been assigned a profile of one of the biggest stars in the sports world right now.

"Okay. Sure. Thanks, Chandler."

"No problem. I'll email you the specs on what we're looking for from you on this, Haven. This assignment's going to take awhile, so clear your calendar."

"Consider it done."

When she hung up, she sat back and stared out the window of her very tiny apartment, stunned that she hadn't been kicked out the door. She stared at the boxes in her apartment, already half packed. She'd been mentally prepared, set in her mind that she was going to head back to Oklahoma to be near her mother, her roots.

Where memories of her dad were.

Now she had to change her focus.

Why had she agreed to do this? This wasn't what she wanted to do anymore.

Was it?

She sat on the bed.

Follow your dreams, Haven.

She still heard his voice so clearly in her head. Maybe he was trying to tell her something. She didn't know if this was her dream anymore, but she'd agreed to take this job.

With Trevor Shay, of all people. She hadn't seen Trevor since her dad's funeral. She wondered how he'd react knowing it was her doing this assignment.

He'd probably ignore her, just like he had in college.

No, wait. He'd specifically asked for *her.* He'd agreed to the interviews, so this time, she wouldn't allow him to pretend she didn't exist.

She got up and went to her closet to grab her suitcase.

Her and Trevor Shay. God, she'd had such a crush on him in college, back when she was tutoring him. All those nights they'd spent shoulder to shoulder, when she'd done her best to try and convince him to focus on his books when all she'd really wanted was for him to notice her as a woman.

He'd been more interested in trying to finagle a way to get her to do his homework.

Now she was going to be in the driver's seat.

She stared out over the boxes, debating whether to unpack them.

She'd leave them, see how this assignment went. If it didn't work out, if it didn't light the fire under her after a few days, she'd call Chandler and tell him she was out.

But she'd give it a try. For her dad.

HOPE IGNITES

LOGAN McCORMACK HAD TO HAVE BEEN DRUNK OR
out of his goddamned mind to have agreed to let a movie crew film
on his ranch.

Why he thought it had been a good idea was beyond him. But
Martha, the ranch cook and house manager, was starstruck, and
when she'd heard who the lead actress was—some name Logan had
already forgotten, alongside some freakin' heartthrob-of-the-
month as her costar, Martha gone all melty and told him it would
be good for business.

Plus, the production company had offered a buttload of cash,
and he wasn't the type to turn down extra money. Since they'd be
filming on the east side of the property, which was mostly hills and
grassland and nowhere near their cattle operation, they'd be out of
the way. At the time it had seemed like a good idea.

They'd come in a week ago, a convoy of semis and trailers and
black SUVs. Logan had been working the fence property and had

seen them driving in. Hell, it had looked like some Hollywood parade. The whole town had shown up at the gates to the ranch to witness it. He'd gotten all the gossip when Martha had served up dinner. She'd talked it up nonstop, her voice more animated than he'd heard in a long time.

"I'm pretty sure Desiree Jenkins and Colt Stevens are on our property as we speak," Martha had said as she'd put the salad on the table. "Are you going to go check it out, Logan?"

"Why would I want to do that?" he'd asked, way more interested in eating than he was in the goings-on at the east property.

"You rented them the land. It's your responsibility to make sure they're settled in."

He'd said no, and Martha had argued. And when Martha argued about something, it was best you just do whatever she wanted, because she wasn't the type to let a topic die.

"I'll go see about it in a few days." That few days had turned into a week, and Martha had been nearly apoplectic that he hadn't checked it out yet. Which could affect his dinner, since Martha in a snit meant she could take to her room with some kind of mystery ailment and he'd end up eating baloney sandwiches instead of a hot meal.

So after he was done with his work the next day, he climbed into his truck and drove over to the site. Crews had already finished building the set for . . . whatever movie it was they were filming. Some post-apocalyptic futuristic something or another, supposedly set on another planet. The sparse vegetation, scrub, and hills of the east property would work just fine for it, he supposed. He'd signed the contracts and deposited the check, but hadn't bothered to pay attention to the name of the film. He wasn't much of a moviegoer. To go to the movies meant heading into town, and he'd rather sit on the porch and have a beer at night. He liked the quiet. If he wanted to see a movie, he had a television and one of those subscription accounts. That was good enough for him.

Martha was right. It already looked like they'd built a small town on some of the flatlands out there. He parked his truck on the rise, popped open the beer he'd shoved in his cooler, and leaned against the hood of his truck to watch the hustle of people moving back and forth. Trailers had been set up as living areas, though these trailers looked way more expensive than anything Logan could afford. They were more like big houses on wheels. Probably what the stars lived in while they shot the movie.

An SUV came up the road, dust flying behind it. A couple of burly guys wearing all black and sporting dark sunglasses rolled out of the vehicle.

"This is a closed set."

Unruffled, Logan stared at them. "Okay."

"You aren't supposed to be on this property."

"I own this property."

One of the guys in black frowned at him. "You're the property owner?"

"Yeah."

"Got ID?"

Logan let out a short laugh. "I'm not about to show you my ID Like I said, I own this land and you're renting it."

"We'll still need to see an ID," burly guy number two said.

Logan folded his arms. "Yeah? You can kiss my ass."

His attention turned to a slight woman—a girl, really, running up the hill. She wore jogging clothes, tight pants that just went past her knees and a sleeveless top that hugged her slender body. She had dark hair pulled back in a braid. The guys suddenly stepped in front of Logan as if he was going to pull a gun on the woman.

When she reached them, she stopped, drawing in several deep breaths.

"What's up, Carl?"

"Saw this guy parked up here and came to check it out. He says he's the property owner but he won't show ID to prove it."

She finally straightened and stretched her back. "Is that right? And are you the property owner?"

"So it says on the ranch deed."

She walked over and held out her hand. "I'm Des."

Logan shook her hand. "Logan McCormack."

"Nice ranch, Logan."

"Thanks."

"Have you been down to watch filming yet?"

"Why would I want to do that?"

She quirked a smile. "I don't know. I thought maybe you'd find it interesting."

"Are you working on the film crew, Des?"

Her lips curled into a smirk. "You could say that."

One of the big guys stepped forward. "Miss Jenkins?"

"It's okay, Carl. You and Duke can take off."

Carl shook his head. "Not a good idea."

She shot him a look. "And I said I'm fine."

With another serious death glare, the guy named Carl and the other guy got into the SUV and drove back down the hill.

"Are those your bodyguards?"

She laughed. "No. Well, sometimes."

"So you must be the star of the show."

She shrugged. "Well, I'm the lead. I don't know about star."

"What are you doing out here?"

"Taking a break. And getting some exercise."

"Not really a gym on site for you to work out in, is there?"

"No. This is better. You must love it here."

"It's home."

She leaned against the front of his truck, grabbed his beer from his hand, took a long swallow, and handed it back to him. "Thanks."

"I don't recall offering it to you."

She turned to her side. "You're not very friendly, are you, Logan?"

"I try not to be."

"Yeah? And why's that?"

"It keeps people away."

"Oh, so you don't like people."

"I didn't say that."

She laughed, and he liked the gravelly, raspy, sexy sound of it. Which he shouldn't.

"Do you have any more of those?" she asked, eyeing his beer.

"I might."

When she cocked a brow, he added, "Front passenger floor of the truck. Help yourself."

She went around and grabbed a beer, bringing him another one, too. "Yours looked about empty." She popped the top and took a long swallow.

"You sure you're old enough to be drinking those?"

There went that laugh again. "I'm sure." She gave him a sideways glance. "Are you old enough to be drinking them?"

"Funny." He took a long swallow.

She leaned next to him, against the truck, and looked out over the valley.

"Just how big is this ranch, Logan?"

"It's pretty big."

She shot him a look. "Pretend I'm smart and just tell me."

"It's a little over a hundred thousand acres."

"Holy shit. That's a lot. No wonder you could afford to lend us a small piece of the pie."

"I didn't lend it. I'm renting it to your movie-making company. Which means I make money. Working a ranch is costly business."

"I'm sure it is. Though honestly, I wouldn't know."

He took another swallow of beer as he studied her. "City girl?"

"A little of that, and a little country. I've been around. Never lived on a ranch, though."

"Where are you from?"

"Just about everywhere."

"Military?"

She tilted her head and looked up at him. "What makes you think that?"

"I don't think anything at all. Just guessing."

"Good guess. Yeah, my dad was army. We moved around a lot."

"So you've seen the world."

She didn't smile this time. "You could say that."

"You probably still see a lot of it, being an actress."

"Sometimes a lot more than I want to." She took a couple sips of her beer and kept her gaze focused below, where the movie was being filmed. And she stopped talking.

Logan didn't know what to make of Desiree Jenkins. She couldn't be more than mid-twenties at best, which put her firmly in the close-to-ten-years-younger-than-him category. Scrubbed of makeup, she looked like a teenager, but there was a worldliness in her eyes that made her seem a lot older.

She sure was pretty with her long dark hair and wide eyes that he couldn't quite get a handle on, color-wise. Every time she shifted position, so did the color. At first they seemed blue, but now they were more like a brownish green, with little flecks of gold in them.

"You're staring."

He frowned. "Huh?"

"You're staring at me. Do I have dirt on my face?"

"No. I'm looking at your eyes. The color of them."

"Oh yeah. My dad told me I had chameleon eyes. I figure they're just hazel, with a little of every color in them. Pretty cool, huh?"

"Huh. I guess so."

She leaned back against his truck again. "Not much impresses you, does it, Logan?"

"Nope." But her eyes did.

"So tell me about your ranch. What do you do here?"

"Work."

"Wow, so descriptive. I'll bet you're a great conversationalist at parties."

"Don't get to a lot of parties around here."

"Maybe you don't get invited to a lot of parties."

"Can't say that breaks my heart any."

She rolled her eyes. "Anyway, about the ranch?"

"We work cattle. We also have horses, but they're wild mustangs so we don't mess with them except to feed them in the winter."

"Okay. Do you raise the cattle for beef?"

"Yeah."

"You didn't strike me as a dairy farmer."

"Really. And what does a typical dairy farmer look like to you?"

She shrugged. "No idea. Not like you. You're more the rugged, work-the-land type, not the milk-the-cows type."

He wasn't sure whether to take that as a compliment, or whether she'd just insulted dairy farmers. Either way, it was obvious she had no idea what she was talking about. Then again, he didn't know shit about movie making. But he wasn't spouting off about that, either.

"Well, I gotta go."

She pushed off the truck and handed him the empty beer bottle. "Thanks for the drink. You should come down and watch filming."

"No, thanks. I'm plenty busy with my own work."

"You might find what we do interesting."

"I'm interested enough in what I do."

She cocked her head to the side, revealing the soft column of her neck. He didn't want to be interested in her neck, but he was.

"Afraid you might linger a little too long? Maybe get bitten by the acting bug?"

He laughed at that. "Uh, no."

"Then come on down and watch us work. I'll make sure the big burly guys won't bother you."

Martha would have a fit if he got an invite and he didn't say yes. "Martha, my house manager, is a big fan."

"Bring her down to watch a day of filming. We're doing a big dramatic scene tomorrow. She'd probably love that."

"She probably would."

"I'll have to warn you there's a lot of standing around and wait-ing in between takes, but I promise you the end result is always worthwhile. You and Martha come on out to the set. I promise it'll be fun."

There were a million reasons this wasn't a good idea. But then there was Martha, and he hated the thought of cold sandwiches. "What time?"

"I'm usually in makeup by six a.m., so we should start shooting by eight."

"You get up that early? I thought all you movie stars slept 'til noon."

"Now who's funny? I'll let the crew know you're coming." She lifted her arms over her head, stretched, then kicked off into a run, waving at him. "See you tomorrow, Logan."

Why the hell he'd agreed to that, he had no idea. He had more than enough to do, and losing a day would put him behind.

But at least Martha would be happy.

DES MADE IT BACK TO THE FILM SITE AND RAN STRAIGHT into Theo, her director.

"Des. Where'd you go?"

"I took a run to get some exercise. Did you need me for something?"

"Yes. We need to reshoot one of this morning's scenes. I told you not to disappear."

"Sorry. I'll head over to makeup and hair."

"Too late now. I've already dismissed the crew for the day and the lighting isn't right. We'll pick it up later." He walked with her as she headed to her trailer. "I wanted to go over tomorrow's scenes with you, though. How about dinner tonight? My trailer?" He put his arm around her shoulder.

Her skin crawled and she immediately wanted to shrug him off. Theo was a notorious, disgusting, very married womanizer who liked to hit on his leading ladies, especially on location. But he was also a brilliant director, so one had to take the bad with the good. "I need a shower after my run, Theo. And I've already made plans to run lines with Colt over dinner. You're welcome to join us, though. We could knock out discussion about tomorrow's scenes then."

Theo paused, then shook his head. "No, that's all right. We'll do it in the morning during prep. I'll see you then."

"Okay. See you tomorrow, Theo."

She stepped up her pace before Theo came up with any more pervy ideas.

"Cornered you, did he?"

She smiled as Colt Stevens, her costar caught up with her. "Why weren't you here to save me?"

"Sorry, babe. I was on the phone. I saw Theo hook on to you as soon as you got back on set. Did you have a good run?"

"I did. Did you have a good phone call?"

His eyes gleamed. "I did."

Des looked around to make sure they were alone. "And how is Tony?"

"Pining away for me, as always. I wish he could be here."

"I wish he could, too." Des wrapped her arm around Colt's waist. "Why don't you just come out of the closet and be done with it already?"

They'd reached her trailer. Colt opened the door for her and Des stepped in. Colt followed and shut the door. "Oh, right. Smokin' hot movie star who gets all the sexy roles comes out as gay."

Des shrugged. "So? It's the twenty-first century, Colt. And you kiss better than any leading man I've ever worked with. I doubt any of your future leading ladies would be deterred."

Colt sat on her sofa, stretching out his long legs. "Thanks, babe. Tony thinks so, too."

She laughed. "Seriously, though. We have chemistry through the roof and it shows on screen. If you can pull that off, who cares who you love off screen?"

"Well, I sure don't. And you don't. And probably most of America doesn't give a shit, either. But my management team does care. And they say no to coming out."

She plopped onto the sofa next to him. "I'm sorry. You should be able to live your life freely and not have to parade around with a bunch of women you don't care about while Tony is stuck loving you behind the scenes."

Colt let out a sigh. "I know, love. But it is what it is, and I guess it's going to stay that way for a while. Maybe someday we'll be able to change that."

She pushed off and stood. "Hopefully sooner rather than later. I want you to be happy."

"I want you to be happy, too."

She gave him a smile. "I am happy. I'm living my dream here."

"Sure you are."

"Did you get dinner ordered?"

"Should be here in about fifteen."

"Pop open a bottle of wine for us, then. I'm going to hop in the shower."

Des stripped and got into the shower, washing away the body makeup from today's scenes and the sweat from her run. She thought about Colt. They'd known each other since before either of them had gotten their first film role, when they'd bunked together in a one-bedroom apartment in Hollywood. They'd become fast friends and had stayed that way. She'd found out right away that Colt was gay—hard to hide that kind of thing from your best friend and roommate. And when they'd started getting roles together, they'd bonded and supported each others' careers. Fortunately, they'd also been lucky enough to score roles in films together. Though it was hysterically funny to film love scenes together, they were actors and professionals. And because they were so close, they had a natural chemistry. They were comfortable together, and lit up the screen. They were often linked together in the gossip circles, which Colt found amusing.

So did Des. She didn't mind bearding for him, and often went out to premieres and to dinner with him to give him a cover when he didn't feel like playing the role of a straight guy with some other woman.

Until she'd met Jason and had started a relationship with him.

Which had recently gone up in flames. As did most of her Hollywood relationships. Actors were self-absorbed dicks. Except for Colt, of course, who she was now free to hook up with again. At least on the surface.

She got out of the shower and put on a pair of shorts and a tank top. The smell of dinner made her stomach clench. She was hungry, so she hurriedly combed out her hair and went into the main room of the trailer, where Colt was laying out forks and plates.

"Chinese food?"

"Yeah."

"All that salt. I love looking puffy in front of the camera."

Colt grinned. "You couldn't look puffy if you tried. Sit down and eat."

They ate and chatted about the day, and roughed out tomorrow's scenes between bites.

"I met Logan McCormack, the owner of the ranch, today," she said as she grabbed a fortune cookie.

"Yeah? What's he like?"

"Incredibly sexy, in a brooding, loner cowboy sort of way."

"Really. Would I like him?"

She laughed. "I think you'd love him. And Tony would kill you."

"Hey, I'm devoted and madly in love and you know that. Doesn't mean I can't ogle."

"I invited him to the set. He said his house manager is a big fan, so he's going to bring her tomorrow."

"Hmm."

She looked at Colt. "Hmmm what?"

"You're interested. Now I really can't wait to meet him."

"I didn't say I was interested in him, only that he was interesting."

"Same thing, isn't it?"

"Not at all." She cracked open her fortune cookie and popped a piece into her mouth as she unfolded the fortune and read it.

Your life is about to change in new and exciting ways.

She'd believe that when it happened.